Caught in the Shadows

Also by C.A. Haddad

The Academic Factor
Operation Apricot
Bloody September
The Moroccan

Caught in the Shadows

C.A. HADDAD

ST. MARTIN'S PRESS   NEW YORK

CAUGHT IN THE SHADOWS. Copyright © 1992 by C.A. Haddad. All rights reserved.
Printed in the United States of America. No part of this book may be used or
reproduced in any manner whatsoever without written permission except in the
case of brief quotations embodied in critical articles or reviews. For
information, address St. Martin's Press, 175 Fifth Avenue, New York, N.Y.
10010.

Design by Glen M. Edelstein

Library of Congress Cataloging-in-Publication Data
Haddad, C. A.
    Caught in the shadows / C.A. Haddad.
      p.   cm.
    ISBN 0-312-07666-5
    I. Title.
PS3558.A3117C38   1992
813'.54—dc20   92-4525
                                                                 CIP

First edition: August 1992

10 9 8 7 6 5 4 3 2 1

For Jonathan

Caught in the Shadows

1

WHEN I was five years old, my mother was convicted of killing my stepfather. I remember it, but I remember it vaguely, the way one remembers nursery school. To say my mother's conviction made no difference in my life would be dumb. But the difference it made is something I cannot assess.

Through my early years a slight haze of guilt clouded all my happy times. I was too young to analyze the guilt. But I do know it had something to do with not being able to save my mother. You see, I testified at her trial. That much I remember. I was dressed in my favorite plaid dress, and I had on navy blue knee socks. A man in a uniform took my hand. He led me up the aisle of this courtroom and sat me in a big seat next to the judge. From there I could look down to see my mother. I think she tried to smile at me, but it was hard to tell because her eyes were so sad.

And then two men started asking me questions. The questions were all about my stepfather William Townsend II. Was he nice to me? Was he good to my mother? Did he ever hit me? Did he hit my mother? Did he scream a lot? Did he ever threaten to kill me? Was my mother's life in danger?

I sat mute on the stand. I remember that. And I remember my mother bursting out, "Please! Leave her alone!"

I was dismissed. But even way back then, I knew there was something I should have said. It's just that I could never quite capture what it was.

I saw my mother once after that. She said that she was going away, so I would have to have a new mother. My mother made me promise to forget all about everything, to pretend that none of this had ever happened, and to go on with my life. Someday, she promised, we would meet again, and everything would be all right. I remember thinking how silly and strange her words sounded to me, especially the part about going on with my life. I was only five years old. I didn't know I had a life.

That's when I moved to Sioux Bluffs, Iowa, and began my new life with my new mother Winnie McKennah. I became Elizabeth McKennah legally. This I remember very well. Mom, as I soon enough took to calling Winnie McKennah, so good was she to me, took me to the county court house over in Carsonville and had my name legally changed from Elizabeth Diane Peters to Elizabeth Diane McKennah.

My years in Sioux Bluffs were contented ones. My new mother spent her life trying to make me happy, trying to help me forget. I had plenty of questions, of course. I distinctly remember trying to find out what relation Winnie McKennah was to my mother, Jane Peters Townsend. Was she a sister? Aunt? Cousin? "We're all related in God," my new mother would say to me. "We're all one family, Becky." "Becky" is what she took to calling me because she said she always wanted a daughter named Becky. I only learned later in life that Becky derived from Rebecca, but my mother said it was close enough to Beth for it not to matter. She was like that. She brushed aside any inconsistencies in our life together.

As my mother, Winnie McKennah involved herself in

everything that affected me, from the PTA to Sunday School to the Girl Scouts. There were questions that other children asked about my mother that could have only come from their parents. But even I noticed some discrepancies. My mother was much older than the other mothers attending school open house nights. Her hair was gray, and she was always very correct, prim and proper. Worst of all, she had no husband. Every woman in Sioux Bluffs had a husband, except some of our teachers. My mother once made the mistake of telling some of the women, when pressed, that her husband had died in the war. Since I was born in 1961, the women spent the better part of six months desperately trying to figure out which war my mother was referring to.

Meanwhile, I learned to keep my mouth shut about the past. "It's our business and nobody else's," my mother stressed. And I couldn't help but feel she was right. It was bad enough having to deal with having no father. What if I told all my friends that I was adopted and my real mother was a murderer? That would certainly cut me from the birth-day party list. Furthermore, even if Winnie McKennah wasn't as young as the other mothers, or as pretty, she still was my mother and I loved her. I especially loved her when I was in high school and absolutely nobody asked me out on a date. My mother assured me that when the time came, boys would discover me. I was still waiting for my Christopher Columbus as my senior prom came and went. Imagine the humiliation of sitting home on that night of all nights!

I never considered myself unattractive. I was five feet six, stocking-feet, with reddish brown hair, brown eyes, a few embarrassing freckles, and a size-eight body. I was, in other words, average. But there was something about me and boys. One of my girlfriends put it best when she said, "Boys think you don't like them." In truth, it wasn't that I didn't like boys so much, it was just that I was uncomfortable with them. Why, I don't know. They were just creatures like the rest of us.

When the time came for college, my mother assured me

I could go to any college I wanted—within reason and a two-day drive. "Money's no object," Mom stated. She was always that way, never letting me worry about our finances, even though I knew they must have been tight. She didn't work when I was younger. Only when I entered high school did she take a job with the law firm in town as a legal secretary. I used to visit her, and that's where I was introduced to what was to become the love of my life: computers. Mom used a word processor in the law office. It was nothing like the ones we have today. This one was difficult to use and the instructions that came with it would have confused even the IRS. My mother hated it. She would lose documents and erase documents and misfile documents. But she would never admit it to the partners. Instead, after supper we would both sneak back into the office and try to find them. It was a wonderful world for me. What was inside that computer became my life. It was a puzzle really, a maze, one that stretched from Sioux Falls to the ends of the earth, even in 1979 when I started college.

I entered the University of Illinois in September, 1979. In June of 1980 I married Yuri Belski. My mother nearly dropped dead. Yuri was a Russian Jewish immigrant from Chicago. He was four years older than I was and already working toward his Ph.D. in computer science. He was my teaching assistant for one of the first computer courses I took. My friends all called him Super Nerd. But he was the first man who ever took an interest in me, and I fell in love. We had everything in common—the fact that we were both out of it socially, the fact that we were both computer hackers, the fact that we were in love and in lust with each other. Our bodies were a puzzle we were constantly trying to figure out. Then suddenly, we began to hit the jackpot each time we made love. No wonder we had to get married.

Of course, I could have simply moved in with Yuri. That's what he asked me to do. But I wasn't that kind of girl. So he proposed marriage. When I happily called my mother with the news, she was scandalized. "A foreigner," she kept

4

saying, "and a Russian to boot! How can I hold my head up in Sioux Bluffs?"

"We can't hold the wedding in Sioux Bluffs anyway," I tried to comfort her. "Yuri wants to get married by a rabbi." I don't know if she fainted or the phone went dead, or what. But there was a definite silence on the other end of the line.

We got married in Chicago by a reform rabbi who kept calling me Rebecca. I'm sorry to say Yuri's family was much more accepting than my own mother, who wouldn't even taste the stuffed cabbage that we had for our reception, or the borscht. I know that she tried to be as pleasant as possible to Yuri, though she did whisper to me right before the ceremony, "Does he always walk around with four pens in his pocket?" Hey, I was happy. At least he wasn't wearing his pocket protector.

It was a great marriage while it lasted, and it lasted straight through my college career and beyond into our embryonic careers. We had some fantastic evenings together. We both learned to cook. We became night owls because we had to stay up late to have access to the computers we needed. We loved playing games together and doing crosswords and acrostics. There was so much we had in common. Why then didn't it last? We moved to California.

We both got positions with a company out there called Dynotech. Naturally, Yuri's position was much better than mine, as he had his Ph.D. I was merely one of the programmers. Frankly, my job wasn't what I wanted at all. Dynotech at that time saw the future in business, so I was writing financial software. Meanwhile, Yuri came to California, saw the ocean, and suddenly decided that he didn't know what life meant. "It means working for a living, getting together enough money to eat and have a roof over our heads, and maybe taking a vacation every now and then," I tried to explain it to him. But by then he was listening to different siren songs than I. Slowly, we stopped playing games together, halted the acrostics. Finally we stopped making love, that most wonderful of all puzzles. Meanwhile, I was working away at this lousy job, trying to support us both, while Yuri was involved in his existential crisis. It got to me.

Frankly, I was probably not as understanding as I should have been. But Yuri was too young to have lost himself so soon. And I was too young to devote myself to work I hated. There was a fault line between us, and it wasn't the San Andreas. Then one evening Yuri mentioned something about man's need for serial relationships, while I repeated my fantasies of love everlasting. And that was it.

In California partnerships are easily dissolved. Yuri bought out my share of the Danish modern. Slightly dazed by my departure from a marriage that had lasted a good eight years, I kissed him good-bye and headed back toward the Midwest. I figured if it was good enough for George Babbitt, it's good enough for me.

My mother was glad the marriage had failed. "He wasn't the right one for you," she said. How infuriating her condolences were! "I suppose now you'll take back your maiden name," she added, a bit too smugly.

"No, Mother," I replied. "I like Belski. Becky Belski has a nice ring to it, no pun intended, and I plan to keep on hearing that ding-dong."

"But—" she faltered. "There are no Belskis in Sioux Bluffs."

"What makes you think I'll be living in Sioux Bluffs?" I snapped, realizing by then that I probably shouldn't have come to her for comfort in the first place.

"This is your home."

"This is your home, Mother," I stressed. Then I looked at her, really looked at her, and my anger fled. She was old and tired, sad, yet hopeful. I sat down beside her and threw my arms around her. "I'm sorry, Mom," I apologized. "I'm just—you know."

"Yes." She held me. "You're young. The young are always on the move."

I held her hand. "I'm looking for something in Chicago."

6

"Chicago?" She sounded doubtful.

"Yes. Why? What's wrong with that?"

She gazed at me as if I should know something that I didn't. Then she smiled. "Nothing. I just thought maybe you'd want to try Des Moines."

I shrugged. "Too isolated. Besides, there'll be plenty of opportunities in Chicago."

And there were. It was just that for the first several weeks I didn't stumble upon anything I found particularly fascinating. And I knew that fascinating was the sort of job I had to have. I didn't want anything as mundane as financial software ever again. So while I sought out the unusual, I stayed with Yuri's parents. They weren't happy about the divorce, but they weren't monumentally upset either. It seems in Russia divorce is almost as commonplace as in California. They were sweet enough to assure me I would always be family.

Fortunately, I didn't have to overstay my welcome and test their assurances. My third week out I found something I thought I might be interested in. "We need a hacker," I was told. "Can you hack?"

Hacking is exactly why I went into computers in the first place. I pertly pointed that out to my prospective employer.

The company was called Resources, and it was based in Evanston, Illinois, which sits right on top of Chicago's northern border. If you've heard of it at all, it's probably because the Women's Christian Temperance Union was formed there. Little, prim, gray ladies still abound in Evanston. However, drinks are now being served. The city even has a liquor store, and the Northwestern students light up the bars that exist. In other words, Evanston has gone the way of all flesh.

The little gray ladies would not have approved of Resources, if they knew about it. Resources labeled itself a research firm. It did do research. Most of it bordered on the illegal. We delved into people's private lives via the computer.

In the olden days we would have been known as a private investigation agency. But none of us sat in cars with our cameras at the ready to capture an instant of illicit rapture. Now we checked the suspects' Visa bills to see who was charging what and for whom. There were about ten of us at Resources. We sat in front of sophisticated computers, breaking into other companies' computer networks to get the information we needed. Perhaps modesty would become me better, but within a year I had received two raises and was Nat Fergessen's top-of-the-line hacker.

Computer hacking is a young person's game. Nat Fergessen, our boss at Resources, was not a young man. He was pushing fifty. Office scuttlebutt had it that Nat was a lawyer. Because our work at Resources skittered on the edges and into illegality, we all sort of had the feeling that Nat must have been a disbarred lawyer. But I certainly wasn't going to come right out and ask him about it. Nor could I find information on his putative disbarment in any file I found access to. But because Nat was a lawyer, because of his connections, we did a lot of our work for the legal profession. This is how I became involved in the Aberdeen case.

The Aberdeens hit the paper and the local news at ten well before Resources got its hands on them. Daryl and Lionel Aberdeen were used to being in the papers, but usually they made the society pages. They were both stalwarts of what passes for "society" in the Midwest. I sort of took a personal interest in them because, while Yuri and I were planning our wedding, Lionel and Daryl were planning theirs. Theirs was held at the Drake, ours was held at Yuri's apartment. Theirs was outlasting ours by about two years. Theirs was not ending amicably.

It was just a wild guess of mine that the parting between the Aberdeens was less than felicitous. I made that surmise when Daryl called police from their mansion in Kenilworth to report she had just shot a prowler. It turned out to be her husband.

It was a sad situation. Right next to her bedside was a

copy of Dominick Dunne's *The Two Mrs. Grenvilles*. Worse yet for Daryl, Lionel recovered. He accused her of attempted murder. "He could have been a prowler," she was quoted as saying.

Well, who doesn't love scandal? I followed the story of the Aberdeens as voraciously as the next tabloid reader. But as suddenly as the story flared up, it died. The Aberdeens and Daryl's family the Mellons—no, not those Mellons— were people of great influence in Chicago.

The next we, the public, heard of the two lovebirds, they had both filed suit for divorce. The charge? Extreme mental cruelty. Certainly, Lionel had cause. I can see how being shot could create doubt in a husband's mind as to his wife's disposition toward him. But what would be Daryl's side of it? That Lionel cruelly recovered? I was as ready as the next person to enjoy the carnage that this case would engender.

Nat called me into his office one fine, bright morning—it was about ten. I never showed up until ten. But then, as I always explained to Nat, I worked into the evening hours when others signed off from their own networks, which gave me easier access.

Nat looked at his watch as I entered his office. I sat down. I was wearing my usual work clothes, sweatsuit and sneakers. I find that taking quick twenty-minute walks helps clear my brain. One can't sit before the screen all day. "Do you have a suit?" Nat asked me.

"A suit?"

"Yeah. One of those things women wear to look respectable."

"A suit." I pondered the question. "I have one that I bought for job interviews."

"Yeah. I remember. It was gray. It made you look like a virgin."

Apt enough. I hadn't slept with anyone since my magnificent Yuri started trying to find the meaning of life. Oh, not that I hadn't tried my luck on Rush Street, but my knack for not attracting men seemed to be sticking with me. Sometimes I even had fantasies of flying out to California just for a healthy session of carnality with Yuri. But would I stoop so low? Or was it merely a question of being too cheap to spring for the round-trip airfare? Anyway, I had my computers. Maybe I could find someone on one of their bulletin boards.

Nat unlocked his desk drawer. "I'm giving you three hundred dollars. If anyone asks, it's for office furniture. Go out and get yourself a good-looking suit. Try Loehmann's first, please. I'll want the receipt and the change."

"I always do my shopping at Marshall Field's," I protested.

"Then I pay you too much. Loehmann's. And get back here as soon as possible, looking respectable."

I was going to ask for mileage on my car for the trip out to Morton Grove, but I decided not to push my luck. I liked my job at Resources too much. I did find a suit at Loehmann's for $250. But then I had to buy shoes and nylons. Also, I felt I needed a haircut. Since the salon I used was near Marshall Field's at Old Orchard, I stopped in at the cosmetic counter and had my face redone.

Five hours later I showed up in Nat's office, looking very respectable. He didn't seem to notice. He was too busy sadly examining the bill I handed him for the rest of my makeover. I wanted to tell him it was only money, but men can be strange about bills.

I sat primly in his office while Nat made a phone call. When he put down the receiver, he leaned over the desk and said, "You know, most of the people in this office, you can dress them up, but you can't take them out. You're dressed up. You get what I mean?"

"Uh—"

"Act like a normal person."

"But I am a normal person, Nat."

"Yeah, I know. Just a small-town girl from Iowa who has larceny in her heart. Look, we're hitting the big time now. So when I introduce you, shake hands, smile, say, 'Pleased to meet you.' After they reply, 'Likewise, I'm sure,' you sit down and shut up. Or maybe smile slightly. No. Forget that. You'd just look like an idiot. I want you to try to look intelligent.''

"Nat, all this flattery. I just can't stand it. Where are we going?''

"To Cohen, Kahn, Cohn and Kahane.''

"Couldn't they decide how to spell it?''

"Yeah, with a sense of humor like that, we're going to lose this case.''

"What case is that, Nat?''

"The Aberdeen divorce case.''

I started salivating.

2

WHEN we arrived at the law offices, we didn't see Cohen,
Kahn, Cohn or Kahane. We saw Bellini Reese, the preemi-
nent and most expensive divorce lawyer in Chicago. Entering his office would have made me, had I been a client,
immediately worry about the bill. The floor was wall to wall
Persian carpets, lapped on top of one another. On the wall,
Reese had the comfort of a Modigliani, a Klee, and, yes, the
ever-present David Hockney. Here I lost my respect for his
taste in art for art's sake, unless the Hockney was a gift he
felt obliged to display.

The furniture, when I sank into it, was office—durable,
comfortable, leather. Kleenex boxes in needlepoint cozies
were strategically placed within easy reach of wherever one
sat. Divorce and therapy obviously went hand in hand.

Since we were alone when we first entered the office, Nat
and I sat in hushed reverence, admiring this display of
well-garnered wealth, until the side door opened and this
impeccably tailored gnome entered, smiled brightly at us,
and said, "Nat, and you must be—"

I stood, reached for his outstretched hand, and stammered, "Becky Belski, divorced already." He laughed. I liked him.

Nat gave me one of his meaningful looks, indicating I should sit down and shut up. So I sat and listened while Bellini, as he told me to call him, and Nat discussed old times at the University of Michigan law school, a reminiscence brought on by the untimely passing of one of their fellow graduates from a heart attack. "It's going around these days," Nat commented brilliantly.

The social niceties taken care of, Bellini looked around him, preparatory, I thought, to opening the case up to us. I was dying to know which side of the Aberdeen divorce he was representing. I hoped it was Lionel. That would be easier. After all, he had been shot. Daryl Aberdeen was the shooter. I leaned forward expectantly. Bellini smiled at me. It was a very comforting smile. Did I dare ask him how much he billed an hour for that smile? No, I daren't. "We're waiting for my associate," he explained. He sighed. I guessed that he was used to waiting for his associate. Finally, he flipped on his intercom and said, "Ms. Wilson, is Michael anywhere in the building?"

Then he smoothly turned and asked Nat about his golf game. Before Nat could finish describing the glories of his new golf cart, the door to the office burst open like a shot, as they say, and our attention was directed to what had become center stage. There stood—be still my melting heart—a classic example of pure, unadulterated, ethnic hunk, so common to Chicago, with its influx of immigrants from every corner of the globe, and so attractive to those of us who are born white bread. He even had that sort of stupid look on his face that one can appreciate only if one is looking elsewhere along the body. "I'm sorry, Bellini. I was in the law library and lost track of time."

Bellini dismissed his excuse with a short, insincere smile. "Michael Rosen, my associate; Nat Fergessen and Becky Belski of Resources."

I stood to shake hands. Michael Rosen had a good handshake, firm but not oppressively so. I fell back into my seat and smiled when he sat down in the chair next to mine. I smiled until all his papers slid from his file. I knelt down to help him pick them up, only to find my body being treated like a soccer ball by his head as he crashed up against me. I tumbled over onto my backside, legs splayed, and couldn't help but think how much more appropriate my sweatsuit would have been, had I known there was to be physical combat. Between Michael's profuse apologies and my gracious acceptances, once I scrambled onto my knees, thus snagging my nylons, we managed to gather his papers and return to our seats. As I straightened my skirt over my developing run, I noticed Bellini staring at Michael Rosen with a look of patience tried.

Michael seemed not to notice, or perhaps he was used to it. In either case, he got out his long legal pad and was ready to write.

"This is going to be a difficult case," Bellini began.

Michael was writing. I looked over and saw, "Difficult case."

"Michael, not yet," Bellini told him.

Michael Rosen settled back in his chair and made an effort to compose himself.

Bellini continued. "We're representing Daryl Mellon Aberdeen."

One question answered, a second one popped into my mind. "How?" I asked.

Bellini smiled. "Both the suit and the cross-suit are for mental cruelty. Daryl is a dear girl, a sweet child, yes, a little on the dumb side. All that inbreeding. But no woman is going to pick up a pistol and shoot her husband for no reason. Daryl, at this point, is not willing to discuss her reasons. We have to assume she was provoked. Right now all Daryl wants is a fair, equitable settlement for the time and energy she has put into this marriage. Since the dear ones did not have a prenuptial agreement, it'll be up to the court to decide who gets what, unless—and this is where Resources comes in—we lawyers go into court with a settlement already in hand. Now, I've made a good start getting Daryl what she needs to embark upon a new life with the support agreement. However, we are operating under the handicap of the unfortunate incident of unauthorized pistol use."

"She shot her husband," I straightened the words out for him.

"Allegedly," he noted. "But the shooting is only part of it. This is going to be an intricate case. We're talking money here, and property, and families. Both the Mellons and the Aberdeens lace the North Shore—Wilmette, Kenilworth, Lake Forest. Their friends are mutual and intertwining.

"Now at this point you may be wondering why I called you, Nat. What can you do for me that I can't do for myself? From a lawyer's point of view, the process of discovery is slow and time-consuming. Sure, that means more billable hours. But clients don't mind paying when they see results. I want to get Daryl the settlement she's asking for. So what I want Resources to do is discover enough of what went on in that marriage to assure that neither side wants to go into open court with any of the sordid details. Assuming there are sordid details. And that's an assumption I've found one can always safely make.

"I originally thought that this was going to involve legwork. But Nat says you can do it all by computer," he addressed himself straight to me.

"We can do an awful lot by computer," I assured him. "We can certainly establish precisely the network of family and friends surrounding the—uh, unfortunate couple."

"Arrest records? Bank statements? Charges?"

"Certainly. If anything's found its way into a computer network, I can get my hands on it," I promised.

"At this point, I don't know what sort of information I'm going to need to get my client what she feels she deserves. So the more information you can gather, the better. Michael will liaise with you. He's already prepared a list of people we would like you to explore, people who might be viable witnesses for our side."

I looked at Michael and smiled. It was wasted. He was searching for the list. I was afraid there was going to be another avalanche of papers.

"Michael," Bellini said to his associate, "why don't you take Becky to your office so you can go over what we talked about earlier?"

Michael had his pen in his mouth when he tried to say, "Good idea." But we got the point anyway.

I stood. The skirt of my suit fell silkily over my slip. Bellini stood also. I went over to the desk to shake his hand. I was wrong about him. He wasn't really a gnome. He must have been a good five feet four. "We'll meet again, I'm sure," he said to me.

I smiled and turned. I gave Nat a wink, then marched to the door that Michael was holding open for me. He sort of looked as if someone had just kicked him in the stomach. He was bent over, making sure the files didn't fall again, at least not in the office.

A second later, we found ourselves in the outer office. Ms. Wilson inspected Michael with some amusement. Michael still had the pen between his teeth, so I had to guess at what he was saying. I was sure it was something about following him to his office, so I trailed along as we went down a skylit corridor, walking on plush beige carpet until we hit the elevator bank. Down one floor the carpet wasn't so plush, nor were the offices spaced so far apart. We stopped before one that said Michael Rosen, Esq. Somehow I just knew his mother had bought the plaque for him.

He opened the door for me, and we went inside. Michael did have a window, but that's the only comparison one could make with Bellini Reese's office. The rug here was institutional. But the desk was nice, wide and wooden. Michael had a high-backed brown leather chair behind it and two comfortable armchairs before it. He also had a bookcase where he kept law books and a series of novels that focused on the law. "My hobby," he said, as I walked to the bookcase and searched through the titles. "I spend some of my weekends going to garage sales, looking for these books."

I turned back toward him. Quite a change had overtaken Michael Rosen since he'd left Bellini's office. He seemed calm and confident and not a bit flustered. I smiled. He seemed to understand what I was smiling about. He shook his head. "I don't know what it is, but every time I'm in Bellini's presence, I act like an idiot."

"Maybe it's a technique he's perfected with previous associates," I suggested.

"No. I think it's me and how I got this job. You see, he knew my mother in high school. He was sweet on her, she says, but she thought he was a little putz."

"So maybe he sensed her contempt, and he's taking it out on you now." I kept coming up with explanations.

He shrugged. "I act like such a fool in front of him."

"Aren't there other lawyers you can work with?"

"But I want to be the best damned divorce attorney there is," Michael said with some intensity. "And there's no one better to learn from than Bellini Reese."

"Hmm," I said thoughtfully. "There's so much pain involved in divorce."

"Yes," he agreed. "My mother says that's why I've never been married."

Or it could be the reason he never married was his mother. After all, he had mentioned his mother twice within five minutes. "Do you live with your mother?" I wondered.

"God, no! I live right off Addison, a few blocks from Halsted Street. And you?"

"Evanston."

"Ah, right. That's where Resources is." He checked his watch. "Listen, do you want to discuss all this over drinks and maybe an early dinner?"

Tempting, but—"What's the time frame on this Aberdeen investigation?" I asked professionally.

"Hey, we're lawyers. Time means nothing to us," he assured me.

I smiled. There is, occasionally, humor in truth. I agreed to go with Michael Rosen. After all, it would be almost like a date, something I hadn't had for—oh well, never mind. Let's just say it was like high school again, where I was always available. Not that I didn't go out at all. The guys from Resources often got together for drinks when we felt Nat was overworking us. But somehow our labor grievances and our personal lives faded when someone brought up the latest development on the hard disk or whether mouses would always be a sign of computer illiteracy.

I expected drinks and dinner with Michael to be a variation on a theme. After all, either of us would be able to deduct the meal, though I was sure he had more leeway in that department than I. But the evening with Michael turned out to be more social than professional. I suppose that was my fault, as I kept asking Michael questions about himself. His answers were highly amusing in a self-deprecating manner. It was like listening to a comedy routine. Humor in a man can make up for a lot of other faults—not that Michael had any major faults I knew about, except wanting to make his way in the world as a divorce lawyer.

When he asked me about myself, I told him I was happily divorced from a wonderful guy who was in California, trying to find himself. We talked about my love of computers because I couldn't really talk about any other love. "Yeah," he sighed. "It's hard. There's no time to really make connections anymore."

He sounded as lonely as I sometimes felt.

When we left the restaurant, which was Peruvian and located in Evanston, I asked Michael if he wanted to come up to my apartment for coffee. Michael stopped dead on the sidewalk. "What does this mean?" he asked me.

Men!

"It means either you want coffee or you don't."

He smiled. He took my hand. "Yes. Why not?" he said.

I blush over my own boldness. I hadn't really been propositioning him. Honestly. But here I was, a virginal two years without Yuri or any other suitable male companion, when Michael Rosen came into my life. Call it timing. Or call it a feeling of general well-being after drinks and a bottle of wine at dinner. Yes, once we got to my apartment, I'm afraid the coffee never got brewed. Until morning. Instead, our blood, perhaps excited by the spicy food, led us to fall into bed for an evening of unbridled lust.

Michael had a knack for unbridled lust.

It was a night to remember. Sex-starved as I was, I barely let poor Michael get any sleep. But he rose to each occasion, and the next morning we woke up satiated if not refreshed.

We also woke to the realization that we hadn't done a thing on the Aberdeen case. So while I showered, Michael made a quick dash to his car and the corner rip-off grocer, as he wanted something more than water for breakfast.

I sprayed perfume over the bod before I got back into my working clothes, in this case my sweats. Michael was already at my kitchen table, with his pad and orange juice, milk, and cereal. A health nut. No wonder he'd had so much stamina last night. I was tempted to ask if he learned these habits at his mother's knee, but I didn't want to ruin my new vision of him. So far, during our night of passionate sinning, he had avoided all mention of his mother. Maybe I had misjudged him after all.

He looked up and found me watching him. We smiled at each other. I felt a warm glow suffuse my body. No, it wasn't passion. It was just, well, you know how it is. With some people, I suppose, you'd rather not see them in the morning. But it wasn't that way with Michael. I liked him sitting there at my kitchen table.

He frowned. "I don't have copies of these names," he admitted. "Stupid of me not to make them."

"That's okay. We can run over to Resources and copy

them." And then I noticed how many names there were. I tried not to look discouraged, but there were pages and pages. The Aberdeens obviously led busy lives.

"Would you like me to explain who all these people are?" Michael asked.

"Let me look them over first. You don't, by any chance, have birth dates for any of them?"

"No."

"So you're going to have to give me the approximate ages, if you know them. I don't want to waste time looking up aunts and uncles with the same name."

"A lot of them are juniors or thirds and fourths."

I took the list from his hand and started reading through the names.

"What's probably going to happen," Michael said, "is that you'll do all the investigative work, prepare a dossier on each of them; and then I'll go and get a deposition from the ones who'll advance Daryl's case. Of course, we need to know what the others will be saying too, because we don't want Lionel to be able to spring any surprise testimony on us."

I was listening with half an ear while Michael described tactics. Meanwhile, I was eyeing the list, moaning to myself at the similarities of the names and probably of the people. I already knew the type of networking I would discover: same godparents, same church, same prep schools, same yacht clubs. My eyes slid down the alphabetized list. I was becoming more depressed every minute. This was going to be one hell of a boring assignment. And then my eyes stopped.

I floundered, then found the name again. I felt a sweat break out over me, and the sweet smell of my perfume rose with my panic. I saw him oh so clearly in my mind. He had been double my age, with curly brown hair and a big smile. He was always asking me if I wanted to go outside and play catch with him. I loved him. I adored him. I had never known anyone so beautiful.

I had forgotten all about him, about all of them, until—

"Becky, what's the matter?" Michael asked. He put his hand on my forehead, then took out his handkerchief and wiped my forehead dry. "What is it? I know. Low blood sugar. You need something to eat."

I couldn't tell Michael. I wouldn't tell Nat. I had reconstructed my past, leaving out my real mother's incarceration for murder. I was Becky Belski, simple Iowa girl from Sioux Bluffs. And yet here on the list my past rose up to me with the name of my stepbrother, William Townsend III.

3

HOW many years had I pushed the past aside and never thought of it? The murder had happened twenty-four years ago. My mother shot my stepfather, and after that I never saw Billy again. Or had I? Was he at the trial? Had he been there in the house when my stepfather was shot? Had I?

Everything was so vague. Everything! It was as if I had deliberately blotted it out of my mind. And while I could remember Billy, I couldn't in the least recall my stepfather.

Except sometimes in my dreams I saw a figure, tall, straight, stern. He was rushing down the stairs toward us, toward me, no kindness, no pity, no compassion. I couldn't see his face. There was a big, round window on the stairs, and it cast the light behind him as he descended. The sunlight swept through his hair, giving him the appearance of an avenging angel. And then I would wake up, never knowing who the figure was or what he represented.

I stood and let the list of names fall from my hand. "I need to lie down," I told Michael. He helped me to my bed, the bed that just last night had seen our far-flung passion. Now it felt like a deathbed. The bell was tolling.

"What should I do?" Michael asked worriedly. "Do you need a doctor?"

"I just need to rest for a few minutes. I saw a name, that's all, someone I once knew."

"On the list?"

"Obviously on the list, Michael!"

"Well—"

"Don't worry. It won't compromise my integrity," I assured him, feeling better now that I was lying down and had vented a bit of anger.

"I wasn't—"

"My investigation will be very thorough."

"Look, Becky—"

"Michael, take the list to Resources, have it copied, place it in my mailbox."

"What if your boss—"

"I never come in before ten. He won't expect me. It's easier to gain access late at night."

"Then I'll come by tonight after I've finished work. Is that okay?"

"Yes. I think I'd like that." I smiled weakly but bravely up at him.

Michael was still wavering. But he left, convinced by my continuing assurances that I would be okay. And after a short nap, I was okay. The nightmare was gone. Only the name on the list remained.

I tried to sort through my feelings about that name. What was it that I was hesitant about? After all, Billy and I had been friends. Had been, until my mother murdered his father. Instead of fainting at the sight of his name, I should be intrigued. Wouldn't I like to know what had happened to him as much as he might like to know what had happened to me?

If he ever gave me a thought. Which I doubted. He was presumably married now, with children, and had put all of this behind him, as had I. It was probably as dim a memory to him as it was to me. Except Billy was ten when his father had been shot and I was only five, so I'm sure he remembered more of it than I, who could recall practically nothing.

I did try occasionally to piece that time of my life together. I would wake up some mornings and go into my mother's bedroom and ask her if she knew what had happened to me when I was a little girl. And she would repeat the basics: My mother shot my stepfather; she was sent to prison; she died. And so there I was with my new mother in Sioux Bluffs and wasn't that okay?

Of course, it was okay. No one could have a better mother than Winnie McKennah, and for some reason I would always feel guilty after these sessions, as if I were rejecting her for a past I couldn't remember. So after a while, I simply stopped asking. It was easier to put the past aside completely.

But now this name on a list had drawn me back a quarter of a century. Maybe that's what my mother had been afraid of when I decided to relocate to Chicago, that somehow I would run into my past again.

I got into the office about eleven. When I checked in my mailbox, the list of names was there. I got to work. Nat stopped by to ask how it was going. "It's just preliminary now; you know that," I scolded.

"Nothing that I can feed to Bellini?"

"I thought I was to liaise with Michael Rosen."

"Ah, that kid," Nat said derisively.

"Kid?"

"Or as Bellini calls him, the klutz. You know how it is, you owe someone, so you do them a favor. Michael's a favor, from what I understand. He's not worth much except for matinee value."

"Matinee value?"

"Bellini keeps him at counsel's table so the ladies of the courtroom can swoon."

"Umm. Perhaps Bellini underestimates Michael."

"Bellini never underestimates anyone. He's very good at sizing people up. He liked you."

"Maybe it was the suit."

"So what can I give him?"

"Of the names I've checked so far, more than half are divorced. It doesn't bode well for the stability of the Aberdeen social circle."

"Arrest records?"

"Give me a chance, Nat. I've only been on this for a couple of hours."

He backed off. I returned to my supposedly restful screen, partitioned off from my fellow workers by gray sectioning. The only time we were aware of one another was during our free throws to the baskets, where we dumped our soda cans and candy wrappers. Good health and computers simply do not go together.

In between waiting for the information I was searching for to pop up on the screen, I thought about what Nat had said concerning Michael Rosen. I resented Bellini thinking of Michael as a matinee idol with nothing between the ears. And how could he call Michael a klutz? Certainly, Michael wasn't a klutz in bed. I would have noticed. I think. My experience, such as it was, had been limited to Yuri before last night. Still, I had achieved a state of bliss with Michael that is referred to in various salacious magazines as—oops, here came my records.

However, I would concede that Michael did have one major fault. Not many people want to grow up to be a divorce lawyer, certainly not the best divorce lawyer in the country. It seemed to me that there was more to aim for in life. If one had to be a lawyer, one could at least be involved in civil rights. I remember, even with my own no-fault divorce from my formerly beloved Yuri, that there was pain, the pain of eight years down the drain, if nothing else. Divorce is the death of dreams. Neither my mother nor Yuri's family could make up for the fact that I no longer was a part of somebody else. I was alone, as my mother has been alone all these years in Sioux Bluffs.

At least she had me, I thought. I wondered. If I had had

a child with Yuri, would that have been some consolation for his loss or would it have simply caused problems between us, as children did with so many other divorced couples?

I wondered if Bill Townsend had been torn between his mother and his father. Did Bill live with us or his mother? His mother, probably, because I could remember so little about him. I thought of picking up the phone and calling my mother in Sioux Bluffs to tell her the news. But I didn't. It always discomforted her when I made any reference to my rather scarlet past as the daughter of a murderer. And Winnie was getting on in age. She had already been upset enough by my divorce, though not as upset as she was about the marriage to begin with.

It was after seven when I could trust myself to get to work on William Townsend III. By then I was sure Nat Fergessen would be safely ensconced in his lovely, Skokie three-bedroom home, defrosting something in his microwave. The charming Pearl Fergessen had stopped cooking the moment her last child went off to college. This was probably why Nat arranged for a business lunch each day. Certainly, he wasn't losing any weight from the lack of her culinary activities. But at least he wouldn't be here to bother me now.

William Townsend. There were tons of them. Why couldn't I remember his middle name? It would be, yes, there, Buckman. I remember. He used to call me Elizabeth Diane and I used to retaliate with William Buckman. How could I have forgotten? I searched. Wonderful. He had a driver's license. Big help that was. Car registration. Birth certificate! Father, William Buckman Townsend II. Mother, Sarah Ann Mansfield. Date of birth, April 19, 1955. My fingers flew over the keys of the computer, as I tried to unlock that bit of my past that was Bill Townsend. Finally, I hit that jackpot. I found his place of employment and broke into the personnel files. The computer spewed forth its data. William Townsend III, hired as a commercial artist by Dano, Associates. So he was in advertising. He made pretty good money; not that he needed it, judging from his home address in the eastern part of Wilmette, right near Lake Michigan.

Bill was unmarried. Strange. The S was blackened, not the D for divorced. This was probably the reason for the insurance company's intensive medical checkup. Bill was totally healthy. I was glad to hear it. But I was more interested in the health form's information on family members. Father deceased, 1966, murdered. Oh, lord. How embarrassing to have to put that down. Poor Bill. Mother, deceased, 1963, fall.

Fall? Father, murdered; mother fell. This certainly must have given the insurance company pause. It gave me pause too. Here I had been worried about Bill being torn between mother and father after the divorce. It never occurred to me that his real mother was already dead. And if Sarah Townsend had died only three years before her husband, then when and where had my mother met and married the man?

My screen blanked to black. I had been sitting there for five minutes, contemplating Bill's deceased parents. I could have kicked myself. Resources operates commando style. Like breaking and entering, when one violates someone else's computer files, one does it and gets out fast. Yet, here I'd sat on this file for over five minutes now, probably more like ten. Someone could be tracing me. Then Nat would really need his connections in the legal arena. Still, there was one more thing I had to get from Bill's medical form.

Siblings: Alan Mansfield Townsend, b. 1945. Still living. The older brother. I didn't remember him. And me, his stepsister? I wasn't mentioned at all.

I got out.

The buzzer sounded, and I jumped. I thought I had been caught with my hand in someone else's computer files, but it was merely Resources' front door bell.

I wasn't alone in the office, so I didn't have to go to answer it myself. Matter of fact, so involved was I in finding out all about Bill Townsend, I had forgotten that Michael

Rosen was coming around tonight, until one of my fellow toilers called my name.

I stood and backed away from my partition. Taking a few steps forward, I came face to face with Michael. He was in a gray pin-striped three-piece suit. I was in gray sweats. When his mouth dropped open, I had an idea of how I must look to him. I have a habit, when I'm working, of sticking pencils through my hair until it looked as if I were wearing a bird's nest on top of my head. "Becky?" he asked, as if he didn't recognize me.

"Michael." I smiled and quickly tried to comb my hair with my fingers. "Gee."

"You said to stop by."

"Yeah." God, why couldn't I be Superman and have a neat outfit in the phone booth? "Uh, Michael, why don't we go over to my apartment and discuss what I've discovered." I grabbed my research and shoved it into the canvas satchel that served as my briefcase. How pitiful it looked next to his burnished leather. I slipped on my old beige raincoat and snapped my fannypack around my waist. I was ready to go anywhere, except out with Michael Rosen.

As we were waiting for the elevator, Michael said, "How nice to be able to go to work dressed so—um—casually."

"I look like a slob, don't I?"

"Slob? Uh—"

"Pretend I'm a client," I suggested.

Since Michael had his car outside, he suggested I leave my bicycle chained in the vestibule. As I slid into his red Porsche, I wondered if perhaps we didn't have different value systems. "Nice car," I complimented, when he settled into the driver's seat.

"All the girls like it," he assured me. He looked at me. "Do you want to change, perhaps, so we can get something to eat? I've been taking depositions all day and I'm really starved."

I didn't want to tell him I'd already had a Butterfinger and two Baby Ruths for dinner, so when we reached my apartment, I said, "Why don't you wait here in the car? It won't take me more than five minutes."

"You can do it in five minutes?" he wondered.

"Here." I shoved my canvas satchel at him. "Read some of the research I've got."

I dashed up the stairs to my apartment, not even bothering to check the mail. I knew that somewhere in my apartment I had something to wear other than the suit I'd bought yesterday, something preferably knit so I wouldn't have to worry about ironing. Yes, here was a black knit skirt, always respectable, and a white turtleneck. God, was I going to look hot! I threw them on, then remembered what I'd forgotten. My bra. Okay, off with the turtleneck, on with the bra. Jesus, when did that white turn so dingy gray? Tomorrow I would take a lunch hour and buy some sexy lingerie, if I made it past tonight with Michael. Now, I faced the challenge of all women. Where was I to find a pair of pantyhose without a run? Sure, I had some but they were all stuck in that plastic sack for delicates that my mom gave me for my birthday last year. It was so hard to get around to doing a delicate wash when there were all my sweats to get through.

Damn. But hope was at hand. Here was a fresh pair, straight from the package. The only trouble was they were purple. I know what happened. I picked them up by mistake and had meant to return them. When was that? Yeah, last year. Well, I guess returning them was out now. Would they really look purple in the dark anyhow? I slipped them on, then rushed to the bathroom to see what could be done about my makeup. First I had to brush the hair off my face.

I washed my face, getting the turtleneck wet, then did a quick two-minute job with my brushes and creams. I was ready. Grabbing a hip-length sweater, I dashed down the stairs and breathlessly reentered the Porsche. "Better?" I asked Michael.

He looked me over and smiled. "I hate purple."

Wouldn't a real gentleman have pretended he didn't notice the color of my pantyhose?

We went to Carmen's for deep-dish pizza. I had resolved not to speak to Michael the entire evening, but it was sort of hard, as we went over several of the names I had investigated. Then Michael gave me fresh information on the ones he wanted me to concentrate on.

By the time the pizza arrived, I was too thoroughly involved in the Daryl Aberdeen divorce case to really care about Michael's rude comment on my nylons. "What's your case going to be based on?" I asked him. "I mean, she did shoot her husband. It's there in black and white on the police blotter."

Michael sweetly took his napkin and wiped the beer foam off my upper lip. "People can be provoked to violence," he told me.

"So? How was she provoked?"

"I'm not at liberty—"

"Oh, Michael! Stop being such a prig. Tell me."

Michael considered it. "Let's just say there were drugs and violence and miscarriages involved."

"Oh lord."

"It's not a soap opera."

"But it will be if it gets to court," I pointed out.

"Bellini thinks that neither family will let it go so far. You know how these people like to keep things dark and hidden. Becky?"

It was those words, "dark and hidden." For some reason, when Michael said them, that house popped into my mind, that house with the staircase and—Oh God, who was it coming down the stairs? What was happening to me? Why did I want to know now? I didn't want to know!

"Becky?" Michael took my hand. "Are you all right?"

I shook off the shadow. "People's lives can be so disastrously complicated," I said rather mournfully.

"Thank God," Michael replied. "Otherwise, I wouldn't be making a living."

I didn't argue when he picked up the check for the pizza. He'd probably charge it to Daryl Aberdeen in any case.

We drove back to my place in his Porsche. I was glad I had brought my sweater because it was getting chilly. Soon the damn snow would be falling, and we would be slushing through it for seven months. For a moment I thought wistfully of California, and of Yuri.

"You're lost again," Michael noted.

And I had been lost. Here we were, already parked in front of my apartment. "Do you want to come up?" I asked him, wondering what his answer would be.

"I'm glad you asked," he said.

I kept the lights very low so he didn't see the dingy gray bra. Yet I didn't keep them too low to miss his exquisitely beautiful body. Men have all the luck. They're so slim and trim, with no bulges except the one that matters, while we poor women are left to fret over our roundness. Yes, the angular definitely appealed to me.

To say we fell asleep in each other's arms would make the evening more romantic than it actually was. True, the sex was great. Michael was a warm and comforting lover, whose hands seemed to know how to sweep joyfully across my body. However, our postcoital bliss was compounded by a long work day, a large pizza, and a pitcher of beer. Sleep was irresistible, even though Michael did bitch a bit about having to fight the traffic early next morning into the city.

I didn't hear the phone when it rang. I was lost in dreamy thoughts of entangling bodies. I suppose that's because Michael and I were so intertwined. But Michael grabbed it. I noticed because his elbow came down on my breast. "Who?" he said first. Then, "Oh, God, sorry. Just a minute, please. Sorry, I thought I was home," he whispered, as he handed me the phone.

"Hello?" I said.

"Becky?"

"Yes?"

"This is Joel Gibbons, from the Sioux Bluffs police."

My heart stopped. "Joel," I said. We had gone through

high school together, then he went into the army, I to college. Please God, let it not be anything about—

"I'm sorry to have to be the one to tell you, but—"

"No!" I said, shooting up in bed.

"It's your mom, Becky. She had an accident as she was driving home from her bridge game. Doctor Taylor thinks you should get up here pronto."

"She'll be okay?"

"Uh—"

"Is she dead, Joel!"

"Not yet, Becky, but—gee, it doesn't look good."

"All right. I'm coming up there. I'll—I don't know how I'll get there, but I'll be there."

"What is it?" Michael asked, as I put down the receiver.

"My mother. She's been in an accident."

Michael helped me pack some things. He was the one who got together the clothes he thought I would need, and my cosmetics. I was too busy crying and fretting. "How are you going to get there?" he asked.

"Drive."

"Becky, you're in no condition to drive."

"I'll be all right. It's faster. By the time I got a plane to Des Moines and drove over to Sioux Bluffs, it'd take twice as long."

He tried to convince me otherwise. Then he made me promise to call him as soon as I got to Sioux Bluffs. By three-thirty I had hit I-88, heading west.

4

BY ten o'clock I was in the hospital with my mother. The whole drive west I had tried to figure out how my mother could have had an accident. The roads were perfect. There was no sign of rain. Her bridge partners all lived within two miles of her. I couldn't understand what had happened.

When I arrived, I found out. My mother had suffered a minor stroke, which caused her to lose control of her car. She had been going over the town's only overpass, had struck steel on the side of the road and then careened down onto the grassy shoulder and into a field. Since there were other cars on the road, help came almost immediately. But she had gone into shock and then suffered another stroke. "But people recover from strokes," I told Dr. Taylor.

"Let's hope so, Becky," he said to me, and I just knew he didn't believe she would recover. The bastard!

My mother was in intensive care, and she was hooked up all over the place. Right then I hated doctors more than lawyers. Which made me think of Michael. I called him as promised and asked him if he would please phone Resources for me and explain what was happening.

Then I waited. I wasn't alone. All my mother's friends were at the hospital, waiting with me. I know they meant to be kind, but I didn't want their company or their quiet chatter. I just wanted to be with my mother. But she was unreachable because of all the machines surrounding her.

And then, just as you see on television, the reassuring beeps died into one lone tone, the green line fell flat, and those damned nurses and doctors raced into my mother's room with more machines. Through the window I could see her body convulsing as they worked on her. They just couldn't let this final indignity pass her by.

But she was dead.

Lord, how did I make it through those first three days between visitation and burial? For one thing I called Yuri. For the first time in my life I realized how terribly alone I was. He was the only one I had to turn to. And he came, God bless him.

Everyone attended the funeral. Sioux Bluffs is a small town. My mother had lived in it for twenty-four years. She had made herself a part of a community, which is something I couldn't say about myself. So she had the sort of burial everyone wishes for, surrounded by people who cared about her. Thank God Yuri was there to stand between me and the funeral director, who tried to sell me the plot next to my mother.

But then Yuri left. He had to get back to California. He was now a member of a think tank that used computers to predict the future. I was proud of him. He had managed to combine his philosophical longings with his science. He had a purpose in life. I didn't know what I had, except being nosy about other people. I no longer even had a mother.

"Will you be all right?" he asked.

"I don't know," I confessed.

"Call me. Any time. You know that."

I hugged him tight and didn't want to let go. But I was alone.

Though not for long. I still had to confront the lawyer and

worse, the real estate agency. My mother's will was simple. She left everything to me, except for a few bequests to her friends who had admired this piece of furniture or that platter. There was nothing I would miss. The lawyer promised to wrap up my mother's affairs, whatever that meant. The real estate agent was a bit more pushy. "Bad to let a house stand unoccupied," she told me. "With winter coming, the animals will get in, make their nests all over the place. A house needs people. Of course, if you're planning to move up here—"

But I wasn't, as she very well knew. Except to visit my mother's grave, there would be no reason to return to Sioux Bluffs at all. There would be no more Thanksgivings or Christmases, no New Year's sherry, no Easter basket under my bed, where she had always put it, even last year, including my favorite milk chocolate bunny.

Tears came to my eyes, but there was no time to cry. Decisions had to be made. By me. When I called Nat after my mother died, he told me to take all the time I needed. But then he phoned after the funeral to wonder when I might be back. Dear Nat. Life goes on.

Finally, I decided to attach a U-Haul to the back of my car, take what I wanted from my mother's house, let the real estate agent sell the house and an estate agent arrange for the sale of my mother's property. The only problem was that I'd have to go through everything first.

In my mother's closet I found every card I had ever made her, all my school photographs, all my commendations, all the letters I had written to her from college and beyond. Oh lord, what was I to do with these? I couldn't throw them out, but what would be the point in keeping them? I shoved the box aside. I'd decide later. In the study where my mother kept her typewriter, I found her checkbook and bank books. She had a healthy balance, but then she was always a thrifty woman. I found correspondence from her friends who had moved south to Phoenix or Florida. And there in the closet were stacks of ledgers, accounting for every penny the woman spent. I shook my head. Obviously, I was adopted. I never kept track of anything.

At the bottom of the closet, behind a pile of old rubber boots with flannel linings, lay a gray metal box that looked very much like a safe deposit box. I took it out, only to find that it was locked with one of those baby locks that took a key almost as thin as aluminum foil. I was bemused. My mother had only costume jewelry, but she always had this fear that someday a prowler was going to step into the front of the house while she was out in the back, working in her garden.

When I had sorted through everything else, I took the metal box down to the hardware store and had another high school buddy cut off the lock for me. "I guess it's okay," he said, "seeing as your mom's, well, passed on."

"Thanks," I told him. I picked up the box when he was finished and started walking out.

"Aren't you going to see what's in it?" he asked.

"Why else would I have you cut off the lock?"

"Well, maybe you should open it here, in case there's another box inside with a lock."

Obviously, gossip was slow in town that day. I smiled and departed. I didn't even open the box in the car. I waited until I got home. Then I set it down on the kitchen table and lifted the lid.

My poor friend would have been very disappointed. The gossip value was nil. It was simply another ledger, and underneath that a few aging, brittle newspaper clippings.

I took the ledger out and opened it up to the very first page. "June 1, 1966. $100 rec'vd from Alan Townsend."

While I was still trying to figure that out, in the debit column I noted a long list of expenses: shoes, dresses, doctor's exam, food, movies.

Why was my former stepbrother Alan Townsend sending money to my mother?

So meticulous was my mother that she had written down

the shoe size and the dress size. These were not the sizes Winnie McKennah wore. She was never quite that small.

My eyes blinked as they fell down the page. Every month a check from Alan Townsend; every month an itemized expense list. My frugal mother always came out a few dollars ahead. The money left over was placed in a joint savings account for Winnie and Elizabeth McKennah. I flipped through the pages of the ledger. It was all here, my braces, my dancing lessons, my piano lessons, my clothing, my allowance, everything. And as the years passed, the monthly allowance from Alan Townsend increased as my mother struggled to keep up with inflation. My college also, received from Alan Townsend: tuition, books, room and board. And then in May, 1983, the checks stopped. I had graduated from the University of Illinois in May of 1983.

I sat back in the kitchen chair, dumbfounded. Why would my stepbrother, a stepbrother I didn't even remember, unlike Billy, pay for my upbringing? My mother had, after all, killed his father. Had my adoptive mother been—but that was ridiculous! Winnie McKennah was much too moral a woman even to consider blackmail!

Wasn't she?

I put the ledger to one side and gazed at what remained in the metal box. There sat a pen, a silver pen still attached to a certificate. I unfolded the certificate. It read, "To Winnie McKennah for twenty years of meritorious service." It was signed "William Townsend II, President, The Skyline Agency." My stepfather, Winnie McKennah's boss? Curiouser and curiouser.

Because when I thought about my adoption—and I hadn't really thought about it all that much once I learned my real mother was dead—I assumed that Winnie McKennah was someone the state found to take me on. I did ask her why she had adopted me, as little girls who are adopted will, and she always told me because I was the sweetest little girl she had ever seen. For me, that was enough of an answer. Now I realized I should have dug deeper.

I put the pen aside and picked up the aging newspaper articles. The edges crumbled in my hands. Hesitantly, tentatively I opened up the first one. It was an announcement of the wedding of William Townsend II to Sarah Ann Mansfield in September, 1944. Townsend was in uniform. But Sarah Mansfield was in an extravagant lace gown. The wedding was held at the Green Point Country Club, bordering on Lake Michigan. I read carefully to see if I could spot Winnie's name in the list of attendants or guests, but she wasn't mentioned.

The second article was newer, easier to unfold. The year was 1963, the article relatively short. It was an obituary notice for Sarah Mansfield Townsend, who had died tragically at home in a fall down the main staircase of the Townsends' Kenilworth estate.

Violence and the Townsends seemed to go hand in hand.

Two articles, the certificate, the ledger. They created more of a puzzle than they helped solve. I wished then that my adoptive mother had sat me down when I was old enough and explained everything to me. But she had chosen not to. So the questions I now had I alone would have to answer. And I had the resources, pun intended, to do it.

5

EVERYONE at work was very solicitous when I returned. Even Nat managed to look mournful for a few minutes while he commiserated. That was just before he asked me if everything was all settled and I was ready to get back to work. "I hesitated to give the Aberdeen case to anyone else, but we've lost two weeks."

And I've lost a mother, I wanted to scream at him. But I knew what he meant. Someone else could have just as easily extracted the superficial statistics, but he might have missed a follow-up contained in the same file. It was better to have one person with a sharp eye dedicate herself to the work. "I'll make up for the time, Nat," I promised him.

"I don't mean to push."

"What else do I have to do?" I snapped.

"I'm sorry, Becky. We all mourn with you."

And I think he meant it. But what Nat didn't realize was that, with the puzzle of my past before me, I had been rejuvenated. There were secrets to be uncovered, and I would go about it like a bulldozer, leaving no patch of earth unturned, no matter whose bones I dug up.

Michael called, sweet Michael. But I had no time for him. I was working fourteen to sixteen hours a day. Many of my friends on the other side of the Resources partitions came by to urge me to take at least a candy bar break with them. But I was relentless in my pursuit of knowledge. I heard Nat say at one point, "Leave her alone. This is therapy for her." How right he was. It was family therapy.

It was amazing how I could do my job and deal with my own problems at the same time. I had Lionel and Daryl Aberdeen to thank for that. Children of extreme wealth, they both grew up in mansions along Lake Michigan. You wouldn't be able to see their houses from Sheridan Road, which rides along the lake, because there are trees and gates and side roads distinctly labeled Private to keep out the beach traffic. But the houses were lavishly there. Nor were their owners transients such as one could find in the western suburbs of Chicago. These were North Shore people. Their families had settled near the Second City when Chicago was hog butcher to the world. Their wealth came from insurance, real estate, commodities, definitely commodities, all the exchanges, candy, steel, the rails, even one meat-processing heir. They were merchants and country gentlemen.

I found two loci of geographical interest: Kenilworth, a few blocks of prime real estate less than five miles from where I lived, and Lake Forest, four suburbs north, where most bankers made their home, taking the METRA express into the city and back again. Lionel was from Lake Forest, Daryl from Kenilworth. Their families knew each other, of course, but the children didn't really become chums until Lionel went to Colgate and Daryl attended Vassar. That's when they began to see a lot of each other.

From college both returned to Chicago, where Lionel joined his father's insurance firm, while Daryl dabbled in interior decorating. One year after their return to Chicago, they were married. I read the stories off microfiche from various newspaper sources. One of the ushers was William

Townsend III, my stepbrother. In attendance were Alan and Tricia Townsend, the first clue I had that my older stepbrother was married.

The newspapers weren't of further use until the shooting. So I had to rely on charge slips and insurance claims to find out what kind of marriage the Aberdeens had. Daryl was a prodigious spender; Lionel was no slouch himself. Brooks Brothers and Burberry add up. As far as medical claims, Lionel seemed completely healthy. But Michael was right about one thing. Daryl had suffered through two miscarriages in the last three years. That was strange in itself. She married when she was twenty-three, but waited until she reached thirty to try for a child. After all, it's not as if she had to work and save to be able to afford a house or anything. I knew if I got married again, the first thing I would do was have a—

But marriage wasn't in my future. Meanwhile, I had my computer to keep me warm. And I did find another interesting article about Lionel. He and his crew had won the Green Bay yacht race, sailing from Chicago to Kenosha, Wisconsin, and back again in the fastest time. There he was with his crew, holding the trophy. One of his crew was William Townsend III.

I pushed myself away from the computer. I had gone as far as the computer could take me on the Aberdeen case. Now I would neatly print out my report with little boxes and charts, all the graphics I had picked up in my CAD courses.

Meanwhile, I had my own discoveries to contemplate.

The trouble with using a computer is that some people don't have the good sense to store all their records in it. The computer, in other words, was little help in my mother's case. Everything that had happened to her had happened twenty-four years ago, except for her death, which I take it, from what Winnie McKennah said, occurred in prison. The only hard information I could get about my mother came from the newspapers that had been microfiched. There were pictures of her standing next to William Townsend II, my stepfather. It was funny. I couldn't even remember him. My mother? Well, there was something in her smile, so radiant on the day of her wedding, that was very familiar to me. She wore a suit and a little pillbox hat. A few of the papers just had the announcement and the picture. But then there was the local paper that had—oh my god—a picture of all of us: my mother, me, my stepfather, and Bill Townsend. Here the story gave paragraphs to my stepfather, his forbears, his breeding, his accomplishments, and the fact that he was a widower of less than a year. Oh my. The writer hadn't liked that much. I took out a pad of paper and noted down the woman's name. What I was planning to do with it, I had no idea. After fulsome paragraphs about the great William Townsend II, there was a short paragraph about my mother, Jane Peters. Mrs. Peters was a widow who up to a few weeks ago had been working as an executive secretary at The Skyline Agency.

The Skyline Agency was the Townsend firm. My mother had been a secretary there. Winnie McKennah had given twenty years of her life to The Skyline Agency. The pen in the cash box was a tribute to her dedication. So they must have known each other. But my mother was young, so very young in that picture, younger than I was now.

At least that solved one problem, why I was never sent to live with my father after my mother was convicted of murder. My father was obviously dead.

Now came the painful part. I searched the newspapers' indexes for further mention of my mother. Needless to say, she made them all on January 5, 1966, the day after she shot my stepfather.

There were pictures of her with the police, looking dazed. In the body of the story, which was long though not quite as juicy as it might have been, my mother claimed self-defense.

Very few stories followed this. I assumed that was due to the Townsend influence, not to lack of interest. After all, here was a society murder case, and everyone likes to see the rich suffer. The trial came. And now I was shocked. Instead of pleading innocent by reason of self-defense, my mother pled guilty to second-degree murder with mitigating circumstances. What brilliant lawyer had suggested that? At her sentencing hearing, people were called to testify: a doctor, friends of the Townsends, family. I was called to testify. I "sat mute on the witness stand, only able to cry." But the other witnesses had more to say. The dead Bill Townsend was "something of a bully," "not a gentleman," "perhaps a bit overbearing." The doctor had several times previously had to prescribe sedatives and tranquilizers for my mother. "I lived in deadly fear of my husband," my mother testified in her own defense. "For myself, for my child."

And yet no one said what went on inside that house, especially on the day of the murder. Neither Bill nor Alan, my stepbrothers, was at home. Bill had been at a friend's house, getting ready to return to prep school. Alan was in his last year at Princeton. Only I could have reported what went on. But I was "mute." As the prosecutor noted in his summation before the judge, "Even her own daughter has nothing to say in her defense."

But one didn't have to be a genius to read between the lines of what his social circle had to say about Bill Townsend to discover that my stepfather was a wife-abuser. Why hadn't my mother come out with a stronger defense? What kind of lousy lawyer had she hired?

Then I tried to look at it logically. At first my mother pleaded self-defense, but I noted in the story that my stepfather had been shot six times. Perhaps that was five too many. Second degree with mitigation carried a minimum sentence of four years, which was what the judge imposed, so perhaps he realized that William Townsend II wasn't as upstanding as the world had previously believed. Also, all this had occurred before the women's movement gained strength, long before women realized they had the right not to be abused. The sixties were still a time when men believed they had the right to do whatever they wanted to their wives and children. A man's home was his castle, women and children serfs within. Primitive times.

Not that things had changed all that much. Most judges were still male and they still had this male bonding with the abusers in these types of cases. But people, even male judges, were beginning to understand that you just couldn't bat a woman around whenever you felt like it. Sometimes we fight back. And I was sure that was exactly what my mother had done.

I remember, oh so vaguely, the last meeting I had with my mother. I strained even now to bring it back to me. "Forget it all," I recall her saying. "Forget everything that's happened. You'll have a good life now. I've seen to that."

I think that's what she said.

But how could I remember her exact words? It was all so long ago.

"Becky."

I looked up. "Nat."

"Are you busy?" He looked from me to the microfiche machine.

"No." I switched off the screen and rewound the tape. I didn't want him to know what I had been looking up. Which was silly. There was no one who was going to connect me with the Townsends. True, Nat did have my full name, which I always set down as Elizabeth McKennah Belski. But no one ever called me anything but Becky or Becky Belski, or when they were teasing BB or the Silver Bullet. How shocked Nat would be to know of my connection to this case.

"We have a five o'clock meeting with Bellini Reese," Nat informed me.

"Five o'clock?"

"He's in court all day. By the way, he was extremely pleased with the work you did. Needless to say, I gave you all the credit. That's the type of boss I am."

I smiled.

"Anyway, he wants you and me in his office to discuss further action on the case. So Belski, get your buttski back to your apartment and put on that lovely suit I paid for."

"Are you sure I wouldn't look more professional in another new suit? He'll probably remember this one."

"Change the blouse. Be back here at four-thirty. I'll drive."

Lord. Here came another drive to write home about. Except I didn't have a home. All I had was my apartment on Alvina Street. Though at one time I had lived in that mansion on the lake. If only I could remember.

6

WE didn't have to wait for Michael this time. He was already in Bellini's office when we arrived. I smiled at him and he smiled back a little ruefully.

Bellini looked chipper. He must have been in his fifties, but a day in court had done him no damage. I noted that he had a suit rack in the corner closet, which had its door half-open. There was a wrinkled suit hanging on it. He must have changed as soon as he returned from court. "Wonderful work," he said to me, clasping my hand in both of his. His hands were warm, and, yes, comforting. "I'm shocked at how much one can find out with a computer. I must say, it makes me very wary, especially the way you can delve into someone's financial and medical records."

"One day the American public will wake up and demand the reinstatement of its right to privacy," I stated.

"Let's hope not," Nat objected. "It'd put me out of business."

"I thought maybe I could cull your mind for any thoughts you have that might not be in your report," Bellini said to me.

"It's so hard to get ideas from cold, hard facts," I told him. "The whole person just isn't there. No one can be summed up by his or her bank statement or credit rating, not even by medical reports."

"Yes. That's why I'm sending Michael out now to get depositions from all of those we feel will be used by both sides for mutual discovery. Michael, you have had a chance to look over Ms. Belski's work, haven't you?"

Michael nodded a vigorous yes, and held up my report. I held my breath. But it seemed there would be no klutzy maneuver this time. Take that, Bellini and Nat! "So you're going to be interviewing all these people I've done the workup on?" I said to Michael, including him in the adult conversation.

"We're going to depose those who we feel will be of value to our case. That means get their sworn statements."

"Oh, I know what a deposition is," I assured him. I was thoughtful. "I'm just wondering if that's the best way to do this. I mean, for Daryl. After all, she has the most to lose, having shot her husband and everything."

Bellini smiled. "How exactly would you go about it, Ms. Belski?"

I crossed my legs and dug into the subject. "I gave a deposition once. A traffic accident. I had to go to the lawyer's office, where I was sworn. It was all very official and scary. And I was only a witness. I was even advised that I could have my own attorney present, if I wished. Needless to say, I didn't want to say anything more than I had to. I was afraid of being sued, even though I hadn't done anything except see one car run into another.

"You see, giving a deposition is an intimidating process. Unless one is a reckless advocate of one side or another, one is going to be very cautious. In other words, you won't get the dirt or the background noises."

"We already have the dirt from Daryl," Michael suggested.

"Wasn't she shoveling more b.s. than dirt?" came my

quick retort. "No, if I were handling the case, I would soften these people up first by having off-the-record conversations about the Aberdeens, just to get a sense of how useful they might be to the case, for either side."

"And yet you aren't handling the case," Nat noted almost under his breath and undoubtedly with gritted teeth.

"Interesting," Bellini said. "And time-consuming. Poor Michael would never be able to handle both the depositions and the casual conversations within the time frame I've allotted for this case."

"Michael can do the depositions; I can do the conversations. We can coordinate our plan of attack. What I find out, I'll pass along to him."

Bellini sat back, his hands together in a spire. He stared right into my eyes, and I felt he was looking into me, searching for the right answer. "Have you had a lot of one-on-one contact?"

"Only with her computer," Nat, the schmuck, said.

"I'm a very people-oriented person," I corrected Nat.

"Yeah, and all the people she knows are Apples and Tandys. Bellini, if you want a leg man, I'll get you one. But Becky belongs behind a computer screen." Was he afraid of my having any downtime that he couldn't bill for?

Bellini smiled only at me and looked down the length of my body. "She looks as if she has very good legs to me."

Sexist, true, but had I won?

"Let me think about it," he said. "Let me talk to my client and see what sort of expense she's willing to go to. Of course, if we win, we'll ask for legal fees from her ex-husband-to-be. She might like the idea of running up the tab. Michael, why don't you and Ms. Belski consult about a plan of attack, should I decide to go with her Plan B, so to speak."

"Good idea," Michael said. He stood, gripping his files tightly. But as he waited for me to advance before him, he backed up into a chair and tripped over one of its legs. I grabbed him to hold him upright. Then I nodded at Bellini, as we left the office. Bellini had an annoyed expression on his face. Poor Michael. At least Nat valued me as an employee. Or he had until this last excursion of mine. I didn't need to look at him to see he wasn't happy. And as we closed the door on our elders, I could hear Nat begin to rumble. But I would have to worry about that later.

Right now Michael and I took the elevator down to his office, where he became his old confident self again. "Michael," I said to him, as soon as he had picked up his messages and we had closed the door on the outer office, "you've got to get out of this law firm."

"Umm," he sort of mumbled.

"Bellini doesn't respect you. You do dumb things around him. You'll never get ahead here."

"He makes me feel like an idiot, like a little child who's always about to do something wrong."

"And that's exactly the way you act around him. God, Michael, you're better than that."

He looked up at me and smiled. "I know."

"Well then?"

"You don't understand, Becky. Bellini Reese's name is magic. Do you know how many people line up to get him to handle their divorces? Has he ever lost? Well, maybe once or twice. But you've got to realize that both Daryl and Lionel Aberdeen were after him to represent them."

"So why was he dumb enough to choose Daryl?"

"Because it makes the splash, don't you see? If he can get Daryl her bundle after she shot her husband, well then, the line outside his office gets longer."

"And what do you get from all this?"

"My picture in the paper standing next to him."

"Does he ever shove any of these cases he doesn't want off on you?"

"Not yet, because I'm his associate."

"You do the scut work for him."

"Look, don't you tear me down too. I had enough of that upstairs."

49

I came to him and hugged him. "I'm sorry, Michael. It's just—I worry about you."

"Really? You didn't return most of my calls."

"I was so busy with the case. You don't know what it's like being on the computer sixteen hours straight. I don't want to speak to anyone afterward. I just want to put a cold compress over my eyes and go to bed. But I was thinking about you." I smiled.

"Umm," he said, unconvinced. "Then trust me about my career, Becky. All I need is one case, one spectacular case of my own. Then it's Bellini Reese, good-bye. I open my own office, and the clients flow in, along with the bucks."

"Such nobility of purpose," I teased.

"Hey!" Then he saw I was joking and smiled with me. "So what shall we do while waiting for the word from on high?"

"Go back to my apartment?"

"Mine's closer."

"But the only pantyhose I have is the pair I'm wearing."

"There's a Walgreen's down the street. We can get you a pair of pantyhose there. I think they have one in putrid yellow that should appeal to you."

I slapped him playfully on the arm and he grabbed me. Oh god, it felt so good to be held by a man again. Sometimes I just work too damned hard!

Michael and I didn't get around to discussing business that night. After all, we did have to make love, then hippity-hop over to Walgreen's to buy my pantyhose and the basics in cosmetics, then back to his apartment to make love again. By that time we were hungry. After arguing about whether we wanted Thai or Mexican food, we settled for Evanston Italian. Then we drove over to my apartment and made love on full stomachs, after which Michael bitched about being in Evanston, which meant he had to face the morning drive again. "I mean, why did we buy all those things for you if you weren't staying at my place?"

"They're safely at your place for next time," I assured him.

He smiled. "I'm glad there'll be a next time," he told me. And I was glad too.

Michael slipped out of my arms early in the morning. His beeper hadn't sounded all night, so I guess Bellini Reese hadn't made a decision yet. I must admit, after Michael left, far from feeling his lack, I fell back to sleep. I think it was an avoidance mechanism on my part. I didn't want to face Nat after yesterday afternoon. He was bound to be pissed. So it was eleven before I woke and only then because the phone was ringing. It was Michael. I expected a slew of sweet nothings. Instead I got, "Bellini's approved of your suggestion, so we better get together and discuss tactics."

"Resources?" I suggested, knowing I would have to face Nat sooner or later.

"Resources, half an hour."

I tried to sneak past Nat's door, but he had left it open. This meant he could view anyone entering the office and the computer room beyond. "Oh, Becky, dear," he called to me, as I walked past, pretending nothing had happened.

I pivoted brightly. "Nat!" I said, as if delighted.

"Won't you come into my office?" said the spider to the fly.

"Now, Nat—" I began when I was stuck inside.

"You are not a private investigator, Becky Belski."

"We are an investigative-type firm."

"We are a research firm."

"And I'm going to be doing research."

"Becky, if you screw up my reputation with Cohen, Kahn, Cohn and Kahane—"

"But I won't. Please, Nat, this is very important to me. I can't tell you why, but it is. Now, I've never asked you for anything before—"

Nat threw up his hands. "You come in here every month, demanding a raise."

"This is more important than money. This is my life."

Nat sat back and shook his head. "I always subcontract the actual legwork."

"Look, it's not as if I'm going to be working on this alone, where Bellini Reese will be able to single me out. I will be under Michael Rosen's expert supervision."

"Now I'm really worried."

I sank down into Nat's chair, the one he keeps for clients. "Michael really has it all together, except when he's in Bellini's presence. Believe me, I know."

"Does that mean you're boffing each other?"

"Nat, please, I don't delve into your personal life with Pearl and the kids. Don't dig into mine with Michael. Let me just say I have reason to believe there's a lot more to Michael Rosen than the stumbling idiot he becomes in Bellini's presence."

"I hope so, for all our sakes."

"Michael's going to be here any minute now. May I use the conference room?"

Defeated, Nat gave me a go-ahead nod. Therefore, I had everything prepared when Michael arrived. There were yellow pads on the table and two Styrofoam cups filled with coffee, plus packs of sugar and creamer. The Styrofoam passed for our elegant silver coffee set.

Michael looked tired when he arrived. "I'm worried," he confessed, even before he had a chance to tell me how wonderful I looked. Then he started pacing around the conference room. "I'm not a nosy person basically. I know how to take depositions. I'm very good at noting discrepancies. Even Bellini says I'm good at cross-examination. But to just go out and meet somebody and ask general things like what do you think of Daryl and Lionel and their marriage, gee, I don't know, Becky."

"But that's where I come in," I tried to explain to him.

He stopped pacing and stared at me. "Becky, how do you suppose you're going to delve into the Aberdeen case? I was thinking about that as I was shaving this morning. You remember that old 'inquiring minds want to know'? Do you really have an inquiring mind? I understand that's your work, to find out things. But you do it in front of a computer. I mean, here we've slept together several times, but you've never asked me that much about myself. You don't seem curious. And all I know about you is that your mother died. You see what I mean? We haven't even investigated each other. Most women I know would have already inquired about my prospects and the size of my bank account, whether I was ready for a commitment, when was the last time I had a blood test. You know, all the usual dating type things."

"I know all I need to know about you, Michael. You're sweet, you're a considerate lover, your value system is slightly screwy, and you desperately need the approval of your mother, whom you've mentioned too many times."

"Low blow."

"If I need to know more about you, I will definitely ask. But right now we're at the beginning of a relationship that might peter out, pardon the expression. So if I don't know how intense our, uh, friendship is going to be, why should I wonder about commitment? Plus, I make quite enough money to support myself, thank you, so your bank account is of no interest to me. I'm a very practical person, Michael. When I need something, I get it. I'll get you that information on the Aberdeen case. Now, as to our plan of attack, I think we should work it this way: You have a list of people Daryl knows will support her. So take their depositions. Meanwhile, I'm going for the general overview, people who knew both of them and are standing on the sidelines to see where the blood splatters.

"When I was doing my research, I came across a name several times that I think might be a good preliminary source. Abigail Brightly?"

"Never heard of her. She wasn't in your report."

"No. For many years she wrote the gossip—sorry, society column for the *Heartland News*."

"That suburban rag that comes out weekly, stocked with

real estate ads, restaurant reviews, and weekend diversions?"

"And local news, Michael. It had a lot more names in it than either the *Sun Times* or the *Tribune*. Abigail Brightly's column was filled with names. You could tell from reading her that she knew these people. She probably still does."

"Meaning she's not writing the column anymore."

"No, she's handed it over to younger hands."

"Then you're wasting your time. You could probably get just as much information on the Aberdeens from the Episcopal church bulletin."

"We'll see, shall we? Let me follow my instincts."

Michael shrugged. "What can it hurt? But please, Becky, write me a complete report that we can turn over to Bellini. We need to cover our asses every step of the way."

"I know. Nat's already filled me in on that."

After Michael left, I sat around contemplating exactly how I was going to approach Abigail Brightly. It was all well and good for me to assure Michael and Nat that I knew what I was doing. But now I had to do it. In her columns, Abigail seemed so proper, so sure of the right thing to do. I suppose the right thing for me to do would be to intrude upon her first by letter, suggesting that I would call. And yet that would take days, even weeks, should the post office live up to its worst reputation.

The woman was now seventy-six, a widow who lived in Winnetka, not more than twenty minutes from here. Dare I simply call? With a bravado I didn't feel, I snatched up the phone and dialed. A woman's voice, frail yet firm said, "Hello."

"May I please speak to Mrs. Abigail Brightly?"

"Mrs. Brightly isn't buying anything today."

"Excuse me, but is this the Mrs. Brightly who wrote the society column so many years for the *Heartland News*? I'm researching the North Shore, and I would so much like to speak to you."

"Why—uh—may I have your name please?"

What name should I use? Oh hell! "Elizabeth Belski."

"Belski, Belski. No, I don't know that family. But there are so many new people moving in, aren't there?"

Diluting the purity of the blood, no doubt. "If this is Mrs. Brightly, I'd only take a small amount of your time, and I would be ever so grateful."

"Well—yes, why not? I'm always glad to help a fellow writer. Can you come to tea at four sharp? I live at Twenty-three Park Woods. Where are you coming from?"

"Evanston."

"Ah, Evanston. The university perhaps?"

"You've caught me out, Mrs. Brightly."

"A writer and a scholar. That should prove interesting. Now listen, Miss Belski, you have to look sharp. Park Woods is an acute turn to the right just before you hit Park Street itself. Park Street has the light."

"I'll find it. Thank you very much, Mrs. Brightly. I'll see you at four. Sharp."

I put down the phone and grabbed one of the yellow pads. Between now and four I would try to formulate a series of questions, much like formulating a computer program, that would give me the answers I was seeking. Certainly, I would discuss the Aberdeen shooting. But wouldn't one shooting lead to another? And if I pried, wouldn't I be able to turn Abigail Brightly's attention from this most recent shooting back twenty-four years to the day my mother shot my stepfather? I certainly was going to try.

7

BEING a great believer in maps, I had no trouble finding Abigail Brightly's house at all. Park Woods, as I expected, was one of those short streets that go nowhere except into Lake Michigan. There were six houses lining it. I had no doubt that they shared a private beach, maybe even a boat ramp. Number 23 was the middle house, brownish gray clapboard. It almost looked like a postcard from New England, but I suppose that might have been because of its English garden, which, despite the darkening days, still had flowers blooming.

I had dressed for the occasion. I wore a gray skirt topped by a white blouse with a pilgrim collar. Both were left over from my college days. I'm afraid I have neither gained nor lost an ounce since then. I thought it would be overdoing it to wear nylons with seams, so I wore taupe pantyhose and sensible black heels. A wool jacket completed my ensemble. Only at the last minute did I rue not having a pair of white gloves.

As I walked up to Mrs. Brightly's front door, I began to

get slightly nervous, as if I were going to be examined for the Junior League or something. I just hoped this woman wasn't too off-putting. I rang the doorbell. I expected to hear a delicate ding-dong. Instead I got a hearty buzzer. Less than a minute later the door opened, and I was graciously invited into the Brightly house.

I should have known she would have dogs.

We took tea in the solarium, "while it's still nice," Abigail Brightly said. I was freezing. Her cocker spaniel was all over me. "Don't you just love dogs?" she said. I smiled. When she wasn't looking, I planned to kick the little critter in the rump. But, oh goody, the dog found a diversion. Wampums, or whatever she had called him, caught sight of the delicate little sandwiches prepared for high tea. He took a sniff and began licking at them. Meanwhile, Abigail was pouring, one lump or two, lemon, sugar. Then, "Please, have some sandwiches. I'll bring out the cake later."

Oy! to quote my ex-mother-in-law. I reached for one higher on the plate where I hoped Snugums or whatever hadn't gotten his nose or tongue. I nibbled at a corner and pronounced it excellent. "One can only get good fish paste from London," she assured me.

Lord almighty. Might doggy want a sandwich anytime soon? I smiled, taking advantage of the moment to study Abigail Brightly. She was a well-preserved seventy-six, beautiful complexion; and, despite her relatively small stature, she looked good in the plaid skirt she was wearing. "Shall we cut to the chase?" she asked me.

I set down my tea cup but took it up again in fear of her purebred whatever. "I found out all about you from back issues of the *Heartland News,*" I confessed to her. "I liked reading your columns," I flattered. "I believe you're a combination of Edith Wharton and Louis Auchincloss."

She smiled. "I majored in English at Smith. But I'm afraid I squandered my talents at that little rag. I was always a great observer, but I never really had that much ambition. Not like you young girls today."

"Well, we have to be ambitious, don't we, now that life is so uncertain?"

"My dear, I lost my first husband in World War II, my second to an accident on the Edens Expressway. Life is always uncertain."

"I just meant, I think there was a time when husband and family were much more protective of a woman than they are now. Now so often we're left to twist slowly in the wind, not knowing when we're going to be served with divorce papers."

"Hmm." Abigail Brightly sat back in her seat. "I'm trying to decide which subject you're attempting to broach gingerly. Women in modern society? Divorce? Or someone I know?"

I smiled. "The Aberdeens."

"Oh my." She put down the tea cup. "I can't understand why you've come to me, Miss Belski. I stopped writing that gossip column a long time ago. If the tabloid press wants that kind of story, it'll have to look elsewhere."

"I'm not working for the press."

"For yourself then. You have a book contract. Now you have to fulfill it with lurid details."

"I'm working for Bellini Reese, Daryl Aberdeen's attorney."

She didn't believe me. I told her she could verify it very easily. She did so. When she came back into the room, she said, "I'm still surprised that you came to me. I frankly don't want to get involved in what promises to be a very messy divorce case."

"I know. And I have no intention of involving you. I thought maybe we could just—pardon the expression—dish the dirt for a while."

"And why would I ever want to dish the dirt with you, a complete stranger?"

She had a point there. But I tried to reassure her. "I don't want the details of their marriage so much as a history. Why and how did this state of affairs come about? How did two lovely people from good families go so terribly wrong in their marriage?"

"Ha! Have you ever been married, Miss Belski?"

"Yes."

"Then you must know that the operative word in marriage is 'compromise.' He gives, you give. You give more than he gives, but that's life, reality, not theory. Daryl and Lionel—I was at both baptisms—were spoiled children right from the start. It didn't help that both came from broken homes, where marital bed-hopping was the norm. Sometimes I think there's too much inbreeding in our crowd along the North Shore. Too few girls nowadays are running away with the dancing master. No one wants to be poor but happy anymore."

She settled back in her chair and I sighed expectantly, the way one does when one picks up a long novel. "Lionel and Daryl were pushed together by their families. I believe they married because it was the right thing to do, not because they loved each other. But on the other hand, people say love grows. That might have been true for arranged marriages in the past. They had all those years to nourish the seed of love. But now how long does a marriage last? Five years? Six? Ten, let's say, to be generous. And if there's no passion to begin with, well?" She shrugged. "The older I get, the more I believe one should marry for love. Not social position, not money, simply love."

"And there was no love between Daryl and Lionel."

"They played at it. They played house, actually. He was the handsome prince, she the beautiful princess. Their mommies and daddies gave them that castle a few miles from here. I was there for the housewarming. Everything had a label. It was very nouveau. Nowadays there's a lack of class even among those whose birthright it is."

"What went wrong? Besides not having enough love."

"Well, you hear whispers. Lionel was on the exchange, living high, spending high. They were both into kicks, which I understand they got from drugs. Drugs? You know, if the cocktail hour were restored in this country, I think the drug problem would simply fade away. And then, of course, there were other men and other women. The Aberdeens had, I think, about two perfect years before everything went to hell.''

"I understand Daryl suffered through several miscarriages.''

"Is that what she's telling the lawyer? Well.''

I noticed how Mrs. Brightly's lips turned slightly downward; she almost sniffed in disapproval. "They weren't miscarriages. This I got from her grandmother, who got it from her mother. Her first 'miscarriage' occurred when the doctor warned her about the dangers of taking drugs and having a baby. She was so scared she had an abortion. Her second came when she told Lionel about their expectant parenthood and he claimed not to be the father. She was at the time having an affair with Neil Brewster. But Lionel certainly lost any claims to being a gentleman when he threatened to go into court to prove the child wasn't his. Such bad manners. As if it would have been the first time one man raised another man's son as his own. But I think they had begun to hate each other by then.''

I had to agree with her there. "After all, they must have hated each other if she would pick up a gun and shoot him,'' I sadly observed.

"Oh, that wasn't hate, my dear. That was pure, jealous rage. Lionel had just finished servicing Daryl's mother.''

My mouth must have dropped open. Lord almighty, what was Bellini going to do with this! "No wonder they wanted it hushed up so quickly,'' I managed to say.

"Well, Jelly Mellon was separated from her husband at the time,'' Abigail Brightly excused.

The rich really are different from you and me. "You know,'' I said, now that Mrs. Brightly was on a roll, "the shooting reminded me of an event you wrote about some twenty years ago.'' She looked at me curiously. "It seems to have some of the same elements," I continued. "The Town-send shooting?"

"Oh no, my dear, no, no, no. No similarities whatsoever. Lionel is basically a perfectly harmless boy. He's a sinner, yes, but not an evil one. While with Bill Townsend, well, there were always rumors about him."

"Really?"

"Yes." She leaned forward. "You know the Townsend story is one I have often thought would make a good novel."

"One that you might write?"

"Certainly I have the time now to do so. But I value my friendships too much to betray confidences. I like to report only glad tidings."

"And yet your stories on the Townsend shooting were an excellent example of the use of innuendo."

She laughed. "Well, one tried to enable people to read between the lines. Not that she didn't deserve what she got, by the way."

"Who?"

"Jane Peters, Townsend's second wife. She was his secretary. How terribly common of Bill. And she wasn't even his personal secretary. No, that was the loyal Miss McKennah. Jane Peters was in a secondary position, a receptionist almost, from the way I understand it. A widow with a young daughter. She wasn't one of us at all."

"And yet she caught William Townsend's eye."

"Oh, she caught it all right. Most of us just wondered how soon she caught it. He married her eight months after his first wife died in that tragic accident."

"Oh? Now I missed that. What happened to his first wife?"

"Oh my. I don't know if I can bring it all back or if I even want to. There were so many rumors at the time. Daphne Mansfield, as I understand it, threatened to try to take custody of the children away from Bill Townsend. Not that it would have mattered in Alan's case. He was, I believe, either a sophomore or freshman at Princeton when his mother died. But poor little Billy was only nine or ten when his mother died. Died." Abigail Brightly shrugged. "Sarah Mansfield fell down the stairs and broke her neck."

"What a—a shock."

"Yes. For that to happen on Christmas Eve, of all nights. I heard about it early the next morning. That I can remember clearly because I was making pancakes for my own sweet grandchildren. Daphne Mansfield, Sarah's mother, had spoken to Chloe Cauterell, her best friend. Daphne was saying all sorts of wild things. Chloe called me, naturally, as I was the chronicler of our times. Albeit a modest chronicler."

"What was Daphne Mansfield saying?"

"That Sarah had been pushed. Oh, my dear, now that's a story your Bellini Reese should get his hands on. If it hadn't been for Daphne's husband, she probably would have had Bill Townsend up on charges of murder. *Quel scandale, n'est-ce pas?*"

"Because she knew something?"

"That was the problem. Who could know anything? Sarah was dead. She couldn't say how she fell down the stairs. Billy was asleep when it happened. Alan—you see, that's what aroused Daphne's suspicions. Well, she never liked Bill Townsend in the first place. No, I guess in the first place she did. But then, over the years she saw how he treated her daughter. He was a real pig. Anyway, Alan was home from Princeton for the holidays. And when he heard his mother scream, he came out of his room and found his father at the top of the stairs."

"Maybe Sarah Mansfield had too much eggnog that night," I suggested.

"My dear, the Mansfields were not great drinkers. Not that they did toxicology testing then, but I will bet you anything there wasn't a drop of alcohol in Sarah's blood. In any case, Bill Townsend claimed his wife tripped and fell as she was carrying Christmas presents down to put beneath the tree. And it could have happened that way, one must concede.

She sighed. "The poor children, though. Poor Billy especially. To see his mother lying dead at the foot of the stairs and then just two years later to see his father lying dead also, shot, murdered."

"But—"

"Yes?" Abigail Brightly waited.

"I thought Bill—Billy wasn't home at the time of his father's shooting."

"It's true that Daphne Mansfield, after her daughter's death, insisted Billy be sent to boarding school, which was especially smart after the haste with which Bill Townsend remarried. But I remember, it was winter vacation when his father was shot, and he was home. Maybe not in the house at the time. That could be true. But oh, Billy was simply devastated. If Alan hadn't flown home and taken him in hand, I don't know what would have happened to Billy. Billy was always the sensitive one, while Alan was a take-charge sort of person. Alan stepped immediately into the mess and cleaned it up."

"I thought the police did that by arresting Jane Peters."

"Yes, but I meant the family, the business, the estate, all that sort of thing. Alan took care of it as if he had been born to take charge. We all admired him for that."

"Meanwhile, Jane Peters was left out in the cold."

"You have to realize, Miss Belski, that we take care of our own. Jane Peters was not one of us. Oh, she tried. She joined this ladies' auxiliary and that, but she had been, after all, just a receptionist in her husband's office. And we always suspected, since they married so quickly, that she had been carrying on with Bill Townsend even before Sarah took her unfortunate fall."

I smiled. "Now that you've told me why Daryl shot Lionel, why do you suppose Jane shot her husband? At first she claimed self-defense."

Abigail Brightly grimaced. "Yes. It might very well

have been self-defense. Bill Townsend was—not a very nice man."

I waited. But she seemed unwilling to go further. "Meaning?" I had to ask.

"If you had met him, you would have liked him. He was a great glad-hander, which, I take it, is why he did so well in business. He made a good first impression. But—quite frankly, the man was a bully. He bullied his friends and he bullied his women. I remember being at a dinner party once with Bill and Sarah. We were all old, old friends, so there was no need for him to pretend to be someone he wasn't. He spent the evening belittling poor Sarah. She was getting old, her dress was out of fashion, her hair was graying rapidly, you know the sort of things men can say to make you feel awful. She smiled brightly throughout the evening, pushing each little remark aside with some gentle chiding. But there were tears in her eyes. I never invited Bill Townsend into my house after that. He liked to push people around, and that really bothered me."

"Maybe he liked it so much that he pushed his first wife down the stairs and goaded his second wife to the point where she would pick up a gun and shoot him?"

"Very probably," Mrs. Brightly conceded with a grim smile.

"And yet no one spoke in—" I had almost begun to say my mother—"in Jane Peter's defense. You couldn't have been the only one to note Townsend's character flaws."

"Well, as I say, she wasn't one of us. And in any case, she soon enough changed her plea from self-defense to guilty of murder in the second degree. So what was there to say?"

"You've told me about Billy and Alan. But what about Jane Peter's child?"

"Oh, her child," Abigail Brightly said dismissively. "She was probably farmed out to relatives. Alan might know what happened to her, if you're interested." She put down her tea cup and leaned forward. "You know, we've spent more time discussing the Townsends than the Aberdeens."

She stood. "I hope I've helped you somewhat, Mrs. Belski. It would be best for Lionel and Daryl to settle out of court. Life is too messy to appear between the pages of a trial transcript, isn't it?"

After thanking Abigail Brightly for all her help, I got into my car and made myself drive away before I pulled off the road and thought. The mystery of my mother was becoming clearer to me. She had obviously been bullied and abused. Why then was she railroaded with no one in particular rallying to her defense? And who had disposed of me?

I don't know if at that moment I decided to set out to clear my mother's name. I do know that I was determined not to let the issue die until I found out everything. And using the Aberdeen case as a cover for my own investigation of the Townsends was as good as I would get.

8

I naturally turned over everything I had learned about the Aberdeens to Michael Rosen. He was dumbfounded. "Bellini has to know about this right away. Talk about a client misleading her lawyer. I mean, she told us she had only meant to threaten Lionel with the gun, to get him to stay away from this other woman. She never told us who the other woman was!"

Bellini was graciously willing to receive us. It was to Michael's credit that he said, "Becky's found out something I think you should hear immediately." He could have said, "We've found out something," or even "I've found out something." Wasn't Michael too nice to be a lawyer?

So I sat down and told Bellini about Abigail Brightly. Then I told him that the woman with whom Lionel was having an affair was Jelly Mellon, Daryl's mother.

Since he wasn't in court, Bellini allowed his mouth to drop open, much as mine must have done. "Her mother?"

"I understand that Jelly Mellon was separated from her husband at the time," I said in mitigation.

"Oh, that makes it okay then," Bellini replied sarcastically. He shook his head. "I think this is what they call a serious rupture in the fabric of American society."

"And they're probably all Republicans," I commented, adding to our disillusionment.

"However"—Bellini perked up—"this certainly adds spice to our case. What judge, what jury, if it comes to that, couldn't understand a young, delicate flower like Daryl being so unnerved by learning of her husband's attachment to her mother that she would pick up a gun and shoot the bastard, defending her side of the mother/daughter relationship, if nothing else. Yes! I like it! Michael, make a note. Check around and find out the status of Jelly Mellon's marriage. Are they just separated or has the legal disentanglement begun? We might be able to grab another case here."

"I hope the husband's side," I said.

"Hmm. It certainly might present a conflict of interest to represent Jelly." He sat back and contemplated the situation. Then he leaned forward. "Becky, go sic yourself on the rest of them."

I refused to take this dogification personally.

"Dig up the dirt. You seem to have a nose for it."

"Thanks ever so."

Bellini was surprised by my tone of voice. "That was a compliment," he assured me. "I'm going to call Nat and tell him how pleased I am. Now, Michael, how are the depositions going?"

I had to listen to poor Michael stammer and watch him sweat until Bellini dismissed us both. When we were out in the corridor, I gave Michael one of my looks. "Well, I couldn't help it," he protested.

"You can help it, Michael! For godsake, take a Dale Carnegie course or something! I think the Evanston Park District has courses in assertiveness. Or maybe take up martial arts."

"You think I'm a—"

"I think you're perfect, Michael, absolutely perfect. However, that's not the way you act before Bellini. Be forceful, be positive.''

''If I could only get that one big case,'' Michael repeated like some mantra.

''The one big case won't come to you if no one has faith in you. And people can't have faith in you if you don't have faith in yourself. Now shape up! Being warm and sensitive and caring is all to the good, but sometimes you have to just go out there and kick ass.''

''So, I guess I won't ask you out for dinner and dessert because obviously you won't respect me in the morning.''

By that time we were in his office. I leaned over and gave him a kiss. ''I'm sorry,'' I apologized. ''I just hate to see Bellini's effect on you. Anyway, we have to have dinner. We have to discuss our next plan of attack.''

During dinner Michael made various suggestions about whom I should see next. None of them especially appealed to me. Not that gardeners and live-ins didn't have their merits in this case, but I had my sights set on Bill Townsend III. ''He's Lionel's friend,'' Michael pointed out.

''Know thine enemy. Besides, he grew up with Daryl and Lionel. He went to the same parties, the same schools. How do you know he won't be objective?''

''Because men stick together,'' Michael said sharply. I pouted. He gave in. ''You've got the nose,'' he relented. Then he looked me squarely in the face. ''And a very pretty one it is. Did you have it fixed?''

''Fixed?''

''You know, did you have a nose job when you were a teenager—like everyone else?''

''No.''

''Hmm. So you've always looked WASPish?''

I smiled and didn't know if now was the time to tell him I wasn't one of the chosen people, though we in Iowa do like to think of ourselves as special. Fortunately, I was saved by the coming of the check, which Michael promptly picked up. We went to my apartment this time because, as

Michael explained, "I have to get back to work tonight anyway, so I won't have to worry about that awful drive down in the morning." Should love really be complicated by the commuting patterns into the city?

The next morning I was up bright and early, despite my protesting body. It wasn't used to seeing the semidawn at seven o'clock. But there was work to be done on the computer, and I wanted to get to Resources early. I had to check in with the Social Security Administration. I wanted to find out who had been working in William Townsend's office when my mother—and my adoptive mother—had been working there. Unfortunately, the Social Security Administration didn't help me as much as I'd expected, so I called personnel over at The Skyline Agency. I thought I'd take the direct approach. Needless to say, the secretary at the other end of the line simply couldn't give out that information. "Not even for a hundred dollars?" I wondered.

The pause was rewarding. She had a coffee break at ten-thirty. We arranged to meet in the corner coffee shop of her building, both bearing envelopes. Then I had to call Michael, who was already at work, bless him. I explained my predicament. "Unethical, no," he said. "Costly, yes. And yet if you think the information will help the case?"

The Aberdeen case, no, but it sure as hell would help mine. Feeling slightly guilty, I said, "Michael, isn't it much less than you bill an hour?"

He told me how to get the money and warned me of the strict accounting I would have to do, protecting my sources, of course. I hoped by the time the accounting came, I could somehow fudge over the issue of who got the money and what information she gave me for it.

But, as one of my favorite lines in literature and life has it, I'll think about that tomorrow. Today I put in a call to the advertising firm where Bill Townsend worked as a commercial artist. Except he didn't work there anymore. "He freelances now," the receptionist told me. She gave me the number where I might reach him.

I dialed and, when a man answered, I tried to connect his voice with the Bill Townsend I knew as a child. But nothing was left of his pre-adolescence, if this indeed was Bill. "May I please speak with Bill Townsend?" I asked.

"Speaking."

"This is Becky Belski. I'm doing some work for the law firm of Cohen, Kahn, Cohn and Kahane."

"Oh lord."

"In reference to the Aberdeen versus Aberdeen divorce case?"

"Oh? Thank God. I thought I was being sued or something."

"I believe you know both parties in the case?"

"Yes, I do, but—"

"It would really be helpful if I spoke to you about Daryl and Lionel Aberdeen. Perhaps you can clear up some of the finer points of their marriage for me."

He laughed. "Ms.—uh—Belski, was it? I have absolutely no intention of speaking to you about Lionel and Daryl. What's happening is very sad, but not at all unusual, except for the money involved. Whom are you representing, by the way?"

"Daryl Aberdeen."

"Oh. Well, she's a sweet girl, and I'm just sorry things didn't work out for her and Lionel."

"Look, we're not trying to develop an adversarial situation here. The lawyers for both camps want to come to the court with an agreement already wrapped up. This entails some sort of mediation. Both partners must be made to see the light and not use the courts to get even with one another. So it would really help if we had more insight into their characters. That's all I'm asking for, just to find the light of humanity among the charges and countercharges."

"Well—"

"What about lunch?" I suggested. "We can limit our conversation to an hour. If I begin to make you uncomfortable, we can eat in silence or change the subject to the Cubs or the Bears. Okay? Lunch? My treat?''

''An hour, huh?''

''An hour.''

''Mélange. Do you know it?''

''Plaza del Lago shopping center.''

''One o'clock.''

It was going to be a busy day. The first thing I had to do was rush home to change. That's when I bumped into Nat. He was just coming in. ''Great job you're doing,'' he yelled after me. I didn't turn around to see if he was being sarcastic or not.

I thought the best thing to do was make good use of the suit Nat had me buy for my first appearance before Bellini Reese. It paid to look professional to the extent that people then had to take you seriously. This goes to show you what a sad state the country is in, when dressing is more important than what's in a person's mind, which in the case of most people who wear suits is absolutely nothing of lasting value.

Such was my prejudice. I noted it was not shared by the secretary from The Skyline Agency's personnel office. She was wearing, as she promised, gray pinstripes. But then so were half the other women in the coffee shop. Fortunately, she was looking around her surreptitiously, so I figured her for the guilty party. I walked over to her and said, ''Personnel?''

She nodded. I slid into the seat next to her and took an envelope out of my bag. It contained used twenties. ''What do you have for me?'' I asked.

''Everyone who worked in the boss's office between the years 1955 and 1966, when he died.''

She didn't even know he had been murdered.

''Who's the boss now?''

''Alan Townsend,'' she said, as if everyone knew.

''And what kind of boss is he?''

''I've only been working here a little over a year, so I've

seen him maybe twice, once at the Christmas party, when he shook my hand in the receiving line. I understand he's quite aloof.''

"Thanks," I said, about to take my leave.

"I only did this because I knew the information couldn't harm anyone."

"You're right. It can't harm anyone. It can only help."

So she had her hundred and I had my list. I went back to Resources to check it out. The secretary had been thorough. I had the names, addresses, and telephone numbers of everyone who had worked in William Townsend's office at the same time my mother had. Winnie McKennah, Jane Peters, naturally, but also Clariss Taylor, Susan Bradshaw, and Megan Wilder.

I spent the next hour and a half tracking them down as far as I could. Unfortunately, that wasn't far enough. I started with Susan Bradshaw because she was about the same age as Winnie McKennah. I figured they might have been fast office friends. Winnie had received her twenty-year pen and certificate in 1964. So she had been about forty when I was thrust upon her. No wonder the young mothers of Sioux Bluffs found her such an odd phenomenon. Susan Bradshaw was a few years older than Winnie, and her last known address was Niles. Susan Bradshaw was also married. So she might have had reason to stay put.

I dashed into our reference room and pulled out the suburban phone book with Niles in it. Bradshaw, Philip, same address. Thank you, God.

Megan Wilder and Clariss Taylor were more of a problem. They had been younger than my mother, both unmarried. And neither was in the phone book at the address on the paper. So I would have to institute a search for them, via their social security numbers, should they still be working. This was something that on other occasions I could turn over to one of our part-timers. But then someone, perhaps Nat, might ask what all this had to do with the Aberdeen case. Therefore it behooved me to do my investigating on my own.

But that would have to wait. Right now I needed to wend my way through lunchtime traffic up to Wilmette, where my stepbrother was meeting me for lunch. Whatever happened to the young boy with whom I played catch? I would soon find out.

9

IT was funny how I recognized Bill Townsend the instant he entered the restaurant. It would be silly to say that an ten-year-old boy doesn't look any different from one who's thirty-five, but in Bill's case it was true. He had the same sort of impish eyes, the same brown curly hair. I stood when I saw him and raised my hand to catch his attention. He looked at me and smiled. Did he recognize me, too? For just that moment my heart stopped.

But when he walked over to me, all he said was "Ms. Belski, I presume?"

"Call me Becky. Please."

We sat down. "An hour," he warned me. So we ordered right away. Mélange is dedicated to California cuisine, so I had angel hair pasta with sun-dried tomatoes, while he had fish with broccoli and cauliflower. Fortunately, there were breadsticks to fill up on. We started chomping immediately, while I continued to stare at him. "Is there something wrong?" he asked me.

"Your newspaper photos don't do you justice."

74

"My newspaper photos," he mused. "I can't remember being photographed for any newspaper."

"The yacht race?"

"Oh."

"The Lyric Opera benefit?"

"Right. I suppose when I think newspapers, I think trouble."

That gave me the opening I wanted, but no doubt he would find it strange if I immediately started asking about his father's death. So I returned to my alleged purpose for being here, the Aberdeens. "Certainly it was trouble for Daryl when she shot Lionel."

"Yes," he agreed. "The press eats that sort of thing up."

Another opening coming too soon, damn it!

"You know both of them, don't you?"

"Forever," he confessed. "Birthday parties, prep schools, trips to Europe; and we all went to college within hiking distance of each other, Lionel to Colgate, Daryl to Vassar, I to Amherst. Then we came back home to try to make lives for ourselves."

"Lionel and Daryl married almost immediately."

"A year or so out of college," he corrected me. "They had been seeing each other, and everyone felt marriage was the sensible next step. We all were clinging desperately to the idea of perfect love at that point."

I waited, not knowing what to make of that statement.

He smiled. "You wouldn't understand," he suggested. "We—none of us had that stable a background. Daryl's mother was embarrassingly promiscuous. She's on her third marriage. Lionel's father died in a boating accident on Lake Michigan; his mother remarried some foreigner who had these ridiculously European views on child rearing. Either that or he wanted Lionel out of the house permanently. I guess all of us at prep school and boarding school had parents who couldn't seem to get it together in the happiness department. So we all swore to each other, when we discussed these things, which we did when something

75

particularly shitty happened, that our lives would be lived in perfect harmony with our needs for, um, love and security." He smiled wryly. "What did we know?" He laughed, a soft little chuckle that I found very appealing.

"And your marriage?" I asked. "Is it anything like Lionel's and Daryl's?" Of course, I knew he had never been married. At least that's what the computers said. Still, I couldn't help but be naturally nosy about my stepbrother.

Bill took in a deep breath. "I swore when I was young never to marry, and I've seen nothing around me to make me change my views. Though I am a great believer in serial relationships." He looked at me so directly that I felt my heart skip a thump. Was Bill, my own stepbrother, coming on to me? Or was it just his way to flirt with every woman he had lunch with?

"Tell me about Lionel and Daryl," I said quickly. "Whose fault is this whole mess?"

"Fault? Hmm. I think there's enough fault to slather around for years to come, which is the course they seem to have set. Both sides want the divorce, but instead of getting on with it, they're using it as some sort of battering ram to hurt each other." He shrugged. "Lionel's my good friend, but I also sympathize with Daryl. She so desperately wanted a child. Both times it didn't work out."

"One time because she was on drugs and the other because Lionel threatened to claim in court that the child wasn't his."

"She should have divorced him then and had the child. Instead things deteriorated until she—"

"Shot him. For sleeping with her mother."

"It certainly sounds bad for Daryl, doesn't it?" Bill conceded. Then he looked puzzled. "Where did you get all this information?"

"I have my sources," I said officiously.

"Don't be so tough toward Jelly Mellon. She was always a friend to me." He looked up. "No, not sexually," he corrected any misapprehension I might have. "She was a good friend of my stepmother's, and then when my step-mother—well, Jelly always sort of looked out for me, after that.''

Jelly Mellon, Phaedra's closest incarnation on the North Shore, a friend of my mother's? Dear Mom, what did you get yourself into? "After that," I repeated Bill's phrase, feeling now perhaps was the time to broach the subject I had come here for. "You mean, after your stepmother shot your father?''

He looked surprised that I should know, but all he said was, "Yes.''

"It must have been a shock when you heard about Lionel and Daryl. Déjà vu.'' He was silent. I sat there and waited, hoping he would say something. But he seemed to be investigating his fish, flake by flake. So I ventured into the muck again. "Did you like your stepmother? Or was she some sort of wicked witch?'' I myself could barely remember my own mother.

Bill's face lit up with a genuine smile. "I liked her, yes. She was a kind woman who tried to be a mother to me. She had a child from a previous marriage, so it was sort of like a ready-made family for me. My brother Alan was so much older than I that we never really played together. But with Elizabeth—that was her name—I felt as if all of a sudden I was the older brother. I used to enjoy coming home from boarding school for vacations and playing with her. And her mother, my stepmother, would make us cookies and Kool-Aid. I was so delighted because I had never had Kool-Aid before.'' He laughed.

"It must have been devastating when it happened. I mean, when your stepmother shot your father. Were you home at the time?''

Bill turned quite cool. "I was at a friend's house.'' He pushed himself away from the table and looked pointedly at his watch. "Your hour is up.''

As I was paying the bill, I complained, "I didn't learn anything new about Lionel and Daryl.''

"I warned you I wouldn't be helpful." He stood. "I have to get back to work."

"Oh? Where do you work?"

"At home. I'm a commercial artist."

"I'd love to see some of your work."

He smiled. "Why? To ask me more questions?"

"No. Of course not. We agreed on an hour, and the hour has flown. But I do like art."

He looked me over, I mean really looked me over, as if he were trying to assess what was behind my interest, something social or professional. Then he came to a decision. "I live five minutes from here, if you want to duck in and see some of my stuff."

I followed his car west toward Green Bay Road, then north onto First Street. Bill pulled into his driveway and I pulled up behind him. We kicked our way through the leaves to his front door. He lived in a pleasant house that must have been at least half a century old. The porch creaked as we stepped onto it, just right for Halloween. The first thing I noticed when he opened the door was the wood. The place was gleaming with it. I was going to admire it, but Bill indicated that I should follow him upstairs.

I don't know how he did it, but Bill had transformed the entire upper floor into an artist's studio. Walls had been knocked down to give him all the space he would ever need and skylights traveled across the raised roof, letting in the sun. "Beautiful," I complimented.

"I have a friend who's an architect. Of course, that didn't stop the skylights from leaking the first year. You can look around, if you like. I've got to get set up."

Bill had cubbies against the wall, much as they do in grammar schools, but his were long enough to contain his work. I pulled several portfolios out and examined the contents. Some of them were interesting, some totally boring, like all those architectural drawings he made of proposed shopping malls. What I liked were the boats, the fashionable women, food, flowers, and, my favorite, the greeting cards.

Bill was already toiling away when I finished looking. I placed his work back in the cubbies, then sat and watched him, trying to recapture the child I knew. It felt comfortable just sitting here with him. Matter of fact, it felt so comfortable that I didn't want to move, lest he chase me away, banished me forever.

Finally, he deigned to notice me. He looked at me inquiringly. "I've never known an artist," I confessed. "I wanted a taste of the ambience."

He shook his head. "First of all, I'm not an artist, I'm a commercial artist. Second, the ambience is frustration."

"Your work is beautiful."

"My work is functional."

"You shouldn't put yourself down." I stood and looked out his window. The leaves, which had been so many hues just a week or so ago, were all brown now, those refusing to fall from the trees. But Bill still had mums in his garden, holding out against the coming winter. "I like it here," I told him.

"I like having you here," he said easily. Then he examined me, but not as a brother would a sister. "Come to dinner," he suggested. "But no talk about the Aberdeens," he warned.

"Okay," I agreed. "What time?"

"Seven."

I walked out of his house, knowing I was involving myself in something wrong, but I couldn't define exactly what it was. Professionally, I was not betraying my trust. I would give Michael a complete report of what Bill had to say. Which was basically nothing we didn't already know.

Why then was I uneasy? I suppose it was because I found Bill attractive, in a romantic way. And yet, how could I, when he was my stepbrother? Was I feeling the tinge of incest? That would be difficult because Bill and I weren't related by blood, simply by the happenstance of our parents' marriage. Yet the taboo was still there.

The knife-sharp edge of uncertain guilt stabbed me deeper when I returned home to change for dinner at Bill's. Michael had left several messages on my machine, all asking me to return his calls, as he was available tonight. I took the coward's way out. I had faxed him my report from Resources. I would pretend I hadn't returned home in time to catch his calls. Meanwhile, I dressed expectantly for my dinner that evening with a man whom I would have to try harder to think of as my stepbrother.

10

LOVE disorients us. This was a lesson I was fast learning. When I was in high school, I never had the opportunity to study love, not having had a single date. In college I met Yuri, and we fell in love, the gang of us, Yuri, me, and our computers. We were all friends together, and Yuri would have been shocked had I suddenly turned womanly soft and frilly.

Then Michael came into my life, fell into my life as easily as we had fallen into bed together that first night. I knew he was right for me, for that part of me that would always be the clear-sighted professional.

But the clear-sighted professional wasn't prepared for the whammy that was Bill Townsend. No man has ever treated me the way he did. He was quite simply a woman's fantasy. The first night we were together, he did a watercolor of me. It was as if someone had written a poem to immortalize me. I had worn slacks and a tailored blouse over to his place. But when he sketched me, he placed me in a frilly, opaque negligee that I would never have spent my money on. And he captured a youthful innocence in me that I no longer felt. "Who is she?" I wondered.

"She's what I see in you," he replied softly.

Okay, I'm not stupid. I understood that this was a line he had probably used on women before. After all, he had already confessed to being a great believer in serial relationships. But he made me a gift of the portrait, and the next day I dropped it off to be framed. In a week's time it was hanging in my living room.

In a week's time, I thought I was in love with Bill Townsend.

I was horrified, and yet there it was. I had seen Bill three times that week, and each time he swept me off my feet. I couldn't help but compare his idea of a date with Michael's. With Michael, we ate, we talked, we slept together, we talked some more, then Michael fretted about facing the traffic on his drive home. The next time I went out with Bill after the dinner, he took me horseback riding. Horseback riding. I had never been horseback riding in my life! I felt like a little girl on a pony when Bill helped me up into the saddle. Of course, I felt something else when I got off the horse two hours later, but Bill suggested a half hour in a hot tub would cure that. "I only have a shower," I stated.

"I have a tub," he offered with that impish smile of his.

Now why should I criticize Michael for not taking me horseback riding, especially when he worked from eight until eight at the very least? No one except Zorro goes horseback riding at night. Still—

On our third date Bill and I went to an opening at a gallery in River North. Bill seemed to know all the artists there, and it was fun, slightly bohemian. I definitely didn't fit in with his crowd. They were people with a capacity for clever, witty conversation, quick parries and thrusts. I felt out of place until one of them told me I possessed interesting cheekbones that gave strength to my face.

Michael never paid attention to my bone structure. Sure,

he said I had "fabulous tits" and a "fantastic ass," but how could those compare to the strength of my cheekbones?

On our fourth date Bill and I drove to the Indiana Dunes, braving the traffic through industrial areas to walk in the sand together. Bill brought his supplies, and I sat in the sand next to him while he painted, not minding overly much the fact that I was practically freezing to death. "I like being with you," he told me then. "It's like being with myself. Warm. Comfortable."

He brought a blanket along. Now he spread it out and we sat on it together, watching the birds fly above us. He put his arms around me and hugged me to keep me warn. When I turned to him to say something, his lips were there and he was kissing me. He was neither desperate nor anxious. His lips were soft and expressively connected to mine, and I couldn't help but return their pressure. His hand reached inside my coat until it came to rest on one of my "fabulous tits." My hand naturally fell on his hip. But when I moaned for the first time, I became conscious of what was happening, and I pulled away.

"What is it?" he asked me, not angry, just curious.

"I'm not ready for this," I confessed. "There's—I have—"

"A boyfriend," he finished for me.

I smiled. "Someone I'm seeing."

He shrugged. "Just my luck."

"I can't help but find you attractive," I admitted.

"There is an easiness between us," he agreed. "I don't know what or why that is. I thought it might be love."

"Love doesn't come so quickly."

"Love is like a firecracker."

"For men perhaps. And then in a flash it's over."

"Ah," he nodded, "have you had problems with partners who prematurely ejaculate?"

I laughed and he laughed with me. We sat on the blanket and talked about past loves. Bill seemed to have gone through many more than I, but then he was five years older and had never been totally committed, as I had been with Yuri. "Yes, with women somehow it all comes down to marriage. And I will never ever get married," he said with an intensity that surprised me.

"Why not?" I wondered. "It's not that bad, even when it ends in divorce. Better to have loved and lost, et cetera."

"Really?" he questioned bitterly. "Not from my point of view. I've seen too many marriages close up, including my father's. They terrify me."

Bill retreated far into himself. A cold cloud surrounded him, and my warmth couldn't cut through it. So we sat there in silence until the wind turned so harsh that even Bill noticed. We gathered our things and headed back toward home.

Bill dropped me at my apartment and promised to call again soon. "I really like being with you," he stressed.

"Me too," I answered lamely. I was glad he didn't suggest coming up because I didn't know what would happen if he did. I was afraid I wouldn't have resisted him. I was also glad because, when I got up to my apartment, I found my answering machine blinking furiously. The gods must be angry.

Two of the messages were from Nat, the rest were from Michael.

Michael. God, I had been avoiding him lately. Our only contact this last week had been through the phone and the fax machine. Being with Bill, surrounded by the dreamlike quality he brought to my life, had taken the edge off my research, especially my research into my stepfather's murder, but also the research I had been doing on the Aberdeen case.

In between dates with Bill I had managed to question more acquaintances of Lionel and Daryl Aberdeen. What I found was not exactly pretty. I don't know if it was too much money or too little ambition, but everyone in their circle except Bill was addicted to something, whether it was drugs or alcohol or adultery. No one in the Aberdeen crowd seemed to be living a life of purpose. Several were involved in the stock exchange and the commodities markets, or in one large firm or another that dad or granddad had started, but there was a lack of dedication. After all, they all had enough money to live on forever. Further, their primary source of pleasure seemed to be relationships that had revolved around each other since childhood. They ran in a pack, and the pack was going nowhere.

All these reports I faxed to Michael. I figured he could present them to Bellini Reese without my assistance. And now in return I had all these messages from Michael. "Becky, please call." "Becky, where are you?" "Becky, you are neither at home nor in the office." "Becky, are you avoiding me? If so, why? Bad breath? B.O.? Hey, I can change."

I called Michael. "Becky!" he shouted. "The little lost lamb. Can this Bo Peep take you out to dinner tonight?"

"I'm sick of dinner. Let's do something exciting," I suggested, in a way surprised at how glad I was to hear his voice. I thought maybe Bill had totally dulled my attraction to Michael, but not quite.

"Uh, I can rent a few videotapes and bring them over with Chinese."

"Michael, you're incurable," I told him. I sighed. Why didn't Michael have Bill's imagination? It would have solved so many problems for me.

An hour later, he was over at my place, food and tapes in hand. We sat at my butcher block table, which I still loved despite other design fads, and ate and talked.

How can a woman be in love with two men at the same time? I had to wonder because, as I sat there, talking to Michael, I realized I was still strongly attracted to him. Was it the difference between the two men? With Bill we communicated with silences. Michael kept up a constant stream of patter. I loved the funny slant he put on all his experiences. He could see the humor in anything, and he never failed to make me laugh.

I never outright laughed with Bill. I smiled knowingly, and I was happy. But nothing was hilarious.

I thought of writing to Dear Ann or Dear Abby or Tales from the Front to see if anyone else shared my experience and/or my indecision. After all, I couldn't sleep with two men at the same time, could I? No, not Elizabeth McKennah from Sioux Bluffs, Iowa.

While we were cleaning up in the kitchen, Michael said to me, "You know all those surveys?"

"What surveys?"

"The ones that say Yuppies have lost interest in sex?"

"Oh yeah."

"I just wanted you to know that I'm atypical. All week doing research, writing briefs, dropping my files in Bellini's office, I thought about you. I don't know whether it's because I've reached the age where I'm ready to settle down, or if I'm in love with you, or whether I'm simply grateful that someone finds me halfway presentable."

"Michael, stop putting yourself down. You're very good-looking. You've got to know that."

"In an ethnic sort of way, perhaps."

"So what's wrong with ethnic?"

"Why have you been avoiding me this week?"

"Is this lawyerly tactics, trying to confuse me by changing the topic of conversation?"

"Is this Becky tactics, trying to avoid the subject of whatever feelings we might have for each other?"

"I'm not trying to avoid anything," I lied. "I just haven't had as much time to think as you have. My work load's been heavy. And besides, if I were avoiding you, we wouldn't have just broken eggrolls together." I kissed him on the nose, then backed off. "So what movies did you bring?"

He smiled and closed the dishwasher. We went into my living room, and he placed the first tape in the VCR. In the beginning, I thought it was a cheapie foreign film because the hues were unnatural and there was this seedy street scene murkily shot in the way of some artsy moviemaker. Then the title came on the screen. *Ladies in the Dark.*

The first scene had several women making love to one man, who had this enormous—well, what could one call it in polite society? The second scene had several men making love to one woman. The third scene had several men and several women entangled on a floor. All these scenes were connected by women walking down dark streets.

The fourth scene—I didn't quite catch the fourth scene because Michael and I by that time were entangled in our own pornographic coupling. But let's just say our sound track was worthy of the movie flickering over us.

I was surprised at how turned on I was. Little innocent me at twenty-nine had never seen a porno flick before. I'm sure it got repetitious, but then Michael and I got repetitious too. I loved his stamina, twice in the living room, once in the bedroom.

It was only when we were about to fall asleep that he asked me, "Do you think anyone could ever discover that I took out those movies?"

"Probably," I said. "But you can claim you were doing legal research. Michael?"

"Yes?"

"I—" Oh god, I was going to say I loved him. So what stopped me!

"Yes?" He was waiting.

"I'm glad you came tonight."

"Yeah." He was disappointed. "I'm glad you came too," he turned it into a joke.

Dear Michael. What was wrong with me? What did I want from life if not the steadiness of someone like Michael Rosen?

In our sleep, we wrapped and rewrapped ourselves around each other. It was comforting having someone so close.

Early Saturday morning the phone rang. I fumbled to get it. "Becky, it's Bill."

I couldn't take it. Here I was, lying in bed with one of the men I loved, while the other was on the phone. Great! How to ruin a weekend. Step one!

"Listen, my brother's invited me and guest to the Bears game this Sunday. We'd be in his box so you wouldn't freeze to death. How 'bout it?"

His brother? Alan? The one who took charge after their father was shot, the one who wrote a check each month to my adoptive mother? I'd be meeting his brother? "I'd love to. Thanks for asking."

"Who was that?" Michael asked, when I put down the phone.

"Someone who has tickets to the Bears game."

"Jesus. Lucky you."

"Michael, let's do something absolutely wild and crazy today, something we'll regret tomorrow. Like fly to Las Vegas and lose all our money."

"Oh, Becky, I can't. I've got to be in the office at ten to meet with some clients. Bellini wants me to work up a preliminary on them. I'm sorry," he said, when he saw how disappointed I was.

"It's okay," I lay back in the pillows to say. "I just wanted you to sweep me off my feet."

"I'm trying. Believe me."

Save me from myself, I wanted to beg him. But maybe it was too late for that.

11

DRIVING the car he uses to hack about in the wilderness, Bill picked me up at ten. "I hope I didn't disturb anything by calling you so early yesterday morning," he said with a grin.

I was annoyed and amused at the same time. He must have guessed I'd be with that someone else I had told him about. But I certainly wasn't going to admit it. "The only thing you disturbed was my sleep," I said primly.

We headed down Sheridan toward Lake Shore Drive, where the traffic had already grown heavy with people trying to beat the rush to Soldier Field. "Do you like football?" Bill asked me.

That was a tough question to answer, since I had never actually attended a game past high school. In college the best time to access the computers was when Illinois was on the field. And Yuri certainly never dragged me to a game. Besides, I couldn't see the fascination of sitting in a stadium with thousands of people, a fourth of them drunk, freezing my butt, toes, and fingers off, cheering on a team I couldn't care less about, while, if I wanted to watch, I could stay home in front of my television. There I could get a closeup of some coach getting apoplexy over a silly ball his team had missed catching.

"Football, I love it!" I assured Bill.

"That surprises me."

"I'm a positive person, Bill. I try to go into each experience with a smile on my face, even if half an hour later, I know I'll be crying."

"Well, this shouldn't be too bad. As I told you, we'll be in my brother's box, which is heated. Plus, he always has a lavish spread because he entertains clients. The whole thing's a massive write-off for him."

"What does your brother do exactly?"

"He runs The Skyline Agency. Don't ask me about the business. All I do is pick up a monthly check from it as part of my inheritance. You know, it's one of those financial firms that handles everything from bonds and stocks, to real estate and commodities."

"I've heard of it. But isn't that a family firm?"

"Right. My grandfather started it, William Townsend the first. Then my father took over, then Alan."

"But you never wanted to join? Or did Alan—"

"Oh no. I could have joined, I guess. Alan would have seen to it that I was assigned something I could do. He's not the typical older brother. I suppose it's because he's ten years older than I am. He's always sort of protected me."

"From what?"

Bill was silent for a minute, then he said, "There was a lot of shit we went through as children. Our mother died when I was eight; he was eighteen, in his first year at college. I lived at home, naturally. But after she died, Alan made sure I wasn't left stranded among the relatives. I remember vaguely hearing him and my Grandmother Mansfield arguing with my father, and the next thing I knew it was off to boarding school for me."

"It wouldn't have been better to stay home?"

Bill shrugged. "After my mother died, there wasn't any home. Alan—well, after my mother died, he never came home again, not while my father was alive."

"He never came home at all?"

"Nope."

"Not once? That's strange."

"He never got along with my father."

"But you did."

"I never really knew my father. That's a funny thing to say, but I don't really have any memories left of things we did as a family, Alan, me, my mother, my father. Then my father remarried. I told you that Jane was a nice lady, kind, the type of mom who baked cookies and wiped noses. But Alan didn't approve of her, so I always felt guilty liking her. And then when she, well, after the tragedy, Alan finally did come home to take care of everything. He was a senior in college at the time. When I look back on it, it must have been so hard for him, but he arranged for my father's funeral, he set up a caretaker head of the firm until he graduated from Princeton, and he tried to straighten out the legal mess that my father's death had created. That's why I get upset now when friends say Alan is so cold and distant, forbidding even. He's had so much to put up with, I don't think he's ever been really happy. Meanwhile, he's let me go my own way. I don't know if I even deserve the share of the firm's profits he pays me each month. But it certainly has helped support me, especially in my early years as a commercial artist, when I was making nothing."

"But aside from your interest in the firm, you must have inherited quite a bit?"

"Yes, but Alan always told me not to touch it, to save it for rainy days." Bill smiled. "Our mother used to say things like that to us, save your money for a rainy day, let a smile be your umbrella, all the clichés. Alan's a lot like our mother, except nobody can see that side of him except me, and maybe his kids. Well, you'll see what I mean when you meet him."

I was dying to meet Alan Townsend, if only to test any memory I might have of him. It's funny how I remember Bill so well, and yet Alan was just a shadow. Of course, if he never returned home after his mother died, why would I have any but the vaguest memories of him? I must have only met him during the time of my mother's trial.

Bill was waved into a parking spot. We climbed out and felt the strike force of the wind from Lake Michigan. I thanked God we were going to be in a box, as it was cold and moist outside, frost-bite weather.

Bill hugged and hustled me inside the stadium, up to the boxes. There was a guard on duty. We were checked in and sent on our way.

Alan Townsend's box was already filling up when we arrived. There were plenty of men, a few wives, two children, and two people overseeing the buffet. Bill took my hand and directed me toward a man who was much different from him. Bill was tall; Alan was taller, and thinner. He had dark hair, which he parted on one side and combed back, so that it looked almost sleek, except for one lock, which had escaped to fall over his forehead. His eyes were a dark brown, and they were staring straight at me. Far from feeling undressed by those eyes, I sensed that I had been discovered.

"Alan, this is Becky Belski. Becky, Alan," Bill introduced us.

I shook hands. Alan's clasp was firm and businesslike. He held my hand no longer than he had to. "I'm glad you could join us today," he said with a professional veneer. "Please, help yourself to the buffet, and I hope you enjoy the game."

I laughed at my fear of discovery. We were simply greeted and dismissed. Since I had eaten nothing all day except for my morning cup of coffee, I took Alan up on his buffet offer. I tried not to make a pig of myself, but everything was delicious. Bill and I both mingled, though there wasn't much going on of interest. The men, even on this football

Sunday, were discussing business, business, business. So if the IRS asked, I could tell them the box was a legitimate write-off.

I tried to join the women, but I didn't exactly fit in. They were all very polished; and their conversation, while genteel, was a war game all its own. They talked about their children, what their children were doing, what scores their children received on the latest intelligence and achievement tests, which private schools their children would be going to, which skiing hole the family would grace during winter vacation. When talk turned to their country clubs and golf games, before focusing on the merits of indoor tennis, I figured maybe I better sit this whole afternoon out.

Fortunately, at that moment Bill signaled to me. I smiled and joined him. He was with a very well kept blond. She wasn't a brassy blond, just that delicate shade of champagne that I like to believe can only come out of a bottle.

"Becky," Bill said, when I joined him, "this is my sister-in-law Tricia. And," he added, as Tricia and I shook hands, "these two troublemakers are my nephews Evan and Graham."

I smiled at the boys, both in their early teens. "No William Townsend the fourth?" I wondered.

"We're waiting for Bill to produce his namesake," Tricia said, before she turned from us to greet a newcomer.

I was glad when the kickoff came. Everyone sort of settled down in the seats to watch the game. The Bears were playing the Vikings, and the TV in the box picked up the various ensembles those in the stadium were wearing to support their teams. Meanwhile, the waiters were coming by with bottles of wine and beer to refill our glasses, along with cute little hors d'oeuvres.

At half time a new buffet appeared, this one with luncheon meats and hard rolls, and cheesecake for dessert. By that time I was all eaten out, but the men seemed to revive enough for a sandwich or two.

Bill was no exception. He came back with ham on rye and a beer. "Having a good time?" he asked.

"How the hell can you eat so much?" I wondered.

"Hey, it's free."

The second half came; the Vikings were ahead by three points. Each side had three touchdowns and conversions, but the Vikings had been first on the board with a field goal. The men were cheering on the Bears. Since I couldn't care less, I watched Alan Townsend. Now his sons were sitting to one side of him, and he leaned over constantly to speak to them. When he smiled at them, he was no longer some CEO. He was just a father out with his children, albeit a father with tons of money. Anyway, I saw what Bill meant about the two extremes of Alan's character, aloof with outsiders, yet very loving toward his children.

In the last minute of the game, the Bears tried to move the ball down the field. They got halfway before they had no choice but to kick or lose. They kicked, but they lost anyway. It sort of put a damper on the afternoon. As everyone was saying a dejected good-bye, Bill returned to me. "Tricia wants to know if we'd like to come back to their place for a light supper."

Oh lord, if I had to have another thing to eat—and yet, here was the opportunity to become a member of the family again, even if they had no idea who I was. Plus, I'd have the chance to see the house where it all took place, where the first Mrs. Townsend fell down a flight of stairs to her death on Christmas Eve, and the second shot her husband to death three years later, just after New Year's. "Sure. Let's join them," I said to Bill.

If only there were a magical way of leaving Chicago after a Bears game. But no, we were stuck in the traffic crawling up Lake Shore Drive, so it took us over an hour and a half to reach Kenilworth. I discovered with more than a twinge of envy that Alan Townsend and his family had traveled home via limousine. Such is the life of the very rich. My mother must have enjoyed this while she had it. No wonder she married William Townsend when she had the chance. And then for the first time—and I'm ashamed to admit it—it occurred to me that this sort of life would have been mine had not my mother confessed to killing her husband.

The circular drive that led up to the front portico of the Townsend manse was gravel. I didn't remember it. The house was Georgian. I didn't remember that either. The lake I remembered, but there were lots of houses on the lake. Maybe when I got inside, it would all come back to me.

But once inside I was still not struck by anything that seemed even vaguely familiar. A maid took our coats. I turned to Bill to whisper, "Is this the family estate?" He looked at me strangely. "I mean, where you grew up?"

"Oh no," Bill said. "Alan sold that off immediately after my father's death. Too many unpleasant memories. He had a condo in the city until he married Tricia fifteen years ago. Tricia bought this house mainly because it needed so much work. Redecorating is a continuous process with her."

I was made well aware of that when, as soon as we entered what certainly would have been called the drawing room, with its blazing fire, french windows that led out to the backyard, and rather delicate furniture, Tricia smiled and asked if I wanted to see the house. Needless to say, I was polite enough to answer enthusiastically, "I'd love to!"

Not only did I have the opportunity to see the house, I became party to her retelling the adventures she had finding each item in the house. I learned the name of her painter, which architect helped her reconstruct the upstairs porch where she and Alan had their morning coffee in the summer, where she purchased the material for her drapes and who made them. After viewing the house, I had no idea whether Tricia loved her husband or her children, but I knew damned well she loved that house.

Coming down the stairway, I observed again a six-foot portrait of a dark-haired woman in a pale yellow dress. It dominated both the downstairs and upstairs hallways. "Who is she?" I asked Tricia.

"How often I've declared we should move that portrait," she confessed to me. "But Alan insists on having it in the hallway, surrounded by our stained-glass windows, like a shrine. It's totally out of sync with the rest of my decorating, but Alan sometimes is so stubborn."

"A relative?"

"His mother. Ne'er let a word against her pass your lips."

"I never knew her."

"Who did? She died so long ago, but tragically. I think that's why Alan wants her portrait here. It's as if he can't say good-bye."

"And his father?"

"No, there are no pictures of his father anywhere. Not in the house, in photo albums, not even at The Skyline Agency, though he was director there long enough. Alan was never close to his father. Well, he really doesn't talk about his parents at all. I just assume he felt strongly about his mother, since her picture stares us in the face all the time."

"Did you know either of his parents?"

"Oh no. I'm a Boston girl. I was with Filene's as a buyer when I came to Chicago with a promotion to join Marshall Field's. I had several friends out here from Mount Holyoke. They invited me to parties, which is where I met Alan."

"And he swept you off your feet."

Tricia smiled. "Alan's not the sweeping kind. I'm afraid it was more a case of I chased him until he caught me." She laughed. "Everyone thought he was never going to get married. Sort of like it is with Bill. Only Alan married when he was thirty." She sighed. "Both Alan and Bill seemed scared of marriage. I practically had to arrange the wedding around him before Alan realized he was trapped." She gave a light, tingling laugh. "But who can blame the brothers? I guess they were scared off marriage by their father's second one. I understand their stepmother was a real gold digger."

"Who told you that?" I wondered defensively.

"No one's ever come right out and said anything. It's just

the scuttlebutt around the club and the way Alan's occasionally spoken with such bitterness about the haste of his father's second marriage."

"Well, if she were a gold digger, she didn't get much out of it, did she, except a term in prison?"

Tricia shivered. "Horrible story. And I didn't even get all the facts from Alan, who'll never talk about it. I had to hear all about it from other people after we were married."

"Alan seems the antithesis of Bill," I egged her on. "Bill's so," I shrugged, "erratically romantic, while Alan appears to be very much in control of everything. At least that's the way it seemed at the game today."

Tricia sighed and nodded. "But whatever Alan lacks in the wild romance department, he more than makes up for with the children. No child could ask for a better father. I guess he's compensating for what he feels he never got."

As if to prove her point, when we returned to the drawing room, the males of the family were missing. Then we heard their shouts. All four of them were outside, playing touch football, horsing around with each other. It was a game. It was love. "Let's play catch," Billy said to me, when I was five years old. A wave of sadness swept through me. Who had we been? What had happened to us? And why?

Tricia called them in when supper was served. They washed up quickly and joined us in the family dining room, as opposed to the formal dining room. Here there was tile on the floor, not carpet. A very wise choice with children, I should imagine.

We had macaroni and cheese, and it didn't come from boxes. Then the boys were sent off to do their homework while we retired to the sitting room, where coffee was served. We spoke the usual nothings, about the business climate, Chicago sports, winter vacations, until Tricia asked how Bill and I met. I was thinking of something cute to say when Bill answered all too honestly. "Becky is investigating the Aberdeen case. She's working for the lawyer representing Daryl."

"Bellini Reese?" Tricia said. "How well we all know him. He's getting to be sort of like a family practitioner in our circle. You know, Becky, I'm surprised you're involved in something like that. Had I known you were a private investigator, I probably would have been more guarded in my conversation with you. But I thought with a name like Belski you were an artist."

"Not all private investigators are named Mike Hammer, dear," Alan said. He was staring straight at me, and he was not happy.

"I'm not really a private investigator," I tried to ease his mind. "I mainly work with computers. But sometimes computers can only take you so far."

"What a terrible mess Lionel and Daryl are in," Tricia sighed.

"What struck me as being very strange is that everyone I've talked to seems to know exactly why Daryl shot Lionel, everyone but the police."

"It's none of the police's business, is it?" Tricia asked. "They're here to maintain the public order, which in Kenilworth means mainly giving out traffic tickets. What happens within our houses is our private affair."

"I couldn't agree with you more," Alan assured his wife. Boy, was he unhappy.

"The legal system is intrusive," I noted.

"Not if it's handled right," he replied.

I felt I was being challenged, so I stupidly threw caution to the wind. "Of course," I volleyed, "you were involved in a situation like this before, when you were a very young man. And you handled it?"

Everyone sucked in their breath except Alan and me.

"One does what one has to," he returned with a coldness that frightened me. But he had made the point for both of us. And as I left the house that evening, with fond farewells mixed with assurances from Tricia that we'd see each other again, I resolved once more, despite my feelings for Bill, to get to the bottom of my stepfather's death.

"What was going on between you and Alan?" Bill asked me once we were in the car.

How could I tell him that what was going on was the first stage of an all-out war?

12

I had gone about as far as I could on the Aberdeen case. Not only had I dug up as much dirt as possible, I had also used my investigation to delve into a case of far more importance to me. The Aberdeens were my foot in the door of the Townsend household. But now that path was at a dead end until Bellini decided he needed more information.

Nat was aware of the fact that I had little to do for Bellini Reese. He wanted to assign me something new. I knew Nat. He would pile it on until I had time for nothing except sitting before the computer, digging deeper into obscure files that only I could find.

So I made one of those mad decisions that only someone as foolish as I could make. I confessed to Nat that there was something I was looking into on my own and that, while I was doing so, I would pay him for my use of his computers and his office. "You're crazy," he told me. "Does this mean you want to quit Resources?"

"I want a leave of absence."

"I don't understand the concept."

"Nat, this is really something I have to do."

He saw how serious I was. "How can I charge someone for computer time when she's been to my house for latkes at Hanukkah?"

And yet he managed. But he wasn't charging me the full cost, so I didn't feel abused. No, I had my cubby; I had my computer. Now I had to get to work. I made a list of things to do. Find and interview Susan Bradshaw, Clariss Taylor, Megan Wilder. Plus, surely my mother had had household help. Who were they? Where were they?

Jelly Mellon. Bill said she was a good friend of his step-mother's. Could I use the Aberdeen connection to get to Daryl's mother?

A transcript had to exist of my mother's trial, such as it was. Ask Michael the most efficient way of getting it.

What about her lawyer? But what excuse could I use to ask about the case? If I said I was Jane Peters's daughter, that would solve so many problems. Except everyone would know who I was and I could then expect no more help. If Jane Peters was an outsider, Becky Belski was more of one. No one lifted a finger to help Jane when she was charged with murder. Why, twenty-four years after the fact, would they help her daughter? Knowledge of my identity would simply lead to a further coverup.

No, I would play it safe. Becky Belski was a wonderful identity to hide behind. No one could possibly guess I was Elizabeth Peters. Meanwhile, I would continue to see Bill, if he asked. Not that that would be a hardship. Besides, he was my key to the secrets I believed only Alan Townsend held.

And so to work.

Susan Bradshaw was first on my list, mainly because I believed I had already located her in Niles. She had served secretarial duty in the Skyline firm at the same time as my adoptive mother Winnie McKennah. She was about the same age as Winnie, maybe a few years older. Dared I hope that they were confidantes?

From the information I received from my snitch at Skyline, Susan was employed at The Skyline Agency at the time of William Townsend's untimely death. Certainly, the gossip mill must have been working overtime to cover that astounding event, and perhaps the event three years earlier, when the first Mrs. Townsend took her fatal fall down the staircase.

It struck me then how strange it was for Alan to have his mother's portrait dominating his own staircase. I wasn't a psychologist, but I had to wonder at the connection.

But back to Susan. How best to approach her? I could say I was researching a book on the Townsend case. But then mightn't she clam up out of some misbegotten loyalty to the firm? Or even worse, call Alan Townsend and ask if it was all right to talk to me?

Aha! I could be a lawyer representing the estate of Winnie McKennah. Winnie could have left Susan something in her will. Could have, but she hadn't, and would Susan have expected something?

Damn. Perhaps deception wasn't quite my thing.

What would make Susan Bradshaw talk to me?

I sat at my console for half an hour just thinking. Nat came by several times to stare at me. Finally, I thought I had come up with something that might be slightly plausible. At least it was nonthreatening. I would be the McKennah family genealogist. We were having a McKennah family reunion in Iowa, and all branches would be represented, along with a short history of each. Unfortunately, Winnie had been so cut off from us for so long that we hadn't really known what she did in her Chicago years. Could Susan help fill us in? How did I get her name? From someone I wouldn't specify at Skyline.

In truth, my adoptive mother had relatives all over Iowa whom we occasionally saw, but none in Sioux Bluffs. I had a feeling she liked it that way. There were a lot of cousins I never could keep straight, even when they came to Winnie's funeral. But I felt I could fake it.

I would naturally enough be Becky McKennah.

Becky McKennah.

Winnie had called me Becky instead of Elizabeth because she'd always wanted a child named Becky. Susan Bradshaw might make the connection, and I'd be sunk along with my lies. But the same thing could happen if I used Elizabeth. However, who would know my middle name? Diane McKennah. I made my call.

I felt guilty when Susan Bradshaw fell all over herself to be of help. She recognized Winnie McKennah's name immediately and was honestly sorry to hear that she had died. But yes, she would be delighted to fill in the blanks on my family tree. I could come over that very afternoon.

The house in Niles was typical of the Chicago suburbs. The Chicago area is filled with what looked like Monopoly houses, lined up exactly the same, one after another on little patches of lawn with only the flora to distinguish one bungalow from the other.

The Bradshaw house was well taken care of, the lawn neatly cut. The only clue outside that the owners were old was the huge gas-guzzler sitting in the driveway. As I rang the doorbell, I put on my eager, friendly, Iowa face and waited.

Susan Bradshaw was plump and midwestern. She had that empty, white-bread face that one would never find in California or even in Chicago's ethnic neighborhoods. It was old-fashioned, open, and receptive to strangers. I was welcomed into her parlor.

Well, actually it was her dining room. Her husband was watching ESPN in the living room. She poured tea and inquired how Winnie had died, or, as she put it, had "passed on." She wanted all the details. "Then she didn't have to suffer through any operations," Susan said, when I gave them to her.

"No, Mrs. Bradshaw, not that I know of."

"Winnie was always a fortunate women. I myself have had my womanhood taken away from me. I can't tell you what that was like."

Well, actually, she could tell me. And she did. After that we went through her CAT scan and her latest root canal. Feeling faint by that time, I almost thought she was going to have to call an ambulance and take me to the hospital, which I sensed she would have enjoyed. However, her love of blood and gore gave me hope that she would have gotten all the juicy details of the Affair Townsend.

"So tell me," I was finally able to say, when the medical drama was winding down, "what did you and Winnie McKennah do at Skyline?"

I sat back, prepared to spend the night, when Susan Bradshaw started with her first day at the company. Winnie, who had already been there over six months, showed her the ropes. "I was right out of a secretarial course, and this was my first job. I was terrified because I could never take dictation fast enough, certainly not as fast as Winnie."

"Winnie was very successful as a secretary?"

"The best. And dedicated too. They all liked that about her."

My poor adoptive mother. That probably meant she fell all over herself to please everybody.

"How far did she rise in the firm?" I wondered.

"As high as it gets, personal secretary to William Townsend himself!" Susan said with radiating pride.

"William Townsend—William Townsend," I repeated thoughtfully. "Seems to me I've heard that name before. But I just can't quite put my finger on it."

Susan had a little smile on her face. "Well, if you knew anything about scandal in Chicago, you would have heard his name."

"Oh my. Was Winnie involved in—"

"Lord no!" Susan objected. "Winnie was always the soul of discretion, which isn't to say that everyone in the Townsend office was quite that perfect."

I leaned forward. "Now I'm really curious. What happened? You've got to tell me."

As if she wasn't going to tell me anyway. She looked into

the living room to make sure her husband was occupied. Then she said, "It all started with the death of the first Mrs. Townsend. Well, maybe it started a little bit before, but I don't know for sure, and I'm not the sort to spread rumors."

Sure. "How did the first Mrs. Townsend die?" I inquired softly.

"She fell down the stairs in her house, poor soul. She was such a sweet lady. Every year we would meet her at the Christmas party, her and her sons. I can't tell you how upset we all were when this happened. Winnie asked me to take up a collection for flowers from the staff."

"Mr. Townsend must have been absolutely devastated."

"Well—" She leaned back thoughtfully. "I can't say as I know how he felt. But the death certainly put a strain on him as far as the family went. That's probably why he remarried again so soon, to give a mother to those two sons of his."

"You knew the two sons then?"

"I knew Alan Townsend quite well. He was the oldest. When he was fifteen, he started working at Skyline in the summer. Everyone knew he would be taking over the firm. After all, his grandfather and father had run it before him. Of course, no one knew he'd be taking it over so soon. He was always a strange boy, so unlike his father. His father was very friendly, a backslapper some people called him, while Alan was the silent type. He cut quite a romantic figure among the young secretaries, even though he was still a teenager. What was sad was that he never quite got along with his father. Teenaged years and all that. Rebellion sets in, and in Alan's case it seemed to have been aggravated by the death of his mother. Matter of fact, now that I come to think of it, we never saw Alan again after his mother died. I think he spent all the time out east at that school he went to."

"Was there any reason for Alan to be hostile toward his father?"

"Well—" Susan screwed up her face as she thought. "I

had three children myself, so I can tell you raising them isn't easy. Sometimes you have to try to instill the fear of God in them. However, there was something dark in Mr. Townsend's character. Of course, we never knew what went on inside his private office, but before Winnie took over, he let go a whole slew of secretaries. He called them incompetent, while they said some things about him that don't bear repeating. But you know how it is, a man is under so much pressure that he has to release it somewhere."

I could just imagine the way my stepfather released his anger. I was so sick to my stomach, I almost wished Susan would go back to describing another of her operations. "So I suppose that's where I heard William Townsend's name," I said, "his wife falling down the stairs and all."

"Oh, no, no, no," Susan corrected me. "You heard his name because he was murdered."

"Murdered!"

"Shot by a girl Winnie and I knew very well. Maybe Winnie told this story to some of your cousins."

"Could be," I said doubtfully.

"Certainly, we saw enough of police and lawyers at that time for Winnie to remember it. Not that we had much to tell them. But, you see, Mr. Townsend's second wife was a secretary in our office. Her name was Jane Peters, and she was sort of Winnie's right hand, had a desk in the main office with Winnie and everything. Oh, she was a pretty thing, tall with reddish brown hair and freckles, just like yours," Susan noted. Oh God. But she went on with a sigh. "Jane could wear just about anything and look like a model in it. That's what made us all so jealous.

"She was a widow. I remember, when she was hired, we were all afraid that, because she had a child, she wouldn't be able to do her fair share of the work. But she never asked for a day off because of that child. She was a hard worker, I'll give her that, I don't care what everyone else said about her afterward."

"What did they say?"

Susan looked strangely at me until she recalled, "I forgot to mention it, didn't I? She was the one who killed her husband. Shot him all over the place. Six bullets in him. What a shock that was. Here we thought she had it made, marrying the boss and all, living in that huge house in Kenilworth, having all the money anyone could ever dream of. And what does she do, throws it away by murdering him. How do you figure these things?"

"Why ever would she kill her husband?"

"Well. Oh lord. We didn't believe her at the time. Nobody did. But now I think, when I think of it at all, now I wonder if maybe she was telling the truth. You see all these shows on TV about normal-looking men who lead average lives; but when they get home, they treat their wives and children like—well, like nobody has a right to. No one gave a thought to that sort of thing back then. Everyone lived behind closed doors and kept any sort of abuse a secret. But now I have to wonder if perhaps Jane Peters didn't get a raw deal, if perhaps there wasn't something to what she said about Mr. Townsend abusing and threatening her.

"Poor Jane didn't have many friends left by then. I suppose we were all jealous of her. None of us had any hopes of marrying money. And when Jane married Mr. Townsend so quickly after his first wife died, there were whispers going around behind hands that she was already sleeping with him before the death. And certainly, his people never accepted her. To them she was just a nobody who married into money. I think she was probably very lonely." Susan smiled. "If someone can be lonely with all that money to count. I'd like to try it for a while instead of living on our pensions."

"So even Winnie didn't like her?" I said thoughtfully.

"Winnie was very dedicated to the Townsend family. And I think Winnie had a crush on her boss, even though she never said anything. You see, Winnie wasn't married like the rest of us older gals, and maybe she had fantasies about Mr. Townsend. Who knows what's in another person's head? I do know she was a bit miffed when Jane announced to us during our coffee break that she and Mr. Townsend were to be married. And then when Jane flashed the ring, we were all blinded by it. I think Megan knew about the engagement before any of us did.''

''Megan?''

''Megan—ooh what was her last name? Can't remember. But she married shortly thereafter anyway and moved to—where was it, Peoria, I think. Her husband worked in sales for Caterpillar. Wilder. No, that was her maiden name. Capone. How could I forget?'' Susan clapped her hand delightedly. ''We all made fun of her because she was marrying someone named Al Capone. She and Jane were good friends. They were like most young girls who came to work, looking for a husband. Winnie and I were in it for the duration.''

''And yet, didn't Winnie move back to Iowa in—'' I checked my alleged notes—''1966?''

''What a surprise that was,'' Susan said. ''One day she was in the office, the next day she was gone. I got a Christmas card from her that year, asking how everyone was, but she never said a word about why she left. Still, so many things were happening then, what with the murder and the trial and the business being in a sort of limbo. Yes, I remember, Winnie left shortly after the trial. We all had to stay around until then. You know what they say, don't leave town. But then she left, and we never saw her again.''

''Things must have changed at Skyline anyway,'' I suggested.

''The months directly after Mr. Townsend was murdered were confused. No one was really at the helm. We were all waiting for Alan Townsend to graduate. We lost clients in that period also. But Alan was a bright boy—I guess I should say man, since he was our boss. And now I understand the company's doing better than ever. I see his picture now and then in the newspaper at one benefit or another with that pretty wife of his. People are stronger than you think, aren't they? Here he survived two tragedies, one right after another practically. And yet he kept going. I still get the office newsletter and every year a basket of fruit for Christmas. Skyline was that type of firm, family. And families are what's really important, aren't they?"

I thanked Susan Bradshaw for all her help in filling out our family tree. "Good to have someone to talk to," she confessed. "I can't get that old lug away from the television. Not that he watches, he just kind of snoozes there."

I gratefully drove out of Niles, back to my own place in Evanston. I had another lead to follow, Megan Wilder Capone. But what would I ask her? What my mother was like? Had she been sleeping with Mr. Townsend before they got married? How much did I want to know? And what in god's name was I going to do with all this information once I got it?

13

WHEN I arrived home from Niles, my answering machine was again pulsating red. Two messages were from my dentist. One said don't forget your appointment, the other said you've missed your appointment. Where was my twenty-four-hour notice?

Bill Townsend called. He had free tickets to the Cyberline Quartet. He would assume, if I didn't reach him by five, that I didn't want to go, in which case he would go alone and try to pick up someone there. I looked at my watch. It was after five. Good. I hated chamber music.

There were two calls from Michael, one telling me he could be free about eight, the other that he could be free about nine, should I deign to call him and invite him over.

One call came from the cleaners. Was I ever going to pick up the winter coat I left there six months ago, or should charity be the receiver of my beneficence?

I flopped into my easy chair. Life was too damned complicated. I was depressed; I didn't know why. I had entered the shadows of my past life, seeking what? The truth? Knowledge? Justice? Or only memory? It was a mistake. Better I should remain the happy-go-lucky child of Winnie McKennah than to try to reclaim even a portion of my life with my mother, a woman even now, with all my newfound knowledge, I only vaguely remembered.

Along with the depression, I had a bad case of guilt. I had been on the witness stand, yet I had said nothing to save my mother. The fact of the matter was that the only thing I could really remember about the entire incident was just that, saying nothing. I was probably sitting there sniveling while my mother was being railroaded.

More than ever, I truly believed she was railroaded. So why hadn't I been able to help her? After all, I lived in the house with her and William Townsend for well over a year. I must have seen and heard things. Obviously, the man was a monster. All signs pointed to the fact that William Townsend II murdered his first wife, then drove his second wife to murder him. But who could prove it? I needed help.

Michael Rosen, lawyer and friend, was only a phone call away. ''Do you want me to bring anything or do you have something there to eat?'' he asked.

I stretched the phone cord and looked in my refrigerator. ''Sour milk and Lean Cuisine,'' I inventoried.

''I'll stop at the deli on my way there.''

I showered and dried myself to a state of perfumed loveliness and was covered only in my terrycloth robe when Michael arrived. There was something perhaps a bit askew in our romance because he attacked the pastrami on kaiser roll with pickle and mustard before he attacked me. Obviously, food for the soul was less important to him than food for the body. When I complained, he didn't apologize, only said he needed to get his stamina up for me. Frankly, I've never heard it called stamina before.

When we finally got down to the basics of our relationship, I felt there were four of us in bed together, Michael, me, the pastrami sandwich, and the beer he washed it down with. Should I thank my lucky stars that he had removed the onion?

"What did I do wrong tonight?" he asked me afterward.

"What makes you think you did anything wrong?" I asked, knowing how sensitive the male ego is, and thus being prepared to lie to protect it.

"I suppose it was the fact that you kept complaining about my elbows, my knees, my fingers."

"Did I mention your breath?"

"It was eating first, wasn't it? But, Becky, I haven't had anything since seven this morning."

"I haven't had anything since lunch."

"I brought you roast beef with mayo on egg, just like you asked. Perhaps if you had eaten first."

"Oh, Michael, lay off."

"Obviously." He flopped back onto my Dan Rivers.

"Listen, Michael—"

"I await your words."

"I want to hire you." I reached over his body and grabbed my change purse. I pulled a dollar from it. "Will this do as a retainer?"

He looked at it. "A whole dollar?"

"I mean, will this ensure lawyer/client confidentiality?"

He turned to face me. "Becky, are you serious?"

"Yes."

"Um, maybe I better put my vest back on."

I laughed and hugged him. "I don't want to tell you everything."

"Bad start. You should always tell your lawyer everything."

"Yes, but—this is sort of a hypothetical case."

"Sure." Disbelief flirted around his lips.

"Let's suppose someone confessed to a murder she didn't commit. Well, she did commit it, but she had reason to kill the bastard. At first, she pleaded self-defense, but then she was pressured to change the plea to guilty of second-degree murder with mitigation because—because—" I shot up in bed. How the hell could I have been so stupid! My mother pleaded guilty because Alan Townsend promised to take care of her child. Me. Me and Winnie and all those checks Alan Townsend kept sending. How stupid, how blind I had been! "Because she was protecting someone," I hurried on.

"Someone who actually committed the murder?" Michael wondered.

"No. She committed the murder. The person she was protecting, well, she wasn't really protecting as much as providing for that person. Yet, if she had taken her chances, she might have gotten off with self-defense."

"Why did she kill this person?"

"Because he was abusing her."

"And she had proof of that?" Michael waited. "Becky?"

"I don't know if she had proof, but everyone sort of knew."

"Everyone sort of knew, such as rumors, hearsay? Not exactly proof. Did someone see her being hit, did she go to the doctor's or an emergency room, did she call the police, seek shelter, seek a court order?"

"Michael, this was years ago in the midsixties, when we were but babes. You know people weren't sensitive to those things then. Abuse just happened, and hey, it was too bad, but that's the way the world was."

"She killed someone; she confessed to the murder. And now she wants—what, to lodge an appeal?"

"She's dead."

"That sort of makes the question moot, doesn't it?"

"But what if someone wants to clear her name?"

"Well—" He leaned back. "I don't understand. What are you after?"

I shrugged. "I don't know. That's what I'm trying to figure out. Truth? Justice?"

"The American way?"

"Which is for men to abuse their wives and children."

"Oh lord, you remind me of this feminist lawyer I once

113

dated," Michael said tiredly. "Normal people don't resort to physical violence."

I ignored the potential debate. "What if it could be proved that the murdered man's family conspired against this woman and pressured her to confess to murder, even though she could have got off with self-defense? Then what could you do?"

Michael shrugged. "I suppose you could ask for civil damages, if you could prove everything you're saying. What is all this?"

"Something I've stumbled onto. But I'm sort of stymied because no one knows the true story of what happened."

"Well, what about obtaining a trial transcript and taking it from there?"

"The trial transcript!" I remembered.

"If she pled guilty with mitigating circumstances, she would have called witnesses for her mitigation hearing."

"But would a trial transcript still be available?"

"It'd have to be, Becky. You should know that."

"And how do I get one?"

"Find out where she was tried and go to their court-house."

"And maybe try to get my hands on her lawyer's notes?"

"No, you can't have those. That's confidential." He waved the dollar in front of me. "Remember?" he said.

Poor Michael was beat from his long day spent overcharging clients for his time; so I put my roast beef sandwich in the refrigerator, and we fell asleep in each other's arms. I must admit I was exhausted too. Stirring things up is tiring. But I paid for it. In my sleep I had that nightmare again, me sitting silent on the stand while my mother stared at me with her sad, sad eyes. I'll save you this time, Mother, I promised her, before the flow of her falling tears faded into the scream of my alarm.

14

SINCE the murder took place in Cook County, but outside the city of Chicago, I had to go the courthouse on Old Orchard Road in Skokie to file my application for a transcript of the murder case. The clerk was extremely helpful. I was pleasantly surprised, especially when she told me the fee for the transcript would be only four dollars. Then she broke the bad news. Since the case had taken place so long ago, the transcript was stored in their warehouse. "Don't count on it coming in for a couple of weeks," she warned.

Fine, I thought. That would give me a chance to pursue my lead on Megan Wilder Capone.

Megan was easy to find. Susan Bradshaw had given me all the information I needed. Caterpillar, Al Capone, Megan Wilder. And they were still married after all these years.

From what Susan said, I assumed Megan would be about my mother's age or even younger, which meant she would be in her late forties, early fifties. Family trees wouldn't do for Megan. For her I would be Becky Belski with a contract under my belt to write the true story of the murder of William Townsend II for one of the proliferating Chicago magazines.

Her answering machine was on all day, so I couldn't reach her until the evening. When I told her why I wanted to interview her, she said, "Who would care about that old story?"

"Obviously, my editor. And I understand you might have some vital input on the case. You were, after all, best friends with Jane Peters, weren't you?"

"We were pals," she conceded. "Poor Jane."

"If I could only have a few hours of your time. Perhaps I could buy you dinner. I'm in Chicago now. Should I drive out to Peoria tomorrow evening so we can meet? You could make reservations somewhere."

"Well. Okay. I guess if the story is going to be told, it should be told right. Yes. Someone should know Jane's side of it. Come on out. I'll tell you where we can meet right now. Off the highway on Exit Seven there's a restaurant called the Red Barn. It's pretty nice; we won't be crowded. How about six o'clock? Then I can come there straight from work."

"Great. Six o'clock, the Red Barn, Exit Seven," I repeated. I hung up the phone, well satisfied with my day's work.

When I got a call at ten o'clock that night, I knew it had to be from Michael. He was probably just finishing work and wanted to know what I was doing, which at this point was formulating what questions I would ask Megan Wilder Capone. I picked up the phone, ready to hear Michael's exhausted voice. Instead I heard Bill's more romantic, husky tones. "Is this the woman I'm in love with?" he asked.

"Sorry. Wrong number," I told him.

"Don't hang up, Becky!"

"Oh, you mean this isn't a pervert?"

"I'd like to be, if you'd only give me the chance. By the

way, am I under the mistaken impression that you didn't answer my musical call to arms yesterday?"

I sighed. "Violins give me a headache," I confessed. "Especially violins and bass combined. Chamber music is an upper-class pursuit, Bill. Though I guess lower-upper class, since those nobles in the seventeenth and eighteenth century who hired quartets and trios probably didn't have room in their salons for a full orchestra. Give me some funky, lowdown blues."

"Hmm. Let me check the papers. I definitely want to get together with you to wear you down about this other man of yours."

"You obviously need a challenge."

"Well, you have said no for quite a few dates now. And I'm running out of time."

"You're leaving for South America?"

"No. You might have noticed the Christmas decorations that went up right after the Halloween pumpkins came down. This is my busy season. Everyone wants a portrait of himself or his house or his dog, sometimes his horse, though I'm not good at horses. And cats, I hate them. Mangy little creatures. I'm supposed to capture a cat's personality. Cats don't have a personality. I showed one devouring a cardinal, and I had to give back my commission. So you see, this is where I support myself for the rest of the year. But I'm willing to lose a few thousand dollars here or there just to see you."

"I'm flattered."

"I'll check the papers and call you back. Save Saturday night for me."

"Okay," I agreed.

When the phone rang a few minutes later, I thought it was Bill calling me back to tell me where he was taking me. So I was surprised when I picked up the phone and heard Michael groan, "I'm dead."

"Rough day, huh?"

"The worst. We wrestled with Lionel's lawyer today. The

poor sod's sitting there so smug. He doesn't seem to have any idea that his client slept with his wife's mother. Bellini is waiting, baiting, drawing him in. He does enjoy toying with his victims, just like a cat."

"That's the second time cats have come up in conversations tonight."

"Oh?" he perked up. "Who else have you been talking to?"

"A friend."

"Hmm. I was going to call earlier and ask you out, but frankly, I've got to prepare for a meeting tomorrow with our straight-shooter Daryl Aberdeen. She wants to discuss strategy, and of course Bellini is too busy."

"From her pictures, that shouldn't be too much of a burden. She's very attractive."

"Yeah, but don't worry, I have an aversion to lead, especially when it's shot into my body. I just wanted to call and see how you're doing on your case. Notice that you've hired yourself a dedicated lawyer."

"I applied for the trial transcript. They said it's in storage, so it'll take a few weeks. Tomorrow night I'm interviewing someone in Peoria who might know something. I don't know. I don't know where it's all going to lead."

"In lawyer terms we call that the process of discovery."

"I think in human terms it's called that too."

He managed a weak laugh. "Good luck," he told me. I had the feeling he was falling asleep as he hung up the phone.

The next day I went to Nat at Resources and asked if he had something small he wanted me to work on.

"Are you back on the payroll?" he wondered.

"I need to leave here early, but I don't want to sit around and twiddle my thumbs all day, waiting for my appointment," I confided.

He gave me something small. The Evanston library had discovered that all its books with a mention of Theodore Dreiser in them had been disappearing from its shelves. The head librarian wanted to know if it was a conspiracy of one or were feelings against Dreiser still running high among Chicagoans.

I thought I was discovering a pattern when I had to drag myself away from the console for my trip to Peoria.

Peoria is an economically depressed city. Everyone in it says it is bouncing back. All I know is that you could get a huge house and a lot of land in Peoria for the same price you'd pay for a shack in the Chicago area. Still, I wouldn't be in Peoria proper. Exit 7 was outside the city, and the Red Barn was exactly where Megan Capone said it'd be. Since I was half an hour early, I sat at the bar having a ginger ale while happy hour swirled on about me.

At five of six I made my way to the hostess and asked for a quiet table for two. As I was led into the restaurant, I saw that all tables would be quiet. There wasn't much business this early. "I'm waiting for a woman in her forties," I told the hostess. "Her name's Megan Capone." The hostess smiled and said she would surely find her and bring her back when she arrived.

Bread was delivered to my table instantly, along with ice cold water. But I planned not to order anything before Megan arrived.

I saw her coming, the hostess ahead of her. Whatever Megan Wilder Capone had looked like twenty-five years ago, now she looked like a midwestern housewife. She wasn't dumpy or anything. It was just the way she dressed, conservative, nothing flashy or glamorous. She wasn't a woman from the city, but she could definitely be head of somebody's PTA.

I stood to greet her. She held out her hand. "Ms. Belski," she said. "I've never met a writer before."

Neither had I, but I shook her hand and smiled. We sat down. "My husband thinks I shouldn't be here," she confided. "He says writers always twist everything anyone says to them."

I took out one of those microrecorders I had borrowed

from Nat's office. "We can tape the conversation, if you like. That way both of us will be sure I'm getting it straight."

"Maybe," Megan conceded. "Yet it seems so formal to have everything tape-recorded."

"It saves me taking notes. We can eat and talk at the same time. By the way, dinner's definitely on me, so order what you want."

Obviously not worried about her cholesterol count, Megan ordered the skirt steak. "They do steaks best," she advised me. So I followed suit. Naturally, we couldn't have steak without the baked potato and sour cream. While waiting, we would help ourselves to the salad bar. I only hoped I wouldn't be too tubby to fit behind the wheel for my drive home.

"Now," I said, when we were seated with full plates of salad before us, "tell me about Jane Peters and Bill Townsend."

Megan held up her fork. "First, I should tell you about Jane Peters. We started work within six months of each other. I had gone to high school and taken a year at a secretarial school. At first I wanted to be a nurse so I could meet a doctor and marry him, but I soon discovered I didn't have the heart to stick a needle into anyone. I was assured I would get over my squeamishness, but I didn't. I never got the needle into the orange without bending it. It was a great disappointment to my family when I left nursing school for secretarial school. But the only other alternative was to marry my high school sweetheart, and I had no intention of doing that.

"So I was nineteen when I started working at The Skyline Agency, and that as a receptionist, after a whole year of learning how to type and take dictation. That was in—um— 1962. That summer. Jane was already working for one of the partners. She was twenty-three, definitely had fewer secretarial skills than I, so at first I resented her. But one couldn't resent her for long. She was terrified of failure and she tried so hard."

Megan leaned back in her seat. "I take that back. She wasn't terrified of failure so much as just terrified. You know how we all dream of getting married and living happily ever after? Well, Jane had gotten married right out of Lake Forest College to a student from Northern Illinois, who had gone straight from college to insurance sales. I guess they were doing okay. She got pregnant, had a little girl, and then boom, this guy zooms off the expressway on a snowy day and that's it. Fortunately, in this case it wasn't a cobbler whose children had no shoes. He left Jane an insurance policy, one he took out right after the child was born. So she had that cushion. But it didn't mean she would never have to work. She majored in English in college but failed to get a teacher's certificate. So she ended up working as a secretary. She knew how to type, and she knew her English. She was polished, unlike some of the rest of us. We were still young, beautiful maybe, but unsophisticated. Jane dressed as if she came out of a magazine. So the partners appreciated her and the image she projected. The only thing was she didn't really know much about being a secretary.

"Well, what can you do? When someone admits her ignorance to you, you have to be sympathetic, especially when you find out she's a widow with a baby at home. Her child was only one year old when she started leaving her with a babysitter.

"Anyway, when she needed help, she called on me. We became buddies and confidantes. We'd have lunch together and discuss the old biddies in the office and the Skyline partners. They were all married, but we kept hoping someone young would march in and sweep us off our feet.

"That didn't happen to Jane. Instead, she met Mr. Townsend. Old Big Bad Bill, as we liked to call him. He was one of those guys you could really grow to hate, though Jane didn't see it in time. None of us did. But after Jane left, I saw more of him because I moved up to being a receptionist in his office. He was very charming and good-natured, very accommodating when it came to his clients. But as soon as they left, his smile died. He didn't waste any of the wattage on the peons.

"But how were we to know what he was really like? He spotted Jane, whether it was at one of the partners' meetings or in the halls or whatever. He pursued her. If she hadn't been so darned panicky about making a go of it on her own, maybe she would have been sensible enough to resist his advances. Though I have to admit to not encouraging her to fight him off. I was caught up in it, you know, the romance of it all. He wooed her, he wined and dined her, and then he began to buy her things, little things like an expensive scarf, perfume, once a cashmere sweater. I was foolish enough to think it was romantic, and Jane was grateful for the attention, maybe because it meant she wouldn't lose her job. Who knows?"

"Townsend was a widower when he turned his attention to Jane?" I cut in to ask.

"Oh no! He was definitely married. That's what made it so exciting." Megan laughed. "Of course now if my husband had an affair with a secretary, I wouldn't find it so exciting. But from my perspective then, I was caught up in the danger and romance of it. My best friend sleeping with the boss. And it was good for me too. By October I had my first promotion. I took over Jane's former position because William Townsend wanted her in his office where he could see her more often. Oh, how Jane grew to complain about that. She had to work alongside one of the old biddies we were always grumbling about. Winnie her name was. Prim, proper Winnie McKennah. She was a secretary when the word was first invented.

"Jane probably should have been more circumspect. But so should have Mr. Townsend. Thanks to Winnie, it was gossip, gossip, gossip and all about Jane and the boss. It was like, what new piece of jewelry was Jane wearing and where did she get it and for what? You probably know how catty women in an office can be. But after a while, Jane didn't seem to mind. She even seemed to glory in the perks of her relationship. The weekend after Thanksgiving, she came to me and said, 'Guess what Bill's given me to be thankful about?' I guessed a divorce. But no. He had moved her into a condo along the lake, she and her little girl. God knows how many other women he had moved in there before her.

" 'It's a relief,' she said to me. And I knew what she meant. It was a relief to have someone to take care of her. Not that she didn't keep her job and work hard. It's just that on top of her salary, which wasn't much, believe me, William Townsend was paying all her bills. She was safe again. She thought.

"I don't know how she had the nerve to come to the office Christmas party that year. But there Jane was, shaking hands with Mrs. Townsend. We all thought we would die. But Mrs. Townsend had no idea. Or if she did, she gave no sign of it. Jane was just another employee to be greeted graciously. I asked Jane afterward if she were pressuring Townsend to get a divorce. 'We talk about it sometimes,' she admitted. 'But I think Bill's afraid of the scandal.' In other words, he would keep Jane as long as he was attracted to her, then dump her for someone else.

"Except Mrs. Townsend died. She fell down the stairs on Christmas Eve. It was such a shock when I found out," Megan remembered. "I didn't know anything about it until I returned to work on the twenty-seventh. I had taken a day's vacation and hadn't bothered to read the newspapers, not that they would have had anything about the case in the Kankakee papers anyway. But I returned to find a weeping Winnie McKennah and the offices draped in black crepe. Winnie's doing, I'm sure. She was so devoted to the Townsends, like an old family retainer. She was the one who told me what happened. According to Winnie, Mrs. Townsend had been carrying a stack of presents downstairs to place around the Christmas tree when she tripped on her robe and fell. Lots of contusions and a broken neck."

"Lots of contusions?" I wondered.

"I guess she bounced off the stairs on the way down," Megan said, then grimaced. "Not a particularly pleasant thought when we're about to dive into our medium rare steaks."

"What was Jane's frame of mind when this happened?" I asked.

"She was terribly upset for Bill, as she called him. But you could see—oh this is an awful thing to say. But you could see she was considering the possibilities."

"Of William Townsend's marrying her?"

"Right."

"So he must have really been very much in love with her?"

"He didn't confide in me," Megan said with a wry smile. "But Jane believed he was crazy about her, would do anything for her. However, when I think back on it, as I have since your call yesterday, how else was she to justify her relationship with him if not by love?

"I guess she was a comfort to him in his time of need," Megan summed up sarcastically. "You see, it wasn't a game anymore after Mrs. Townsend died. It was as if someone had been hurt. I don't know why I felt that way, but just to see Jane glowing with love and happiness seemed rather obscene when this man's wife had just died in such a tragic accident. And it was only a couple days after the funeral that he took up with Jane again. Sort of like Henry the Eighth.

"Of course, I was too young to think this way then, weighing and balancing their relationship. Back then I was just Jane's confidante. Uneasy confidante, I might add, as the affair continued. There was something about their relationship that bothered me.

"Maybe it was because, with Mrs. Townsend dead, Jane did press for marriage. As I said, I only knew what was happening from Jane's side, but at first she'd say things like they had to be cautious, to wait until the time was right. Then after six months or so, she began talking about how the time had come, that they shouldn't wait any longer, even though I stressed that most people waited at least a year. 'Not if you're really in love,' Jane replied.

"By that time I thought Townsend was just using her, that he would dump her when he was good and ready. Imagine my surprise when one day, eight months after the first Mrs. Townsend died, I came into the office to hear that Jane wouldn't be working there anymore. She had gotten married. I didn't dare ask. I didn't dare admit I knew anything more than anyone else. But Winnie McKennah was in absolute tears, so I assumed Jane had finally had her way and that Mr. Townsend had married her.

"Talk about ingrates. I never heard from the woman after she married our boss. I remember at the time thinking that she probably believed I wasn't good enough for her anymore. After all, she was suddenly Mrs. William Townsend the Second. One of the receptionists in the office was even assigned to keep a social scrapbook. You know, charity among the ultrarich? So that's how I saw more of Jane, in the society pages, dressed to the nines, as it was once put. And then there was that first Christmas party after they married, Jane playing the grande dame, dispensing little air kisses to her former friends and colleagues.

"Do I sound resentful? Yes, I must. At one time we were close friends. I just wish she hadn't dropped me so.

"I saw her once more after that Christmas party. I was in Field's, shopping for a wedding dress, and she was next door in the designer gowns department. It was funny." Megan smiled. "She was thrilled for me, catching a Caterpillar salesman off the streets of Chicago. I told her it was going to be a small wedding in Kankakee, just family. You know how it is, I didn't want her to feel I was leaving her out. Lord, my sensitivities. As if she would have come to my tacky little wedding. But for a while there, it was like old times. I watched her pick up something for a formal dinner party. 'They've seen everything I've worn this season, and I don't have time to fly to New York for something new,' she explained. I thought, how la de da. But then she surprised me. You see, I had gone to Field's just to check out the wedding dresses. Then my mother was going to come up, and we were really going to look. But right then and there, Jane and I picked out a dress that was totally gorgeous and terribly expensive, certainly too expensive for me. She insisted this was the dress I was going to wear for my wedding. And then you know what she did? She charged it on her Field's card and had them take it over to designer gowns so no one would know she was buying a wedding gown.

"So William Townsend paid for the dress for my wedding, and for my daughter's wedding besides."

Megan sighed. "Poor Jane. After we bought our gowns and arranged to have them sent, we had sundaes together. That was in the old Field's on State Street, before Water Tower Place existed. She was not a happy woman. She said something about spending money being her only revenge.

"I wondered then if Townsend was having an affair. After all, what he'd do to one wife, he'd do to another. Jane didn't know whether he was or not. So I asked her what the problem was. For one, she said, they all hated her, his elder son most of all, but also the people at the country club and on all the committees she joined to become a part of his crowd. She said she just didn't fit in. I advised her to give it time.

" 'I doubt if time will make any difference,' she admitted. And then I remember her saying something about the marriage being a mistake, that it would have been better if she had just remained lovers with Bill, as she called him. Why, I asked. And she said, 'Men treat their wives differently from their mistresses.' Well, we all knew that from reading books.

"When I tried to find out what she really meant, she just sort of shrugged it off, saying she couldn't talk about it. 'I've made my bed. I've got to lie in it. For my daughter's sake, if nothing else. With Bill's money I can give her everything. It doesn't matter what I have to suffer through.'

"I had no idea what she was talking about. Until she shot

the guy. We were so ignorant back that. No one ever faced reality. We pretended, even to our closest friends, that everything in our lives was perfect, like we just stepped out of an issue of *Ladies' Home Journal*. We were such idiots. You young girls have it so much better. I mean, there's the dream, but there's also reality. And there are so many support organizations to turn to. Jane had nothing."

"So you believe, as she said, that she was abused?"

"Oh really, Ms. Belski, I don't know what else it could have been. You see, I don't think she ever cared if he was having an affair, and that would be the only other reason for her to kill him, wouldn't it? Or let's say he threatened divorce. That wouldn't matter because Jane was smart enough to get herself a good lawyer. There were no prenuptial agreements then. What she wanted out of that marriage was security for herself and for her child. In the end, she got neither."

15

ON the drive home I thought a lot about what Megan Capone had to say. It was distressing. I had this perfect picture of my mother as victim. The picture wasn't so perfect anymore. My mother was definitely flawed.

First of all, she had an affair with a married man. Certainly, that's common enough, but that still doesn't make it right. Then how could she not break off the affair when that man's wife died, especially in an accident that seemed highly suspicious? And how, if Townsend was abusing her, could she not have the gumption to simply walk away?

My mother was guilty. She was guilty of faulty judgment and bad taste, if nothing else.

By the time I got home, I was so depressed and it was so late that even a hot, hot shower didn't help. I lay in bed and tried to watch one of the late night comedy shows. I flipped back and forth in an effort to find a guest who hadn't appeared just the night before on another show. There had to be someone on TV who could make me laugh. What had Winnie McKennah taught me? Laughter was the best medicine.

Finally, I settled for the news on CNN. Everything else seemed too artificial.

The phone rang. I absently picked it up. My biggest surprise was hearing Yuri's voice. There was something very comforting about hearing from an ex-husband, especially one you still cared enough about to wear his last name as a keepsake. My spirits rose as we exchanged the usual chatter, which included talk about what kind of computers we were using now. "Are you coming home for Thanksgiving?" I guessed.

"No. My parents are coming out here."

"Oh."

"I wanted you to hear it from me before you heard it from them."

I was puzzled. I didn't think I would have been too shocked if they'd told me they were going out to California for Thanksgiving. It was something I thought my psyche could handle, even at this low point in my life.

"I'm getting married over Thanksgiving, Becky. They're coming out here for the wedding."

"Congratulations, Yuri!" I forced myself to enthuse. "What's she like?"

"She works in computer-aided design at our think tank. She does the graphics for our future projections. She's a real fan of science fiction, Becky, and quite an artist besides, so she really gets the feel of the future we're talking about. She's a wonderful woman. I hope someday you can meet her."

"Oh, Yuri. I'm so happy for you. You deserve the best." You had the best, you schmuck!

"And you, Becky? Have you found—"

"You know that you've spoiled me for everyone else, Yuri," I teased.

"There'll always be a place in my heart for you," he said softly.

"You'll always be a friend," I promised. I hung up the phone. I hated him! How could he remarry? How could the last person I had in my life leave me? Was there nothing left for me? Was I to spend the rest of my life alone, just me and my fucking computers?

I picked up the phone and dialed before I even thought about it. A tired, sleepy voice said hello. "Michael, you have to come over here now! I need you!" I slammed down the phone. Then I sat on my bed, stared blankly at the TV screen and wondered. Why had I called Michael instead of Bill?

Michael wouldn't come, of course. He'd been asleep. He probably didn't even connect me with the call. Even if he had, it was late; he was tired; he had work tomorrow. Our relationship wasn't the type where one could make demands on the other, especially at this hour of the night.

My doorbell rang half an hour later. It was Michael, his topcoat thrown over his sweats. "I shouldn't have called," I said guiltily.

"Does that mean I shouldn't have come?" he wondered.

"Oh, Michael!" I tossed myself into his arms. His cold topcoat felt good against my feverish skin.

"What's the problem?" he asked, as he crushed me to him.

"My husband's getting remarried."

"Your husband? I thought you were divorced."

"Yes, but don't you understand? There was always something between us, and now he's giving that something to someone else. Michael, I have been deserted by everyone I love. Tonight has been the worst night of my life."

Michael stepped back from me. "Look around you," he told me. "Whom do you see?"

I smiled through my brimming eyes.

"You haven't been deserted by everyone, Becky. As a matter of fact, right at this moment you are in the room with someone who loves you very much. All you have to do is accept my love."

I shook my head sadly. "Michael, I'm so confused right now, I don't know what to do."

"Then how about getting some sleep. Things'll look better in the morning. My mother always says that."

"She hasn't seen my mornings."

"Come, Becky. You're just totally distraught. Lie down now." Michael led me back into my bedroom and tucked me into bed. I held out my hand; he took off his topcoat and sneakers, then slid into bed with me. He hugged me; he was warm and comforting. We talked, about love and loss and life and loneliness. When we fell asleep, we were locked in each other's arms.

I barely woke when Michael rose the next morning. Matter of fact, I'm ashamed to admit this, but I didn't get up all day. I tried. About ten o'clock I thought hard about getting up and dressed, going over to Resources and asking Nat for an assignment. After my interview with Megan, I had just about decided to let those proverbial sleeping dogs lie. The past was the past. Why rekindle fading nightmares?

Besides, there was so much I couldn't fathom. First, what kind of woman was my mother? I remember practically nothing of her. To me she was just sort of a vague shadow that had floated through my past life—except for that last time I saw her, in the courthouse, when I failed to testify in her defense. At least I think that's what happened. The trial transcript, when it came, would prove the truth of my memory.

Second, Winnie McKennah was perhaps the only one I heard about who thought highly of William Townsend II. Further, I got the impression that she wasn't particularly fond of my mother. Why, then, did she take me in? For money? For the checks that Alan Townsend sent her each month? This I couldn't believe. I wouldn't. Winnie threw herself into motherhood. She was always baking cookies for the PTA, going on field trips, worrying over my homework, supporting me, loving me. So it wasn't for the money that she took me in. She wasn't just my caretaker. I was her daughter in every real sense.

And yet there was so much I couldn't figure out. Like the

Townsend boys. Alan had set up that two-story shrine to his mother. It seemed obvious that he couldn't stand his father, since he never returned home from the time his mother died until his father's death. He disliked my mother. Yet he paid for my upbringing. This brought me back to Winnie as blackmailer, which was almost impossible to believe. Everything I had learned about her pointed to her as more of a loyal family retainer.

And what about Bill? If Alan seemed cold and distant, except with his own children, Bill was warm, romantic, exciting. Still, he was thirty-five years old and claimed he would never marry. Was that because he remembered what his father's two marriages had been like? But he was only ten when his father died.

I suppose the easiest way to solve all my problems would have been to make an appointment with Alan Townsend and demand that he answer all my questions. But somehow, I thought I would last in his office for ten seconds, just long enough to reveal my identity. Then he'd show me the door. After that, Bill would think I had betrayed him by misleading and deliberately concealing my identity from him. Okay, that was basically true, but that didn't mean I still wasn't taken with him, despite the fact that he was my stepbrother.

Of course, if I was interested in Bill, what did that say about Michael? Was I just using Michael because I knew he cared?

So, you see, I couldn't get up. Every time I tried, all these thoughts swirled around in my head. It was too depressing. So I stayed in bed rather than face the day.

Michael called several times to find out if I was all right. It was sweet of him, even though every time he called, I had just drifted off to sleep so I sounded rather groggy. He finally gave me a stern lecture. My husband's remarriage wasn't the end of the world. It was a new start for Yuri, it was a new start for me. No more ties that bind, even emotionally. I would have to look farther afield. He expected me to shape up. He couldn't come over tonight because he had to get a deposition, and this person refused to do it unless it caused everyone a lot of inconvenience, but tomorrow night he would be over definitely to prepare dinner for me. So I should be home and waiting with open arms by eight.

The next morning, after a restless night, brought on by a sleep-filled day, no doubt, I got up bright and early. I looked out the window and realized I was up too early. The sun barely cracked through the dawn. I hated Chicago. It seemed to thrive on diminished daylight. In this it was so unlike California, where the sun hangs perpetually in the sky, California, where Yuri—oh forget it, Becky! I scolded myself.

The trees were bereft of all that was wonderful about them, early spring green, glorious summer fullness, even the colors of fall. Everything was dead and brown and waiting for the snow that would surely fall within the next several weeks.

I suppose that's why Thanksgiving and Christmas dropped into the calendar when they did, so people would have a reason to survive the winter. The holidays would be bleak for me this year. My mother was dead. No more treks up to Sioux Bluffs for Thanksgiving and Christmas with Winnie McKennah. We wouldn't sit around, decorate the tree, gossip about just everyone in town. And Yuri. How could I even buy Yuri a gift this year? His current wife would certainly resent a present from his ex. I know I would. Perhaps I'd send them a plant, something festive that would have no personal connotations at all. God, no one to buy a gift for, even, no one to agonize over and wonder if she or he would like what I had finally selected.

I was almost ready to crawl back into bed and keep my depression company when I grabbed hold of myself, took a lukewarm shower and dressed for the day. I put on my red sweatsuit in honor of the season I wouldn't be celebrating; I brushed back my red-brown hair and applied a quick coat of makeup. Then on went the Reeboks and I was ready for work.

Nat was glad to have me back at Resources. "Computer people aren't supposed to be temperamental," he served notice. "Okay, you're a woman, but I don't expect raging hormones from you either. I can be as sympathetic as the next man—"

And that about summed it up. Men. I spent the day chasing one of them who had decamped, taking with him all the money in a joint account plus all his wife's jewelry, most of it from her side of the family. She wanted to know where he was so she could call the police and have him arrested for theft. At this point, it would be hard, since the trail was only days old, just long enough for her to begin recovering from shock. Her husband wouldn't have built up much of a paper trail yet, but I would sniff around and see what I could find.

I tapped into several of the motel chain reservations systems but couldn't find him. Certainly he wouldn't have applied for a job yet. Nat had already told her to try and cancel all the credit cards. But I could make a few calls to connections I had and see whether he had tried to use the cards.

So I filled my day and missed the dark drizzle that had descended on the Chicago area. Unfortunately, it was still dripping when I returned home to find Michael waiting in his car for me. I checked my watch. Eight-thirty. I waved to him through his windshield. He tried to manage a little smile. "That's okay," he said, as he got out. "I was using my emergency flashlight to get some work done. However, the ravioli felt neglected."

I liked the way Michael cooked. It had a certain efficiency to it. He bought frozen spinach and cheese ravioli and pre-packed marinara sauce. From Foodstuffs he'd collected two Parmesan bread sticks and a delightful tomato salad. He was obviously a healthy person at heart. While he heated the food, I sat at the kitchen table, trying to answer Michael's last question. How many sweatsuits did I have?

"They're all coordinated," I finally told him, when I admitted I didn't know how many were balled up on my closet shelves. "You see, I don't have to wear matching pants and top. Today I just wore red to get myself into the holiday spirit. But I usually switch tops and bottoms, so I'm wearing something different each day. You know, it's just like wearing skirts and blouses."

"Not quite," Michael corrected.

"Don't you think it's boring, having to look like a Yuppie every day? Always striving for success, everything is status, when really all that matters is your brain and what it can accomplish?"

"People won't let you try to accomplish anything unless you look like a successful person, someone they can trust."

"To look good is better than to feel good."

"Or to be good," Michael amended the adage for our age.

After we ate, I consented to make the coffee. Michael retreated to the living room to wait. I'm sure he expected espresso or cappuccino. Would instant really be that disappointing? "Becky," he called, "did you know your light's flashing?"

I thought it was merely a short in the electrical circuit again, but when I made my entrance, balancing the coffee cups, I discovered he meant my answering machine. I sighed tiredly. "It can wait," I told him.

"Uh—Becky, I left this number as where I could be reached."

"Don't you have a pager?"

"Weren't you the one who just advocated simplifying life by wearing sweats?"

I grimaced and pushed the message button. One from my dentist, wondering when I was going to reschedule (the drill was waiting), one from my landlord, giving fair warning that he was thinking of selling this house. Again. One from—Bill, confirming our date for Saturday night. He'd pick me up at seven. He had tickets to a play at Northlight.

There were no messages for Michael, except that he took

the one from Bill rather personally. "Who is Bill?" he wondered.

"This guy I've been seeing," I answered as casually as possible.

"Oh? I thought I was the guy you were seeing."

"Well, I have been seeing you, Michael, but I've also been seeing—uh—Bill."

He put his coffee cup down. "I thought we had a thing going here."

"We do."

"Then why are you seeing Bill?"

"Because he's a friend. He's different. He's very different from you, Michael. He's an artist; he has a romantic nature; and he has time for me."

"In other words, he's not upwardly mobile and he doesn't dress in suits."

"He dresses in suits when we go out someplace nice," I corrected Michael's impression.

"So you've seen this guy a lot?"

"I met him shortly after I met you. You see, this is what comes from not having a pager."

"Pardon me if I've lost my sense of humor. Are you sleeping with him too?"

"Not that it's any of your business, but no, I'm not."

Michael looked so depressed sitting there alone on the sofa that I went over to him and placed a hand on his knee. "Michael, I'm—"

"No!" he said, throwing up his hands. "I'm not ready to be touched. Tell me about this guy again. Why do you like him?"

So I told Michael all about Bill's whimsical, romantic nature, how he was ready to take off whenever he felt like it, how he had great ideas for dates, just how all around different he was from anyone I had ever met. "And he's an artist," I finished. "He painted that portrait of me. It's quite good, isn't it?" I didn't bother mentioning that Bill was also my stepbrother and I hoped to use him as a source, if I continued the investigation into my stepfather's death.

After I finished talking about Bill, Michael stood. Why do men ask these questions if they don't want answers? He walked to my front door and took his topcoat from the stand. He slid into it and sort of gave me a look. Then he walked out the door. And out of my life.

Oh well, another person I wouldn't have think about buying a Christmas gift for.

16

THE play Bill took me to on Saturday night was a revival of Jean-Paul Sartre's *No Exit*. I was glad to see that other people beside myself were caught in a hell of their own making.

I felt so bad about what happened with Michael, but I didn't know what to do about it. Should I call? Should I leave a message on his machine? But even if I did, what would I say? That I would give Bill up, that I wouldn't see him again? Wasn't it already too late for that? The damage was done.

Bill, sensitive, wonderful, sweet, caring guy that he is, sensed something was wrong. When he asked me what it was, I confessed that a person I was seeing had heard Bill set up our date on the answering machine. "He shouldn't be listening to your messages," Bill chided.

"He thought someone might be trying to reach him."

"Does he spend all his extra time at your place?"

"No. He's usually too busy. But he was trying to cheer me up. He made us dinner. My ex-husband is getting remarried, and I was in a mess about that. And now—"

"Romance Number Two down the drain."

"Thanks."

He placed his hand in mine. "Becky, if it's meant to be, it'll be. Besides, what do you see in this guy?"

So I tried to explain to Bill that Michael, despite his lack of romantic impulses and Byronic gestures, was a solid guy, sweet, harried, perhaps with values different from mine, but still there when I needed him, until he heard Bill's voice. "What I really require," I moaned, "is someone who's the synthesis of the two of you."

"How do you know?" Bill wondered. "Maybe I'm complete in and of myself."

"Really? Michael is ready for a commitment."

"Michael's made it into bed with you. I haven't even got to first base."

"Yes, you have," I assured him. "In my fantasies at least."

"A lot of good that does me."

We laughed together, happily, warmly. "You said you'd never get married," I reminded him. "And you, such an eligible bachelor?"

Bill shrugged. "Yes, but why take the chance of wrecking what's turning out to be a perfect life. Besides, can you name one decent marriage?"

"My boss's. Mine was decent until it died."

He grimaced. "I don't have a single friend who's stayed married for more than ten years."

"There's your brother," I corrected him.

"My brother." Bill shook his head in dismissal. "I was my brother's best man at his wedding. I said all the congratulatory things and wished him good cheer as the crowd was gathering in the church. You know what he said to me? He said he wouldn't be marrying at all if people didn't expect him to. 'It's expected so I'll do it,' he told me. Being married is part of his business persona. And he and Tricia have a comfortable marital contract. She's his social appendage, the beautiful society wife. She spends his money, he gets questions about his sexual orientation answered."

"You mean he's—"

"No. He's totally heterosexual, as far as I know. I used to think of him as being asexual because he was always so cool toward anything romantic. I think seeing our father go through two wives did that for him. Alan loved our mother. He hated our father."

"Why?"

"I don't know, Becky. Sometimes when it's just him and me and his sons, he talks about the old days when he was a boy. He mentions the things he used to do with our mother, like riding and skiing. He's ten years older than I am, and he remembers so much more about her than I do. I suppose in a way I was very unaware of things when I was a child. I had this little zoo I kept out in the backyard with turtles and rabbits and bugs of all sorts, and I spent most of my time out there, away from the house. In the summer, when I wasn't away at camp, I used to have a tent amongst my animals.

"When Alan left for college, he gave me his number; and he said if anything terrible happened, I should call him immediately. I didn't know what the hell he was talking about. But I remember him saying, 'Just, you know, with Dad.' " Bill sat there lost in his reminiscence.

"Did you ever figure out what he meant?"

"I was eight. My father was so big. I always stayed out of his way. The house seemed to die when he came into it. But I had my zoo out back and my magical playroom upstairs. Alan never had anything but reality. It killed him when our mother died like that."

"The accident."

"Christmas Eve, and believe it or not, I was asleep. Something woke me, but for the life of me I don't know what it was. And then—I can still hear it. It's like—you know, if you've ever been in a car accident, you never forget the sound of metal hitting metal? I'll never forget the thud of my mother falling down those stairs. I waited for a minute. Then I heard Alan shrieking. I rushed out of my room, and there were Alan and my father at the top of the stairs. Then Alan ran down to my mother and—"

"How awful. You must have felt sick. There she was, surrounded by all those Christmas presents."

Bill looked at me strangely. "Christmas presents? There were no Christmas presents. Just my mother. We had placed all our gifts around the tree earlier that evening."

God! William Townsend *had* murdered his first wife. "What did Alan do?"

"He called for an ambulance. I remember that. My father was in a state of shock. And I remember the police coming because, my god, whoever sees the police in Kenilworth? Afterward is a blur, the funeral, the blackness of it all, then Alan leaving and I being shipped off to boarding school. It was the end of childhood."

"And only two years later, you had to see your father die."

Bill's face deadened. "I was away at a friend's house when my father died," he said evenly, as if it was a lie he had practiced well.

"Thank God for that," I said.

"And your family? No dark secrets?"

Plenty of them, I felt like telling him. But none I can share with you now. Instead, "Oh, let me think of something. Well, I never knew my father, so maybe I'm illegitimate. You know how birth certificates are. They only give the mother's maiden name and the father's name. My mother always said he died in a war; but since I was born in 1961, I'm still wondering which war it was."

Bill laughed, his good humor restored.

He drove me the two miles home. When he parked in front of my house, he asked, "May I come up?"

"Oh," I said, distressed at the question, "I don't think so."

"Is it too soon?"

"Quite."

He leaned over across his stick shift and gently kissed me. I couldn't help but respond to his warmth. He had the sweetest lips, and I wanted to make up for the pain I had caused him earlier by having him recall the darkness of our shared past. His hand slid down my wool coat and pressed against the bulge where he assumed my breast to be. To make sure he had the right contour, he unbuttoned my coat midway and slid his hands into the warmth inside. His fingers played with my nipple. He was driving me crazy. I moaned against his teeth. "Let me come up," he whispered.

He slid his hand out of my blouse and got out of the car. He came around and opened the passenger door. I sort of floated into his arms. We walked up the stairs to the upper floor, my half of the house, and I let Bill in.

He removed my coat and threw it over a chair. Then he held me hard against him so I could feel the tenseness in his body, his desire for me. He kissed me, holding my head gently. I opened my mouth to him and felt his tongue inside of me. His hands slid down along my back and pressed my hips into his. I was delirious with expectations of a night in paradise.

The phone rang. But who cared. I was in Bill's arms, and I wasn't going to leave them for anything. It rang three times before my machine picked it up. "Becky, are you home yet? If not, you should be. I'm coming over there tomorrow. We have to discuss this."

I pulled away from Bill.

He smiled grimly. "I assume that's Michael."

"Or, alternatively, the voice of my conscience."

Bill sighed. He hesitated, then he backed away. He was nothing if not the gentleman. "I'll call you."

I walked to the door with him. "Thanks for the lovely evening, Bill. I mean that."

"You better hurry and come to some decision, Becky. With the holidays almost upon us and people returning to Chicago, my dance card's filling up."

I smiled. "You never gave me an adequate explanation of why you'll never marry."

"You never made that ultimate, intimate commitment to me."

"Almost," I assured him.

I watched him go down the stairs, his curly brown locks bouncing with him. He was so much the man of my heart. Why had Michael called when he did? Why couldn't I just toss away the next few months of my life on an affair I knew would turn out all wrong? Afterward, when Bill dropped me, I would weep and suffer and curse myself for my stupidity. But at least I would have had Bill and that wild fling that had never filled my life before. Bill was romantic. Bill was dangerous. Bill was love.

Then what was Michael?

Michael showed up on my doorstep at ten Sunday morning. I tried to fake happiness at seeing him, but frankly I had spent the night tossing and turning, mourning over my lost opportunity with Bill.

Michael looked rather odd today, even for a Sunday. He was dressed in jeans, a thermal shirt, and a goosedown vest. I thought perhaps there was some dress-up party he was going to. Still, I was mad at him for last night, so instead of asking about his getup, I said, "You shouldn't have called me on a Saturday night, especially since you knew I had a date."

His eyes narrowed. "I hope I screwed things up for you there."

"As a matter of fact, you did."

"Good! You can tell this Bill character that I'll be calling every time he has a date with you."

It was then that I noticed a roll of paper Michael held in his left hand. It looked like plans of some sort, so maybe Michael was going to help someone who was building some kind of addition. Maybe that's why he was dressed so crazily.

He noticed me looking down at the paper. "I have something to show you," he said. He marched into my kitchen. Then he turned to face me again. "Just because you only know one side of a person doesn't mean there's not another side. You assume, because I appear before you as a young, struggling lawyer, feeding off the romantic miseries of others, that there isn't a warm, wild, Heathcliffian side to me. You assume I spent all my time in college taking courses in business, management, statistics. But no, I took several courses in political science, and that's a humanity, Becky! Plus, after I finished law school, I clerked for a justice of the Illinois Circuit Court of Appeals. You're not dealing with some dummy here, who's all one-sided. When my judge couldn't use the freebies he got to cultural affairs, I went. Sometimes alone, just to enlighten my soul. My soul, Becky. I have one. What was it John Donne said—"

"Michael, excuse me if I break this off, but when was the last time you read John Donne?"

"Last night, as a matter of fact!" he threw back at me. "While I was working on my art."

"Your what?"

"My art. Oh, I suppose now you're going to say you didn't know I was an artist, that you couldn't tell immediately when you stepped into my apartment that someone with taste and artistic sensibilities had decorated it."

"Michael, it's fully furnished, pictures included."

"That's only because I've been hiding my stuff away until I can find someone I consider up to the job of framing it. I've brought you an example of my work. I hope you won't be too astonished by the breadth of my genius."

With a flourish, Michael unrolled the paper he had brought with him. The effort was—unique? I tried to hide my shock. And my laughter. But how long could I fake this cough?

"You—you don't like it?" Michael asked tentatively. "I stayed up all last night doing it. It's mixed media."

And indeed it was. Michael had put paste on a posterboard, then pressed magazine pages to it. On top of that he had thrown what looked like tempera. He must have waited for it to dry before he began to rip the magazine pages off, in order to produce a paint and paper collage.

"I got an A doing something like this in fifth grade. My teacher put it up on the board for parents' day. My mother still has it hanging in the hallway. I guess this one didn't turn out as well," he dejectedly admitted.

"Oh, Michael." I put my arms around him and hugged him. "I don't want you to be an artist."

"Thank God."

"I like you just the way you are."

"But not enough."

"What?"

"You don't like me enough."

I pulled back. "I'm confused, Michael. I'm so confused about everything. Oh hell, it's been a rotten year. My mother dying, my husband remarrying, this case I'm working on, just everything has turned out to be not what I expected. And now you're going to play the artist?" I chided.

Michael took a piece of paper out of the back pocket of his jeans. "I've made a list of several art galleries we can go to that are supposed to be really different."

"Michael, I'm not that interested in art. I said he was an artist because that's what he does for a living. What I really said about him was that he was a romantic, that he appealed to the long lost, feminine fragile side of me. You see, I've never really admitted to myself that I had a feminine fragile side. Bill's just so different from any other man I've ever dated." Those noble few. "But you're you, he's he. What's so difficult about understanding that? I don't dye my hair because you prefer blonds."

Michael sank onto one of my kitchen chairs. "So there's no hope. I came here prepared to fight for you, to square off against the foe, but I've lost even before I take the field of battle."

I smiled. I walked into the bedroom and took a scarf of

mine from the top drawer. I returned and placed it around Michael's neck. "You can wear my colors," I told him.

"Your knight in shining armor?"

"Just be patient. If you can."

He put the list of galleries back in his pocket. "I did clear all day for you. What would you like to do?"

We ended up walking along the beach, the cold wind blowing through us, our noses running, our cheeks reddening. A stray dog was chasing across the beach, so we tossed driftwood to him and he brought it back until we were all tired of the game. We saw a mother with her two small children, and we discussed what having a family meant to a relationship. I was holding Michael's hand, and I felt this surge of maternal desire. I wondered then if I were holding the hand of the future father of my children.

Life was so perfect with Michael. If only there weren't Bill.

When Michael took me home, he didn't ask if he could come up. "You have to sort things through in your mind," he admitted. "Three in a bed is a crowd, I would assume, even for the artistic set."

I smiled and started to go. "Becky," he called me back. "I don't want you to think I'm pushing but—what are you doing for Thanksgiving?"

"Oh—turkey on rye, I imagine."

"Would you like to have Thanksgiving with me?"

I smiled. "Yes, Michael. I really would."

He smiled back at me. "Good. I'll tell my mother."

17

AS the last Thursday in November approached, I began to believe I needed a little Thanksgiving. Life had become an emotionally exhausting routine. I saw Bill, I saw Michael. Bill, charming and debonair as always, pressed his sexual advances; I held him at bay. I thought I had come to a decision. Tempting as he was, Bill was a precarious romantic interest. There would be that short burst of passion, a flame to light the heavens; then it would be extinguished, maybe leaving both of us in the dark concerning the human condition, that is, sex and its relationship to love. With Michael, our passion was more in the keep-the-home-fires-burning division. And yet, according to ancient custom, the home fires burned eternally. That was the point of them.

Perhaps it was a fault in me for not wanting to take a chance on one grand passion. But two men at once? Not in today's world. Besides, Bill Townsend was my stepbrother. He was somehow involved in the murder case I was investigating for my own peace of mind. And I believed that somewhere in his life, Bill was as wounded as Alan had been. Whether it was the fact that his friends' marriages all seemed to have been ripped asunder or whether in the far reaches of his mind it was his own father's marriages that so affected Bill, I couldn't figure out. I did know that at twenty-nine I didn't need to be involved with someone who right up front said he made no long-term, till-death-do-we-part commitments. So, in my heart I would like to be the sort of woman who has a fling and walks away, head held high, with just a tiny tear floating out of the corner of her eye. But I knew I wasn't. Plus, I was doubly wary because I realized I had more experience with computers than I had with men.

However, when I was with Bill, it was hard to resist. When he held me in his arms and kissed me, when he touched me, I melted. Something in me just turned hot and organic. At those moments I would beg him not to seduce me. Yes, that was the actual word I used. "Seduce." He laughed. In a way, I thought he was playing with me. He knew the effect he was having on me and he enjoyed his power.

What had my mother called it? Playing with fire. That's what I was doing by continuing to see Bill. I constantly found myself on the verge of that sweet surrender. I'm ashamed to say that when I was with Bill, he drove all thoughts of Michael from my mind. Michael, after all, was not romantic. He was hard-working, exhausted, involved, but most of all nice.

"Nice" is a killer word. Women don't want their men to be "nice." We want wild and passionate, deep and mysterious, handsome in a quirky sort of way. We want someone who can take us or leave us, whom we have to pursue, while we bemoan the breaking of our hearts.

I didn't pursue Michael. It was a joint venture. And yes, Michael was nice. We were friends. We talked about things, dumb things, silly things, ordinary, everyday things. He was sweet, he was comforting, he was there. How could he compare with the emotionally dangerous, out-of-reach Bill?

And yet, I'm not a woman easily swept away by my own emotions. I was occasionally carried away by the tide of Bill's romanticism. But Michael was the rock that snared me before I reached the ocean of no return.

Yes, that was the routine of my life, debating the two men in it—when I had the time for debate. Nat had me working on a slew of missing persons cases. Why is it that, when the holidays come around, people seek out their loved ones? Or their hated ones? Why do the holidays bring out the worst in people?

I considered that question as I shopped for a dress for Thanksgiving. That definitely brought out the worst in me. I couldn't believe I had agreed to have Thanksgiving dinner with Michael before I found out where he would be taking me. Now I would have to face his beloved mother. In what?

Michael's parents lived in Highland Park. Not to put too fine a point on it, Highland Park has the worst reputation on the North Shore. It has a sign marking its borders: "Me City, U.S.A." Its citizens are renowned for raising rudeness to new heights. I have a friend Marla, who grew up there. She told me it would be a wonderful town if someone dropped a neutron bomb on it. I asked Marla's advice on what I should wear to meet Michael's mother. "It's not going to matter," Marla warned me. "When she discovers that Belski isn't your maiden name, that you're divorced and not Jewish besides, you won't have to worry about Michael Rosen anymore. Your relationship with him won't outlast the rising of the sun on the morning after."

"Thanks. But really, Marla, what should I wear?"

"There are two outfits in Highland Park, one day, one evening. For the day you should wear some outlandishly expensive sweatsuit. The suit should be either hand-painted, embroidered with metallic threads, or have silver bullet studs. No? You don't like that idea? Then you can wear something with fringe and cowboy boots, preferably snake or eel skin. Eel skin is particularly popular because then you have an excuse for why your credit cards screw up the town's charge machines, as in 'Oops! It must be all my eel skin again.' "

"Marla, I'm too old for cowboy boots or silver bullets."

"Darling, there are women out there in their fifties, size sixteen, wearing cowboy boots. God forbid they should ever try to mount a horse. Fortunately, they usually only wear them to Kandi's Kitchen, the local lunch thing."

"What about a simple dress?" I suggested to Marla when we were out on our lunch hour, doing Old Orchard Shopping Center.

"Simple? For Highland Park? Dear, a dress for Highland Park has to have beads or embroidery or something sparkly. Also, whatever you wear, whether it be a dress, sweats, even jeans, make sure you complement it with lots of jewelry, preferably gold chains; thick, gold bangles; and dripping gold earrings. Some big rock on your hand would go down well but be prepared to scratch it across a pane of glass."

Needless to say, Marla's advice did not ease my growing anxiety over Turkey Day in Highland Park. She called the night before, wanting to know what I had decided to wear. "I thought a cashmere sweater and a pleated plaid skirt with low taupe heels."

"Oh my God. She'll know you're a WASP when you're walking down the sidewalk. You'll never even get in the door. That's unless, of course, you hide in the bushes until the catered dinner is delivered."

I just knew Marla had to be joking. She herself was going home to mommy, dressed in jeans and a black sweater. "Only because my family's given up on me," she said. "They consider me eccentric."

I don't know why. Marla was making a fortune in commercial real estate. Okay, she wasn't married yet, but did that really matter anymore? Is that the only thing that constituted success?

"Yes," Marla told me when I asked her. "However,

you'll be glad to know that doctors and lawyers are out as hot prospects for the women of Highland Park nowadays. It is appropriate now for a woman to be a doctor or a lawyer. But men have to make more money than that, so they can keep us in our hand-painted jumpsuits.''

Thanks to Marla's bilious send-off, I felt sick to my stomach by the time Michael picked me up at twelve on Thanksgiving Day. I stuck by my sweater and skirt decision. Michael told me I looked wonderful. ''Michael, I really don't feel good about this meeting with your mother. Perhaps it's too soon.''

''Why? We're not announcing our engagement or anything. You're just meeting my family.''

''But, Michael, you always speak about your mother in such reverential tones.''

''I do not!''

''Yes you do! What if she doesn't like me?''

''Darling, she'll love you.''

Famous last words. I couldn't help but feel slightly faint as we left the safety of Glencoe and hit the sign that said Highland Park. For some reason, I was pleased to discover that Michael's old family homestead wasn't as large as Alan Townsend's. It was big enough for all that. Off Green Bay Road and into one of those circular streets that held towering trees and secluded houses, we pulled up before a white clapboard with additions on either side. In the front stood a basketball hoop, hanging high from a metal pole. There were already two other cars in the driveway, a Mercedes and a BMW. Michael's Porsche fit right in. ''My brother and sister are already here with their families,'' he noted.

Oh great. The whole crowd. Well, at least I wouldn't be grilled at an intimate little affair. I let Michael help me out of the car, then carefully retrieved the box of party cookies I'd brought as a hostess gift. Michael smiled encouragingly at me. ''It'll be fine,'' he told me.

''Sure,'' I replied morosely. My mind wandered for a second to the wonderful Thanksgivings with my adoptive mother in Sioux Bluffs, Iowa; how, when my car pulled up, I could already smell the turkey and the cornbread stuffing. I longed for those days with their simplicity of love. But Winnie McKennah was dead, and I was about to walk into Michael Rosen's house.

The first sign that things might not go well came when Michael's sister Debee took the cookies from me, then called into the kitchen, "Mom, she brought cookies that aren't dietetic. What should I do with them?"

"Save them. We'll give them away later," her mother called back.

I was ready to drop dead right there. But no, I endured meeting the rest of Michael's wonderful family, his brother Si and wife Vickie, Debee's husband Barney, and Michael's father. I was introduced to the children too, but they were all romping around so I didn't quite get who was who.

And then the queen entered. Mama Rosen came from the kitchen, her face red from the heat. So at least the dinner wouldn't be catered. "My baby," she called to Michael the minute she laid eyes on him. He walked swiftly over to her and gave her a huge hug. It was obvious they adored each other. Marla was right. I could cross Michael off my list of prospects. "And this must be?" she said, as she approached me. Then she looked me up and down. Yes, I was the only one not wearing a fancy sweatsuit. Even the female children were dressed in them.

"Mother, this is Becky Belski," Michael said, glowing with pride and happiness. At least I thought that's what he was glowing with.

"Becky," Mrs. Rosen said. "Welcome to the family."

Lord! Fortunately, I was saved from making an inadequate response by the maid coming out of the kitchen to call for help. Mrs. Rosen rushed back in. "Come on," Michael said to me. "I'll show you the house."

I finally got to see the original of the infamous collage Michael made for me, which, by the way, I had hung on my wall. Bill saw it. He wondered if it were a recycling reminder. Michael's room was neat and precise. "My mother comes in and dusts it every week, straightens it up," he said.

"Sort of like a shrine," I suggested.

He smiled. We sat on his bed and talked, avoiding the family until we heard his mother say, "Where are those two anyway?" We thought it might be time to get downstairs.

As with any large gathering for Thanksgiving, by the time Mr. Rosen massacred the turkey with his electric carving knife and passed around the pieces—yes, pieces, not slices—the turkey was cold. But fortunately, I like cold turkey. I also liked cold everything else. I could have made a compress of the mashed potatoes, which I needed, as the meal was constantly being interrupted by the children either throwing rolls back and forth across the table or running around, daring their parents to catch them. It was loud, but it saved me from being the center of attention.

Relieved, I thought I had escaped scot free until the coffee was served, the children dismissed, and we all sat around the table as adults. Then the old battleax bore down. Not that the men were paying much attention. Mr. Rosen had positioned the television so he could see the reflection in the dining room mirror. And that's where the men's eyes were focused, on the football game. But Mrs. Rosen managed to relieve me of my life's history, the salient facts, in less than ten minutes. And she was great at summing it up simply too. "Adopted, divorced, computers, Christian."

"Agnostic," I corrected her.

"Oh, and where do they worship?" Debee wanted to know.

Cornered.

"Michael, may I see you in the kitchen for a minute?" Mrs. Rosen asked her son. I was wondering if I would have to walk home or if Michael would be permitted to provide me with cab fare.

With Mrs. Rosen missing, the men dared to stage a retreat to the living room to watch the game face forward. I tried to help Debee and Vickie clear away the dishes, but they told me to go relax, enjoy being single while I could. So I went into the living room and sat down forlornly among the men. I thought they didn't even know I existed until Mr. Rosen leaned over to say, "The best thing in this house is to ignore everything anyone says." He smiled at me. I smiled back.

We left soon after Michael came out of the closet, as I refer to his confrontation with the matriarch. Michael, playing the lawyer, was very conciliatory to all sides. However, when the family begged him to stay longer, he stated firmly that he had to get back downtown because tomorrow was just another day as far as the law of the land was concerned.

We said our good-byes. No one bothered to say, "I'm sure we'll be seeing you again." When we got into the car and were driving slowly off, I asked Michael what had happened in the kitchen. "Oh, Mother mouthing off as usual," he replied.

"Meaning?"

"She had some qualms about your background. But I informed her firmly that she better get used to you because you were going to be her new daughter-in-law."

"You did!" I sat there in awe of his nerve. But then I remembered. "Michael, you haven't even proposed."

"I've been proposing ever since I met you. You just have never given me a definite answer. Now that I've faced down the dragon, does the hero get the damsel in distress?"

I smiled. Does a damsel wear cashmere and plaid?

"I love you, Becky Belski." He waited. "Nu? What's your answer?"

I sat happily in the car, thinking about it. Here it was, a marriage proposal from Michael Rosen. Mrs. Michael Rosen. Becky Belski Rosen. How sweet. How simple. And yet Becky Belski Rosen wasn't quite accurate. If I married Michael, I would be Elizabeth Diane Peters McKennah Belski Rosen. My face fell.

Michael pulled off Green Bay into the Glencoe Forest Preserve. "What is it, Becky? Is it still this Bill guy? Because

154

if you don't think you can love me, please tell me now. My mother is going to be calling every hour on the hour to discuss 'this craziness,' as she calls it. I'm going to have to leave my answering machine on from now until we announce our engagement. If we announce it. Be honest with me."

Why couldn't I just say yes and let the past fade away? But I was caught in the shadows of my past on what should have been one of the happiest days of my life.

Michael took my hand. His felt so strong, and I knew then he would be someone I could always depend on. Didn't he deserve the truth? "Michael, there's something about me you don't know."

"Oh lord. What is it?"

"There's something about me I don't know."

"Multiple personality?" he guessed.

I smiled. "Remember that story I told you, the one where you advised me to get a transcript of the trial—the transcript still hasn't come, by the way."

"Yeah, I remember."

"Until I clear up that past mess, I can't consider a future."

"If you're in legal trouble, Becky, remember, I am a lawyer. And I honestly believe I'm a damned good one. I might be able to help you."

"I'm not in legal trouble. I give you my word on that. Someone I knew a long time ago was, and now I've stumbled upon something that—well I don't know what's going to happen. When I gather all the facts, I'll present them to you; and maybe you can help me."

"How long is this going to take? Are we talking months? Years?"

"Both murders—"

"Murders! Becky!"

"Both happened around the Christmas season," I stated. "Maybe they'll be solved around then too."

"Becky, what are you involved in? Murder can be dangerous. There is no statute of limitations on it."

"Don't worry," I told Michael. "One of the murderers is already dead, and the other—the other died in prison."

"So then, what's the point?" Michael asked.

"Justice. The truth. For my own peace of mind, I want both."

18

MICHAEL was not satisfied with my answer, but I warned him not to press me. So he drove me home.

Marla called late that night. I had to take the call in the kitchen because Michael was in the bedroom. When I told Marla that, after his confrontation with Mama Rosen, Michael had asked me to marry him, Marla was ecstatic. We made plans to spend Saturday shopping together for a bridal outfit, just to look, we promised each other. "I hear they're making some darling white sweatsuits with beads," she reported.

"Not sweatsuits, Marla, leisure wear," I corrected her.

"Only in Highland Park for a few hours and already they're saving a table for her at Kandi's Kitchen."

I giggled all the way back to the bedroom. "Who was that?" Michael asked tiredly.

"Marla."

"I hope you didn't discuss our personal affairs."

"I told her you asked me to marry you. We're going to shop for bridal outfits on Saturday. What would you like to see me in?"

"What's wrong with naked?"

"Skin tones then. I'll check it out."

Poor Michael, when he arrived on Sunday for our hours of total laziness, found me surrounded by bridal magazines, plotting our wedding. "Should we make it a big church affair?" I asked him.

"Church." He blanched.

"That's a generic term for religious institutions."

He sighed. But I did note that he spent quite a lot of time looking over the new styles of tuxedos and wondering who in the law firm he would invite.

So my dreams were caught up in the future. Monday's mail delivery dropped me back into the past. The envelope was thick and brown. The trial transcript had finally arrived.

I ripped open the envelope and began reading, as if it were a long-awaited novel. I wasn't a lawyer, and for once in my life I was sorry about that. I didn't understand a lot of the terms, nor did a dictionary help much. But I did understand that my mother was pleading for her freedom. Today, she might have had a good chance for it. The prosecutors hadn't even charged my mother with first-degree murder. There was no malice aforethought. It was an impulse, an act she was driven to by an abusive husband. But, as I was to discover, it was who that abusive husband was that mattered to the court. We are all equal before the court, except in this case the dead William Townsend II was more equal than others. My mother did not have his social clout. Her death would not have been the same offense against the community that the prosecutor was claiming his death was.

But I made those conclusions only later. First, I turned to my mother's testimony, and here was the problem: In all her testimony she didn't say anything about William Townsend II striking her, beating her. "He never struck you?" the prosecutor asked.

"No, never," my mother admitted.

"Then how can you claim abuse?"

"You don't understand—"

"No. We don't understand, Mrs. Townsend. We don't understand the taking of a man's life at all." At which point the judge directed the prosecutor to let her answer.

"Bill Townsend was a big man," my mother said. "He was six feet two inches; he weighed over two hundred pounds. He never struck me, but he would come close to me, stand close and scream at me. He frightened me. He delighted in humiliating me. He did this when we were in public, when we were with his friends, when we were at home—in bed."

"So to salvage your pride—"

"It wasn't pride. I was afraid of him, of what he might do to me. There was something basically nasty about Bill. He was a—a bully, and he terrorized me."

The defense attorney led my mother through a series of incidents that demonstrated Bill Townsend's explosive temper. A few of the incidents involved the use of a pistol, one of several in Bill Townsend's gun collections. My mother testified how terrified she was when Bill Townsend stood before her with one of his pistols in his hands. "When he was in the midst of one of his tirades, he would hold a gun in his hand, its barrel pointed toward me, playing with it the whole time he was talking. What was I to think? After he calmed down, I would plead with him to lock up the revolvers," my mother said. "I have a little girl. I was afraid she would play with the guns and get hurt. But Bill insisted on having them around, loaded, ready to fire. He said they were the best defense against theft."

"And did he ever use them against a burglar?" the defense attorney asked.

"No. We had an extensive security system. Our house was never broken into."

"What then was the purpose of the firearms?"

"He used them to threaten me. That seemed to me to be their only function. When he got mad, when screaming wasn't enough for him, he would take out one of his revolvers and wave it at me. Once he backed me up against the wall. He held a pistol to my head and threatened to blow my brains out.''

If there were outbursts—and the prosecuting attorney insinuated there weren't, that my mother's testimony was all made up to suit the occasion—but if there were, what did my mother do to cause them?

"Nothing. I did nothing. I never knew when he would blow, what would set him off. He was just a mean—vicious—bullying bastard.''

But couldn't the prosecutor have seen that by now, I wondered. After all, the defense had subpoenaed a good many witnesses to attest to that fact. The defense had to subpoena them because, according to the trial transcript, none of them came willingly.

All these witnesses were polite and restrained. Yes, they were friends of the Townsend family. No, they were not particular friends of Jane Peters. They didn't know her well. It was the first Mrs. Townsend that they were familiar with. Yes, Bill Townsend could be an unpleasant man. That was the word all of them used, "unpleasant.'' How terribly upper class of them. Some even went so far as to concede that he had a "bullying nature.'' The defense attorney took them through several incidents where his behavior toward the first Mrs. Townsend could be considered "disgraceful,'' in the words of one witness. He acted like "less than a gentleman,'' one of his country club cronies put it.

None of them was too aware of what happened during William Townsend's second marriage. "We didn't associate socially with them all that often,'' was how one society matron put it.

In other words, no one could really attest to how Bill Townsend treated my mother, except for her closest friend in that circle, Jelly Mellon. For the prosecutor, Jelly Mellon's testimony was like a hydra's head. Each time she tried to say something in my mother's defense she was cut short. "Hearsay.'' Hearsay, hearsay, hearsay. What my mother told her, that's what Jelly wanted to repeat. But she could only tell what she knew firsthand.

So, although the defense attorney tried to paint Jane Peters as victim, he had a hard time of it. She wasn't physically abused, she was merely mentally terrorized, physically threatened, treated like shit. Should that cost a man his life? Needless to say, the State didn't think so, especially when that man was William Townsend II.

I returned to that section in the trial transcript where the defense attorney took my mother through that final, horrible day. "What set him off this time?" he asked.

"It was about ten o'clock in the morning," my mother recalled. "It was just after the New Year. Outside it was snowing, and so beautiful. My daughter Elizabeth and I were in the house. We'd had a beautiful Christmas, and even now we were admiring the Christmas tree. My daughter asked if we could turn the lights of the tree on just one last time because we were going to take the tree down before her school started again."

"Just you and your daughter were in the house?"

"Yes. No. Bill. My husband was upstairs. We had just turned on the lights when he came down the stairs. He started yelling immediately about the lights. Why had I turned on the Christmas tree lights when everybody knows you shouldn't turn on the lights until nighttime."

"And what did you do?" the defense attorney asked.

"I quickly turned the lights off. I told my daughter to go into the kitchen to play."

"You wanted her out of harm's way?"

"Objection!" from the prosecuting attorney, which was overruled.

"I didn't want her exposed to Bill's temper. When he lost control, there was no telling what he would do."

"And what did he do this time?"

"He started shouting at me about the Christmas tree still being up. It seems it had always been a tradition in his family to take it down on New Year's Day, but I had left it

161

up a few extra days last year and nothing had happened. I didn't understand why he was complaining now. Well, I made the mistake of saying I didn't think it mattered whether the tree stayed up an extra day or two. And he started—he started ranting on about how I wouldn't know what mattered, how I was just a tramp and a slut and—I don't know. I don't know what he said. I know you want me to recall everything, but at that point, I wasn't listening to his words. I just wanted to get away from him until he cooled down."

"And could you get away?"

"He took one of his guns from the lamp table drawer. And he began shooting at the Christmas tree lights. At the bulbs. At the angel on top of the tree. It was madness. He was insane."

Here a legal objection and the disposition of it.

"And what did you do?" the defense attorney continued.

"I stood there, shocked. I couldn't move."

"And did there ever come a time when he turned the gun on you?"

"Yes. He said my face looked like a Christmas tree bulb and that it needed smashing too."

"What did you do?"

"I ran."

"Ran where?"

"Deeper into the foyer, away from the kitchen, away from my daughter. From the foyer, I moved into the study. We have french windows in the study, and my husband kept a revolver on the upper shelf of the bookcase in case anyone should break in that way. He was a fanatic about break-ins."

"You took that revolver?"

"Yes."

"And what did you do?"

"I suppose I pointed it at my husband."

"You suppose?"

"I don't really remember clearly what happened. I just

know he came into the room after me, and he was holding a gun and I was holding a gun."

"And what did he say to you?"

"Nothing. He said nothing. He just looked at me, holding the gun, and smiled this cold, cold smile. I just knew that he was going to kill me."

"And then what did you do?"

"I pulled the trigger."

"Once."

"I don't remember."

"You don't remember," the defense attorney repeated. "Would it surprise you to learn you pulled the trigger more than once?"

"Nothing about that day would surprise me," my mother sorrowfully admitted.

"What happened after you pulled the trigger?"

"Bill fell to the carpet. I just sort of watched him. I was afraid to go near him because he still had the gun in his hand. But when he didn't move, I hurried past him to the telephone, called the ambulance and then the police."

"You called the police?"

"Yes."

The prosecutor tried to twist everything around. He couldn't deny the damage to the Christmas tree or the bullet holes in the wall behind the tree. He didn't even bother to claim my mother shot at the tree. What he did propose was that my mother decided once and for all to put an end to Bill Townsend in order to inherit his estate. She thought she could get away with it by calling it self-defense. And if that wasn't the case, why, when she saw the evidence stacking up against her, did she change her plea from self-defense to guilt with mitigating circumstances?

My poor mother didn't stand up to the cross-examination well. She even admitted that one of the reason she married William Townsend II was for his money. And his social position. Yes, she knew he had a slight temper when she married him, but she wasn't aware of his rages. But the prosecutor hammered away at one point: She made her bed, she could lie in it without, presumably, killing the man beside her.

For a rebuttal witness, the prosecutor called Alan Townsend. Alan testified that he had never seen his father lose his temper, that his father's marriage to his mother was a "caring" one. When the defense attorney asked why Alan had never returned to his Kenilworth home after his mother fell down those stairs, Alan replied, "Because I was given to understand that my father was, at the time of my mother's death, already sleeping with this woman. I didn't wish to return to a house that had been so polluted."

The defense attacked Alan's portrait of his parents' "caring" relationship, but Alan was cool, cold, telling.

I was the defense's rebuttal witness. I, Elizabeth Diane Peters. The judge asked the five-year-old me if I knew the difference between the truth and a lie. But it didn't really matter. Because I remained silent after I answered the judge's questions. I simply said nothing. I did not speak out in my mother's defense. I remained mute. Because second-degree murder is a class-one felony, my mother was sentenced to prison. She was sentenced to the minimum of four years.

Even now I could not remember what it was that I should have said in her defense.

19

I reread the transcript. I thought in my haste to read it the first time, I might have missed something. After all, I did sort of skip over the technical evidence. So now I went over it slowly, well into the early morning hours.

It seemed to me that, aside from Jelly Mellon, all the other witnesses had closed ranks behind one of their own, William Townsend, with no regard to what my mother must have suffered. And was her lawyer that brilliant? Why hadn't he even bothered to suggest that the first Mrs. Townsend was murdered? If Townsend could terrorize my mother into shooting him, why couldn't he have physically intimidated Sarah Mansfield Townsend, causing her to fall down the stairs?

What smacked even more of a cover-up was Alan Townsend's part in this little drama. He outright lied. I was sure of it. He hated his father. I was equally sure of that. He was ten years older than Bill. He had seen the way his father treated his mother. He had to know that the leopard was still wearing his spots when he married a second time. Alan could have spoken up for my mother, but he preferred to see her put in jail.

Why?

Was it only because he hated my mother as the usurper?

He never gave my mother a chance. Naturally, I could understand how he felt. I myself found little to defend in my mother's conduct. She had been Townsend's mistress before his first wife died. She became his wife eight months later.

I didn't even remember the move from the Chicago condo to Kenilworth. But I did remember the Kenilworth mansion. I remembered my room because it overlooked the backyard with all those towering trees. The lawn fell away toward the lake. I remember our playroom, Bill's and mine. He had a train set, but he wouldn't let me play with it because I always knocked the cars off the track. So I had to just sit and watch and beg him to make the engine go through the tunnel with its whistle blowing.

I remembered school. I remembered my nursery school teacher very, very vaguely and the hearts I made for Mommy for Valentine's Day. And oh how I looked forward to the holidays because Billy would be coming home and I'd have someone to play with instead of having to stay all alone with a babysitter. Bill had liked my mother. Even now he admitted as much to me. But Bill hadn't been called to testify. Only Alan.

So Alan got his revenge.

And yet he supported me from the time I was five until the end of my college education. Why? He didn't even know me. He had never even met me, and I didn't know if we'd seen each other at the trial.

One thought kept crossing my mind. Had Winnie McKennah known something with which to blackmail Alan Townsend?

It was a stupid idea I tried to dismiss from my mind. I knew my adoptive mother, and she wasn't a blackmailer. She was straight and sweet and loving, forthright and honest. But how did I get into her hands, and why those checks?

Was it part of the Townsend estate? Did Townsend have a will and was my mother included in it? She had been convicted of murdering her husband, so I assumed her inheritance was null and void, but then did it pass to me? I'd have to check that out with Michael.

This was all so confusing. The puzzle circled in my mind like too much liquor. I finally fell asleep.

When I awoke, it was noon. I probably would have slept longer if Nat hadn't called to find out if I was sick or something. "You know, you're becoming unreliable," he chided.

"But would you fire me just before Christmas?" I challenged.

"What about January second?" he countered.

"Wait until I find a job with health coverage."

I got up and dressed quickly for work. I was over there forty-five minutes after Nat called. It was good to work. I was glad I had the job. It was much better to be involved in other people's problems than in my own. Matter of fact, I perked up quite a bit at work because I remembered Michael and his proposal. When my orange and brown screen was off searching, I stuck my head into Nat's office. "Do you remember Michael Rosen?" I asked him.

He looked up and thought for a minute. "What case was it?" he wondered.

I sighed and tsked. "The Aberdeen case. Michael Rosen?"

Nat screwed up his face. "Oh yeah, the jerk who serves as Bellini's assistant."

"Associate, and that jerk has asked me to marry him."

"Oh—great guy!"

"Oh, shut up, Nat."

"Congratulations," he called, as I walked back toward my terminal. Then he came to his office door. "Hey, Becky, he must have health coverage."

"I haven't accepted yet," I turned back to tell him. Was Nat trying to get out of paying me my holiday bonus?

I called Michael while my computer was trying a random series of numbers to break into an insurance system. "Hi," I cooed at him.

"You sound happy," he told me, contrary to how he sounded.

"I'm in love," I sighed.

"My mother keeps leaving messages," Michael warned. "Are you any nearer to solving this dilemma of yours? We need to make an announcement."

"Oh! Thanks for reminding me. If someone murders her husband, I assume she can't inherit."

"Right."

"But what about her children?"

"Wouldn't that sort of defeat the purpose?"

"Why?"

"Well, let's say her child is a minor, for instance. Then naturally, the mother would have control of the money as guardian."

"But let's say another person was named guardian," I suggested.

"Hmm. No. I don't think so. Unless the child was named individually, I doubt very much if under any conditions he would inherit his mother's share of an estate. Any other beneficiaries could challenge, as I would encourage them to do, if said child tried such a maneuver."

"Okay. Then I guess I have to get a copy of the will."

He sighed. "Becky, why don't you just turn over the papers for this mysterious case of yours, and I'll have my paralegal get the will for you? Then I can check it over and tell you what you want to know."

"No. I want to do it myself."

Michael told me how to go to the courthouse and whom to see to get a copy of a will. "You're riding awfully far on one dollar," he told me.

"How are things going with you?" I asked sweetly. "You sound tired." Of course, he always sounded tired. Was it really worth it to make six figures?

"The Aberdeen case."

"Again?"

"Daryl is moving through various psychological stages from anger, during which she shot her husband, to grief, when she regretted shooting her husband, to remorse, when she realized her marriage was over, to greed, when she found out how much she could get, on to vengeance."

"Vengeance?"

"Lionel's family is urging him to hold firm. Daryl now wants to lay the whole dirty business out in front of the public. She wants the world to know that her husband slept with her mother. Did I mention inbreeding before?"

"Yes, I think you did, Michael. Doesn't she realize that she has nothing to gain by causing more publicity?"

"She thinks she has, Becky. Right now she's the object of press speculation. After all, she was the one arrested for assault with a deadly weapon, not to mention attempted murder. The families had enough influence to get the charges dropped by persuading the prosecutor to go for the accidental shooting business. But still, Daryl claims the incident has made her a laughingstock. Also, it's ruined her social standing. She said something to Bellini about how she was in the rotation to become president of her Junior League chapter, but after the shooting they persuaded her to retire as an officer."

"Well, at least it'll save her wear and tear on her white gloves."

"She also says it's uncomfortable for her at the club. And that she wasn't asked to serve on the Lyric Opera Ball committee. She feels she's being ostracized just because she shot her husband. But if everyone knew why she shot Lionel, she would become the victim instead of the guilty party."

"Hmm. It seems to me it would still be a rather messy situation all around. After all, her name will appear in the paper all over again. Wouldn't it be better to let the scandal die?"

"Well, she says if she's dropped from the Social Register, she's going public."

"Michael, everyone knows, at least most of the people we interviewed knew, that Lionel was sleeping with Jelly Mellon."

"But no one's admitted to it openly. It's like everyone can count to nine but no one mentions it when a baby is born seven months after a wedding. By the way, when do you think we should start our family? Should we give ourselves a year to adjust to marriage or shall we get pregnant right away?"

"We, Michael? I thought only I could get pregnant. Oops! Got to go. My number just came up." I hung up the phone and worked feverishly into the night. I signed out at ten-ten. Nat could hardly complain now that I hadn't put in a day's work.

When I got home, I was happy to find my answering machine only had one blink on it. Obviously no emergency today. I pushed the button and heard my beloved's voice. "Becky, you weren't here and you weren't at work. I assume I caught you midway. I'll call you tomorrow. I'm crashing. Love ya."

Damn. Now that we were officially in love, I really felt we should talk to each other long into the wee hours. Besides, I was all wound up from overwork, and I didn't think TV would help tonight. I needed human communication.

I thought of calling Yuri and telling him about Michael. But no. My ex-husband, sweet as he was, would be vain enough to think I was marrying Michael because I no longer had the thought of him to cling to. Besides, Yuri might be on his honeymoon.

So whom could I call?

Sadness kicked me in the stomach. I knew whom I wanted to call. I wanted to call my mother Winnie McKennah and tell her all about Michael. I started crying. I don't know why I cried. It was just that the terrible burden of her loss suddenly overwhelmed me. It's funny how you think life goes on, but it really doesn't. It sort of stops and starts itself. It definitely doesn't run smoothly.

My life halted several times. I'm sure it stopped when my mother was convicted of murdering my stepfather.

What at this moment struck me as strange was that I didn't remember being turned over to Winnie McKennah. I just remember all of a sudden being with her in Sioux Bluffs, Iowa. I should have recalled when I first met her. In the same way, I should have remembered when my stepfather died. According to the testimony, I was in the kitchen when it happened. I must have heard the shots. But there was no recollection, only the trial, only not speaking in my mother's defense. And that memory was true. The trial transcripts proved that. And then, poof. My mother was gone, and I was in Iowa with my new mother.

I smiled wryly. Maybe I should hypnotize myself.

Certainly, I could note the other stopping points in my life, both my marriage to and divorce from Yuri Belski. Then there was my dear, dear adoptive mother's death. And now my life had stopped this Thanksgiving when Michael asked me to marry him. I sighed happily.

I had to tell someone the good news. I thought of Bill. He'd probably be up and wouldn't mind hearing from me. Though he hadn't called since before Thanksgiving. Of course, that had been less than a week. But I was sure he would want to know. Besides, he had a right to know.

I picked up the phone and dialed his number. A woman answered! "May I please speak to Mr. Townsend," I said formally.

"May I ask who's calling?" and this said in a rather snotty tone of voice!

"Ms. Belski."

"Are you trying to sell something?"

"Mr. Townsend asked me to call him after ten about the commission he's working on of my parrot."

I heard her say, "Bill, it's some Belski about a parrot."

Then I heard Bill laugh. "I'll take it upstairs," he told the woman.

I knew why he was taking it upstairs. He had his business phone up there, and he could switch lines so whoever was with him couldn't listen in on the extension. "Becky," he said, after I heard several clicks.

"Did you notice how well I covered our asses," I bragged.

"I always notice how well you cover your ass."

"Please, Bill, such vulgarity at this hour of the night? I see I've been replaced."

"Not in my heart, just in my bed."

"That's what I love about you, Bill. You always know the right thing to say."

"Actually, I'm just trying to make you jealous."

"Can I retaliate?"

"Sure."

"Michael's asked me to marry him."

He waited. "And?" he finally had to ask.

"Well, there are a couple of things I have to clear up, but I think I'm going to say yes. The more I consider it, the more I like the thought of being married to him."

"You know, Becky, I really liked you," he said softly.

"Liked? Can't we still be friends?"

He sighed. "It's much easier to sleep with a woman than to be friends with her."

"But I want to be your friend, sort of brother and sister. You bring something to my life that Michael doesn't," I admitted.

"It's called passion, Becky. Hey, perhaps in a year or so we can start our affair."

"Bill, if I find some things that we can do together, platonically, will you come along with me and do them? I really don't want to lose you."

"We can try," he said. "Though it'll be difficult switching gears."

"Not too difficult, judging from who you have waiting for you on the floor below."

172

"Oh," Bill waved that away. "It's charity night tonight. The things I do for old friends. I've been listening to a nightful of complaints against society and the world at large. But the woman is in such sad shape, what can I do? After all, we've known each other since we were kids, lived right next door to each other. So how can I desert her now?"

"Did I ever tell you that you and Sir Walter Raleigh have a lot in common? Do I know this maiden you're rescuing with your bended ear?"

"As a matter of fact you do. Daryl Aberdeen."

"Oh God. Not *the* Daryl Aberdeen!"

"Yeah. Remember? That's how we met. You came calling to ask about Daryl."

"I understand from Michael that she wants the world to know about Lionel and her mother. Can't you say something to dissuade her? At some point, she has to get on with her life."

"I think she's trying to do that tonight. But I usually don't sleep with married women, especially ones who might pull a gun on me." And then he was silent, as if he were thinking about the same thing I was, that his stepmother had pulled a gun on his father. "Don't worry, Becky, I'm using all the dirty laundry clichés I know. After all, I remember what it was like being involved in a scandal, if you'll recall. It's a hard thing to live down. Call me when you come up with something—platonic."

We said good night. I wondered how he was going to explain the length of the call to Daryl. Maybe he would come up with some story about the difficulty of this parrot's plumage.

It wasn't until I drank my glass of milk and was tucked safely in my bed that I recirculated through my conversation with Bill. He and Daryl had been next-door neighbors. Jelly Mellon was my mother's best friend among that set. Had Jelly heard the shots the day my mother picked up the gun and killed Bill's father?

20

I didn't sleep well that night. Instead of sheep tossing themselves over the bridge of my mind, I found figures all jumbled together, parading around in my nightmares, figures I didn't even know, though I put names to them: Jelly and Daryl, Bill and William, the dark figure on the staircase, my mother looking at me with sad eyes, the stern, distant Alan. I needed to cleanse myself of this nightmare before I started my new, blissful life as—Ms. Becky Belski-Rosen?

I woke the next morning at eight. This early hour was unheard of for me, but I poured myself some orange juice and dug into the trial transcripts once more. There was the address of our old house, the house my mother and I shared with the Townsends. I took down the North Suburban phone book. Mellon, Arthur, 227 Elm; Mellon, J., 227 Elm. I looked back at the trial transcript. Townsend, Alan, 228 Elm. So it wasn't next door, Bill, it was across the street.

I called the office. Sadly, I knew that if I asked for another day off Nat actually might fire me, but I suppose I didn't think it mattered anymore. My past was becoming more important to me than my present.

Nat wasn't in. His secretary told me he'd be out of the office until about two. I hung up the phone and called my girlfriend and officemate two terminals down. She'd log on for me, the way I had logged on for her several weeks ago when she just had to take an extended lunch hour to find that perfect dress for that perfect man in her life. Of course, she didn't see him after that one perfect night together, but isn't that the story of our lives. She would do some busy work on my computer while I spent the morning snooping.

As I drove into Kenilworth, I wondered if ten was too early for Jelly Mellon. After all, a woman of sin and degradation probably didn't get up in the morning. On the other hand, if I came later, wouldn't she be getting ready to have lunch at the club or something socially similar?

I had deliberately neglected my manners and not called ahead to make known my intention of paying this unexpected visit. I knew she would not receive a stranger. I couldn't even use the Bellini Reese connection, as I understood from Michael that she and her daughter were no longer on speaking terms. I certainly could understand why. At the very least, Jelly Mellon must be in her early fifties. I know I would find it hard to stomach if my husband preferred my mother to me sexually. It was perhaps taking mother-daughter rivalry a giant step past decency.

It was funny when I turned onto Elm. I should have felt a twinge of remembrance. But even when I pulled to a stop at the curb in front of 227 and looked across Elm at the old Townsend house, I felt nothing. Perhaps that's because I couldn't see the house. Trees and a brick wall partially obscured it. Nothing obscured 227 except a black wrought iron fence six feet high. I considered leaving my car at the curb. But then I thought, what if she sics the dogs on me? They could run down the driveway faster than I could. So I drove onto the circular drive and pulled up in front of the portico, leaving my car door unlocked for that fast getaway.

The grounds were lovely. There were flower beds everywhere. Too bad it was that dead time of year when nothing survives except the evergreen. I rang the doorbell.

A servant answered.

A servant. And yet there were no servants mentioned in the trial transcript. Surely, my mother didn't take care of the house by herself. Here was something new to look into, someone who could prove what a bastard my stepfather was. Servants see and know everything, don't they?

"Yes?" this man said.

"I have an appointment to see Mrs. Mellon."

From the look of him, he knew it was an outright lie. "Your name, please?" he asked, nonetheless.

"Ms. Belski."

He retreated. I wasn't even asked to come in. He closed the door in my face.

It didn't matter. I could wait. I paced the portico and kept hold of my dignity.

Around the corner of the house came a woman. She was thinner than I and taller. She had on an all-weather jacket and her silver hair was held back with a scarf. She had the most beautifully flawless face. Either she saw the best plastic surgeon in the world or she was naturally gorgeous. "Ms. Belski?" she said. "I'm Mrs. Mellon. Would you like to come around to the back?"

Servants' entrance? But who cared? The important thing was that she would see me.

She had been outside on her deck when my visit surprised her. On the patio table was a wide assortment of cameras. "No, not to take pictures of the neighbors," she told me with a sly smile. "My hobby is bird photography. I have bird feeders all over the place. It drives the neighbors nuts. They even tried to introduce a bill through the city council to outlaw more than two bird feeders on a person's property. They say I attract squirrels. But you won't find a squirrel ever getting into my birdseed."

I tried to find a metaphor in what she said. I failed.

She looked at me. "Do you like birds?" she asked me.

"I never give them much thought, except when one of them dirties my windshield."

She smiled. "I've heard your name," she admitted. "You're the one asking questions of Daryl's and Lionel's friends. You're working for Daryl's lawyer. What is Daryl looking for? A payoff? A written apology? My head on a platter? I made a horrible mistake. We both did. I drink too much. And I—get lonely. I don't even remember exactly how it happened. But it did. The evening was beautiful. Young man, older woman, a secret to cherish as well as to bury. Lionel did neither. Instead, he threw our liaison in Daryl's face. One time in the midst of marital battle, he told her, 'Even your mother is better in bed than you are.' So what can I do to make up for it; how can I make it so that it never happened? Tell me, Ms. Belski. What does Daryl want?"

"Daryl's lawyer is a man given to compromise, not flamboyance."

"He can be flamboyant when he has to be," Jelly Mellon corrected. "Several of my friends have seen him in action. It's not a pretty sight. I don't want to be crucified on the witness stand. I'm too old for such a sacrifice. Besides, it would be farcical. So, they've sent you as a messenger. Now I'm asking you, what's the message?"

Oh lord. What was I going to tell her? The truth? "Actually, I've come on my own," I admitted. She simply waited. "Not really to speak about this shooting," I continued, "but one that happened twenty-four years ago. One that took place in the house across the street from you."

I could tell from her face that it was dog-siccing time. She sort of sneered at me. "Being so close to scandal myself, I certainly wouldn't relish spading over the earth on a scandal as old as that one."

She turned away as a signal of my dismissal. "Jane Peters was a friend of yours," I stopped her. "You testified for her at her trial."

"I tried to testify. For the most part, I was stopped from saying what I knew."

"Well no one's stopping you now."

"Why should I want to talk about it? It can't help Jane; it can't help anyone."

"It can help me. I'm her daughter."

21

"COME into the house," Jelly Mellon invited.

I followed her through the sun porch into a spacious brick kitchen. She indicated I should sit at the table while she got us both cups of coffee. "It's funny," Jelly said, as she sat kitty-corner to me, "someday I knew you would come."

"I don't know why I admitted to you what I've told no one else," I replied. "Please, please keep my identity a secret."

"I'm good at keeping secrets," Jelly assured me. "Unlike my soon-to-be-ex-son-in-law. But can I ask you why, after all these years, you've suddenly made a reappearance?"

"I've lived in Evanston a couple of years now. Frankly, I probably wouldn't have given a thought to the case, except our firm was assigned to look into your daughter's divorce. And I saw the name Bill Townsend. That sort of brought it all back."

Jelly smiled. "You and Bill were always such fast friends."

"I've been seeing Bill for the past several months."

Jelly's eyebrows lifted. "Romantically?"

"No," I prevaricated. "As a friend. I'm practically engaged."

"And he doesn't know who you are?"

"No. Bill has no idea. If he found out now, he would probably think of it as some sort of betrayal. But it didn't start out that way. It didn't start out as anything more than trying to fill in a very large blank in my life."

"What happened to you, Elizabeth? Where did you go? Where have you been all these years?"

So I explained to Jelly how I was given over to Winnie McKennah, how we lived our life in Sioux Bluffs, Iowa, until I went to the University of Illinois and married Yuri Belski. Then it was on to California and divorce, then back to the Chicago area, where I stumbled upon my past.

"So that's how you just suddenly disappeared. I was worried about you, Elizabeth. I asked Jane if there was anything I could do for you, but she said everything was being taken care of. I visited her several times in prison until she asked me not to come anymore, that it was too depressing for both of us. Afterward, I wrote and wrote, but she never replied. Finally, I just gave up trying to maintain contact."

"She died in prison."

"Did she?" Jelly said. "So that explains it. Funny that we never heard of it here. But that's the way it is, isn't it? When someone is out, she's out. We're good at creating a nonperson. That's the way it's going to be for me, if Daryl has her big show trial. Now everyone just whispers behind their hands. When the whole mess comes out into the open, I'll be deliberately snubbed. It'll be hard, I suppose. But people have lived through worse."

I sighed. "I don't know what I can do about Daryl."

She patted my hand. "It's not your problem anyway. Besides, I suppose we all have to pay for our mistakes."

"What mistake did my mother make?"

Jelly smiled.

"You see, it's a terrible problem for me," I tried to explain. "I remain bereft of memory. I know I was only five at the time, but hearing shots, probably seeing my dead stepfather, how could all of that have simply passed from my mind?"

"What do you remember?" Jelly asked.

"I vaguely remember the house. I remember my mother, naturally, and that she loved me. I recall various things we did together. And a few days ago I thought about nursery school. And there's Billy. I remember playing catch with Billy. But I can't remember my stepfather. I can't remember Alan, though I guess from what I've found out, I never even saw him until maybe the trial itself. And oh, that trial. I got hold of a transcript, and my recollection of it is accurate. I sat mute on the stand instead of testifying about the brutalities of my stepfather."

"Jane was very angry you had been called at all. Her defense attorney did it over her vociferous objections. In the end, it didn't matter because you didn't say anything. I was worried about you, though, and I knew your mother was, too. Strange that you and Bill should have had such different reactions."

"Bill? He was there, wasn't he? He says he wasn't, and everyone else, except Abigail Brightly, says he wasn't. But I think he was."

"Oh, he was there all right," Jelly affirmed. She settled back in her chair. "I suppose you deserve to know the truth, at least the truth that I know. I don't know what good it's going to do you. I guess by now you have a grasp on what basically happened. Your stepfather came down the stairs and went on one of his rampages, shot up the damned Christmas tree."

"He killed his first wife, didn't he? He pushed her down the stairs."

Jelly gave me a cautious look. "No one can say aye or nay on that one. Let's just say he was at the top of the stairs when she fell down them. At least that's where Alan found his father when he came rushing out of his own bedroom.

Poor Alan. He adored his mother and always tried to protect her. But in the end, he couldn't."

"And no one even bothered to accuse William Townsend," I said bitterly.

"Oh, you're wrong about that. Alan's absence pointed the finger in William Townsend's direction. Also, Sarah's live-in actually went to the police and suggested they should investigate the fall further. They didn't, of course. William Townsend was too prominent. But Townsend found out about the live-in's accusations and didn't make the mistake again of letting someone stay in the house with him and his family. Poor Jane had to make do with a daily who came in every morning after ten, when Townsend would be out of the house. The maid had to leave by four. So no one ever saw Jane and Townsend together. Just remember this, Elizabeth: If you're rich and influential, you can get away with murder.

"Anyway, where were we? Oh yes, Bill Townsend playing wild west with the Christmas tree. It's funny. I only really know what Jane said at the trial. But I can well believe that Townsend came after her with a gun. The problem was, as you probably read in the transcript, by the time Jane got her hands on a gun and fired at her approaching husband, his revolver was empty. The prosecutor used this to prop up his murder claim. Men are so dumb. Would you count the bullets if someone were firing at random in your hallway? If Jane had been old money, she probably would have been put on probation. But she was the usurper, the outsider, his mistress while his first wife was still alive. People always want to believe the worst of someone. It's so much more delicious that way.

"I was home the day it happened. I had just returned from taking Daryl up to the stables in Lake Forest. I didn't hear the shots. I understand I probably wouldn't have, since they were made by a revolver. Anyway, sometimes the guys skeetshoot out toward the lake, so I probably wouldn't have thought anything about it if I *had* heard gunfire. The first I knew there was trouble was when Billy furiously knocked on my door and rang my bell at the same time.

"Naturally, I hurried to the door. He came in, crying hysterically, with no coat on, though it was the dead of winter. I asked him what was wrong. I asked him about Jane, about you. It took him the longest time to say anything at all. Then he said very slowly and haltingly, 'My stepmother shot my father. She told me to tell you that.'

"You can imagine my reaction. Even though I knew what was going on in that house because Jane and I were lunch buddies, I was stunned, shocked into immobility. I asked Billy to tell me again. And he said exactly the same words. 'My stepmother shot my father. She told me to tell you that. I'm to stay here.' And then he started crying again and shivering. I was afraid he was going into shock, so I hurried him upstairs and placed him in the guest bedroom, where I wrapped him in blankets.

"By that time, I could see the police and the ambulance, sirens screaming, racing up the driveway of your house. So I stayed in my own house and looked after Billy. He was crying all the time. There was nothing I could do to comfort him, so I just held him, hugged him, and tried to keep him warm.

"And I have to admit to watching out the window, being the curious neighbor. That's how I saw the policeman bringing you over. He was leading you by your little hand. You were dressed warmly in your coat and your woolen cap and you had your mittens on." Jelly smiled. "Your mother must have dressed you before she sent you across. I was torn at leaving Billy; but when the doorbell rang, I had to go down. I must admit I used the opportunity to try to pry some information out of the policeman. The man was not forthcoming. All he said was there was a situation across the street and Mrs. Townsend asked if I would look after her daughter. So there you were. You had this empty look in your eyes. Now that I think about it, you sat silently for days. I suppose that's why we really didn't pay too much attention to you, because Billy was the one who was hysterical. He was the one who needed the doctor. He only started to recover when Alan came home."

"Alan."

"Yes. Someone from the firm had the sense to call him. I'm afraid my husband and I were too involved with the whole grotesque situation to think of it. But Alan came home and took charge. He was always that kind of guy. Cool. Strong. Even then. And he was not one bit sorry to see his father dead."

"Then why did he testify against my mother at her trial?" I wanted to know. "Why, when he knew his father had killed his mother?"

"Something we only suspect," Jelly reminded me. "Besides, what makes you think he was any fonder of your mother? He knew that Jane was sleeping with Townsend when his mother was still alive. Anyway, he took charge of Billy. Billy and he stayed at the Mortons', as Alan and Doug Morton were at Princeton together. You remained with me.

"Alan was extremely busy. He had to make the funeral arrangements, see to the business, take care of Billy, visit Jane at the county jail, and consult with her when she got out on bail. Just to show you that Alan wasn't all bad, he did hire Jane's defense attorney."

"Yeah, the one that convinced her to change her plea from self-defense to guilty to second-degree murder with mitigation," I said angrily.

"Don't ask me about the legalities of the case because I don't know them. Anyway, Alan also came to see me and my husband. He had in his hand a letter from Jane. He begged us, as Jane did in her letter, that we not tell anyone Billy had been in the house when his father was shot. We didn't need much convincing to agree to that. What good would Billy be to your mother in any case? Both he and you were in the kitchen the whole time. Your mother had sent you there when Townsend first pulled his six-shooter. Be-

184

sides, Billy was so hysterical. All we wanted was for him to recover. So began our conspiracy of silence.

"And then I asked Alan what we were going to do with you, because I was really getting worried about you by then. You still hadn't said a word. You ate and you slept and you watched television. But you were silent. We wanted to take you to a child psychiatrist. But Alan said, 'Why mess up her mind anymore than it is.'

"When your mother was let out on bail, we returned you to her, I'm afraid for only a few short months. I was the only one to go over and see Jane that I know of. You were there with her. She was afraid to send you back to nursery school, afraid of what people might say. But you were talking, and you seemed okay again. She told me that you had absolutely no memory of what had happened, and she was glad for that.

"Then her sentencing hearing came. Because of all the evidence, the judge sentenced her to the lightest term possible while still satisfying the sensibilities of the Kenilworth community. It was awful that Jane had to serve any time in jail. And she probably wouldn't have if Bill Townsend had been an ordinary Joe. But he was William Townsend of Kenilworth. So his life supposedly had more value than others. Plus, the judge didn't like the fact that your mother had been fooling around with Bill before his first wife died. Part of his sentencing seemed to be, well, she got what she deserved. It's all so mixed up, but I suppose family murders are like that.

"Alan came in for the trial. I met him in the hallway afterward. I remember I was crying. He told me not to worry, that Jane would be out on probation in under two years. That's the deal her lawyer cut for her. That's why she pleaded guilty. I guess she never made it." Jelly bowed her head and sighed. "Anyway, I asked Alan what was going to happen to you. I remember I even offered to take you in. I had Daryl, after all; and though she was older than you, I thought one more child couldn't hurt. Besides, if Jane was going to be out in a couple of years, well, that wouldn't be too much of a strain. But Alan said you were already provided for. I had no idea that he had arranged for one of his father's secretaries to adopt you. That's very strange, don't you think?''

I did think so. I sat in Jelly Mellon's kitchen and tried to remember when Winnie McKennah told me that my real mother was dead. It must have been early on, because I know I accepted it, accepted Winnie totally as my mother when I was very young. I shook my head. "Everything seems strange now," I admitted. "If only I could remember."

"If you're friends with Bill again, maybe you should ask him?''

"I've hinted around it. He doesn't like to talk about it. Besides, he still claims that he wasn't in the house when it happened.''

"I'm sure Alan drummed that into him, to always say he was never in the house. Maybe he even believes it himself by now,'' Jelly suggested. "After all, it was so long ago, and it was so traumatic for all of you.''

"I think it's the reason Bill never married,'' I said.

Jelly smiled. "I think the reason Bill's not married is that he's having too much fun being single.''

"At thirty-five?''

"He'll always be eligible,'' Jelly pointed out quite accurately. "If you ask me who's most affected by it all, aside from you and your mother, of course, I'd say it's Alan. He did the correct thing by marrying Tricia, but I don't think the marriage is any more than correct.''

"I was at their house once. He's very loving toward his sons.''

"Yes. He was always good with children. You know, Elizabeth, if you really want to know more, maybe you should talk to Alan about it. Although he hated your mother, for some reason, after your stepfather was shot,

186

they worked quite closely together right on up through the trial. Maybe he can fill in those blanks for you.''

"Umm." I wondered. "But he wasn't in the house, was he? Only Bill, my mother, and I were there. Bill says he wasn't, my mother's dead, and I can't remember. In other words, three blind mice.''

"Rather three blind alleys," Jelly corrected me. "I'm sorry." She smiled. "I'm glad you came by, though.''

"You will keep my secret?''

"A promise made is a promise kept. Don't be a stranger.''

I stood. I smiled. "It's nice, you know.''

"What?''

"Hearing my name again. Elizabeth. It makes me feel warm. My—adoptive mother always called me Becky. But I like Elizabeth.''

"You should go back to it then.''

I frowned. "I don't know. I don't know who that person was.''

22

I was so glad in the next few weeks that I had Michael. I still hadn't said yes, I hadn't said no. We just sort of assumed that we would be getting married. We would lie in bed together, Michael sleeping or trying to, while I contemplated our life together. "I don't know, Michael," I would say, "do I love marriage or do I simply love the idea of getting married? Did I like being married before? I'm trying to recall my days with Yuri. You know, frankly, when we were married—"

"Frankly?" Michael would awake to say. "Frankly, I'd rather not hear about your marriage to Yuri. Frankly, I'd rather think of you as my virgin bride. So if you don't mind, would you please discuss all these love musings with a girlfriend."

"Aren't we going to be open and frank about our emotions?"

"Frankly, I hope not."

"Frankly, we have to be able to communicate our feelings. That's part of being in a marriage."

"Is there someone named Frank in bed with us?"

"Don't you even want to know if I love you, Michael?"

But, frankly, by then he was asleep or faking it.

Bill was much more receptive to my "love musings," as Michael called them. Of course, Bill had probably tallied up many more romantic interludes than Michael. Let's face it, are lawyers basically romantic people? Maybe some of them, like those public defenders, at least on their first day at work. Or maybe civil rights attorneys are incurable romantics because of the difference they can make in our lives. But I suppose it would be too much to expect to find a romantic divorce lawyer. After all, how much romance do they see in their offices, excluding those who sleep with their clients.

Bill agreed with me that I should continue to press Michael on the Aberdeen case. "Daryl has this bee in her bonnet, if I may use that old-fashioned expression. She's creating this forties image of herself as the woman wronged. She can't seem to see that if she brings her mother and her husband down, she'll be bringing herself down too. Can't her lawyer make her understand?"

"I've spoken to Michael about it," I assured Bill. "He claims to have discussed it with Bellini, but he says sometimes Bellini likes to get his licks in inside the courtroom itself, especially if he knows that it'll make headlines, as this case certainly would."

Bill sighed. "Are you sure you want to marry this guy?"

Then I linked my arm in Bill's, and we talked about love.

It was easier than we both thought it would be to move our relationship from the romantic and sexually titillating to the platonic. Perhaps there was a core of remembrance in Bill also that at one time we were brother and sister. Maybe that's what gave our relationship such a feeling of comfort.

We spent time Christmas-shopping together. We hit the stores during their off-peak hours. Nat, my boss, was always more lenient around Christmas. That's because we'd be putting in overtime chasing deadbeats afterward. So Bill would call me at Resources after he had finished one commission but before he started another, and we would trail into the malls or head down to North Michigan Avenue and while away the hours in Water Tower Place.

He had more gifts to buy than I did, certainly—and more money to buy them with. Meanwhile, I was trying to find gifts under ten dollars to give to everyone in the office. Also, I was searching for something appropriate to bestow upon Michael's mother. Bill suggested a black silk gag. That's when we were in one of those kinky little shops secluded in the Loop, which I wouldn't have dared enter on my own. I considered the gag. I also considered several other products they were selling. Perhaps there was something suitable here for Michael. Bill suggested toothpicks to keep his eyes open. "Maybe that's why you love him, because he's always half asleep," he offered.

During these happy, companionable times with Bill, I never brought up the subject of his father's death. After my visit to Jelly Mellon, I didn't see the point. I did want to know what he saw that day. I was curious about what we heard or didn't hear in that kitchen. But how was I to get all of that out of him without confessing to him who I was? I preferred being Becky Belski. I think Bill liked me as Becky. I don't know how he would have felt about me as Elizabeth.

I suppose I would have let the dead lie sleeping if I hadn't received one of those ivory invitations in the mail. Ever since I joined Friends of the Evanston Library, and that only because I thought maybe it would help me with all those library fines the computer kept claiming I owed, I had been on several hoity-toity lists. This was strange because it only costs $25 to join the Friends. However, they must have made god knows how much more by selling my name to every charity within a fifty-mile radius.

This ivory invitation, decorated tastefully with an ink drawing of a Christmas wreath, was called A Happy Homeless Christmas. I liked the alliteration, but I had to wonder at the concept. It was a house tour of exquisitely exclusive homes along the North Shore, all proceeds to benefit the homeless. It was definitely questionable whether the homeless would be allowed on the house tour. That would be stretching charity a bit too far.

As with most monetary pleas, I was going to toss this one into the basket. I'm really not interested in houses. I supposed when and if Michael and I bought our own, I would have to look into it, but this was not the time. Also, I had already given to the *Chicago Tribune* Christmas Fund and was wiped out in the tax deductible charity department. But I couldn't help but wonder what sort of house would be on display. What was considered showable?

Two historic houses in Evanston were listed, one where the Women's Christian Temperance Union had held many of its meetings. No, it had not yet been turned into a bar. One house in Wilmette, a lovely Tudor, the invitation promised, and two houses in Kenilworth were being offered. The address of one of them was 228 Elm, the Butcher house, "recently featured in *American Decorator.*"

It was so very genteel of this charitable organization not to mention that the house at 228 Elm was also known as the address where two murders took place. Or officially, one murder, one suspicious fall down a staircase. Two-twenty-eight Elm was the old Townsend estate.

I bought two tickets, one for me, one for Bill.

23

"YOU shouldn't have," Bill said, when I issued the invitation to accompany me on the house tour. He meant it. "I've seen these houses all my life; I've grown up in them."

"But probably not these particular houses," I argued.

"They're all more or less the same," he informed me. "Besides, these people wouldn't have offered their homes if they hadn't wanted to show them off. Plus, there'll be these prissy, wispy blonds in each room, watching over every move we make. You don't want to do this, Becky."

"But, Bill, I've already bought the tickets," I whined.

"Take Michael."

"Michael? When? The houses are only open from ten to four. Please? Pretty please?"

"Oh shit!"

I took that to mean yes.

We arranged a date and time when we would do the tour. I never let Bill know which houses we would be seeing. Since we didn't have to go in any particular order, I would make sure that we came to 228 Elm last. By then he would probably be tired. His resistance would be low. Maybe finally the truth would fall out of him.

I have to admit I also was curious about my own reaction. What would I remember? When I stepped into the house, what trauma would be shaken loose from within me? By then I fancied both of us racing from the house in horror. Lord. Well, we could always say the house was haunted. And that wouldn't be far from the truth.

The day of discovery came. Bill was being particularly ornery by not dressing for the occasion. He could have at least worn slacks and a suitable sweater. Instead he wore paint-stained jeans and a red and black plaid wool jacket. And he would probably know some of the women who lay in wait for their charitable contributors. I myself had on my plaid skirt again with cashmere sweater, a reprise of my Thanksgiving outfit, when everything had turned out so well, except Thanksgiving dinner. But this time I added a string of cultured pearls. I thought I looked very *Town and Country*, if not very rich.

Bill made an enjoyable companion. He seemed to find nebulously derogatory comments to make about each house along the way, and he would make his comments within the hearing of the very proper ladies who had the houses zoned for protection. By the time we got to our fourth house, also known as the "tea house" because we could take tea in the heated sun porch, it was almost a comedy tour. So we were in a good mood when we drove east in Kenilworth and ended up in front of 228 Elm. Then the good times died.

"What's this?" Bill said to me.

"Our last house. Thank God. By now they've probably called ahead and alerted them to our coming."

"Becky, haven't you seen enough houses?"

"Hey, I paid for the tickets. I want to get my money's worth."

A car pulled up behind us, and two younger women got out. They then helped an elderly woman in a wheelchair out. "Come on," I said. "Let's follow them in. We'll be less conspicuous."

"No, Becky. I've had it."

I tried to look puzzled and slightly annoyed. It never occurred to me that Bill Townsend would outright refuse to enter his old house. "Come on, Bill," I coaxed. "We've had such a good time. Let's not spoil it. I'll always wonder what we've been missing."

"Becky, I know what we'll be missing, and I'll describe it to you in detail."

"Oh! You know the house, and you don't like the people who live in it," I guessed.

"I don't know anything about the people who live in this house now. But I used to live here when I was a child."

"Bill!" I exclaimed heartily. "Now's your chance to see your old stomping grounds, to see what they've done to your room and your private hiding places and everything. Come on!"

I pocketed the car key and got out of the car. I went around to the passenger side and tried to open the door. He had kept it locked. But finally he relented. He opened the door and got out. Then he stood and stared at his watch. "Five minutes. No more."

"No less."

We walked up the red brick path together. Bill's uneasiness had dispelled my own. I was more eager than ever to get inside that house.

We arrived on the front steps just as they closed the door on the party with the wheelchair. So we had to ring the doorbell again. The door was opened, and we were greeted by another mannequinlike woman with the standard salutation of "Hello. Welcome to the Butcher house, and thank you for helping the homeless. If you'll join this other group, we'll give you a little history of the house."

"No thanks," Bill snapped. I was shocked because Bill was never rude.

"We're just looking for the architectural underpinnings,"

I covered quickly. "We'll just wander around, if you don't mind."

"The Butcher house," I whispered to Bill, when we were far enough away from our disapproving hostess.

"An appropriate enough name for this house," he said.

I linked my arm in his and pressed it tight. I must admit a little shiver drizzled through me. But as we stood there, looking around the house—and we could see into three of its rooms right from this huge entrance hallway—I had to admit I didn't remember a damn thing about it. There was a total absence of recall.

It was funny how our attentions diverged. I was focused on what could have been the study where the murder took place, though it was hard to tell now. There were no books in the room. Instead it held a porcelain collection, and its walls were done in mock Victorian detailing. Bill's attention was focused on the stairway. I pulled him gently in my direction. "What did this used to be?" I asked.

"My father's study. They've stupidly taken down all the wood and put up plaster. And they've opened up the wall to lead into what used to be a parlor. Look," he led me into it. "My mother used to have her women friends in for tea here while we all played together. They could keep their eyes on us because we played in the back there."

I looked over the backyard, and this I remembered. The trees had grown and some had even been cut away, but I remember where we used to set up the bases for our one-sided game of softball. "You used to play catch out there," I told him.

He sighed. "So often. I was never very good at it. I was so glad when I got to boarding school and we concentrated on soccer." He smiled at me.

We held hands and walked on. From the parlor we crossed into the hallway again. The entrance foyer, where we came in, was two stories, and then the hall itself extended the length of the house. We crossed into the kitchen.

"Absolutely beautiful," I said enthusiastically. And it was one of the largest kitchens I had ever seen.

"My stepmother's doing," Bill said. "When my mother was alive, we ate in the dining room. But my stepmother wanted a big kitchen where the family could gather like real people." He smiled. "Poor woman. Sometimes when I think of her—she was so out of place here."

"You think of her?"

"I try not to think of any of them, my assorted parents, but they have a habit of creeping up on me. Anyway, I remember when this addition was being built. It was such a mess. There was hammering and sawing going on during my vacations. But she finally got what she wanted. They pushed the back of the house out and gave her her bay window so she could look out onto the lake. She was worried about her daughter, you see. She was afraid little Elizabeth would run off to the lake and drown, and no one would see her. When I was home, I always had to keep an eye on Elizabeth." He smiled. "It was fun being the big brother for a change."

"So this is where you ate then, with your stepmother?"

"Yes. The three of us, Jane, Elizabeth, and I. My father hardly ever made it home for dinner. We would have hot dogs and beans, macaroni and cheese, tuna casserole." He nodded. "She was a good cook."

"Nothing haute."

"No. My mother used to be the gourmet cook. I dreaded some of the dinners we ate. I remember one day she served cold tongue. I was so sick, I ran up to my room and locked the door and wouldn't come out. My father was banging on it, my mother was pleading. I threw up all over my carpet. But I stayed in there with the mess coagulating. Later that evening I heard tapping at my window, and I was afraid they had come to get me that way. I knew I would be punished. So I peeked out the window. It was Alan. He had taken the car and had come to the rescue with a hamburger and fries."

"That was nice of him."

"Yes. Alan was like that. He was a great older brother. He always took care of me."

I followed when Bill led us into the dining room. "This is basically the same," he said, "except the display cases are gone, thank God."

"Did your mother have a lot of china?"

"She did but she kept that in drawers. My father had his guns in here, up on the wall. Sometimes when we weren't behaving, he'd threaten to take down one of the revolvers and shoot us."

"Charming."

"It lacked a certain finesse, but it was effective."

"But the guns couldn't have been loaded?"

Bill was very silent. "We thought not," he finally said.

We walked through the living room and out into the hallway. "Ready to go?" Bill asked me.

"We haven't seen the upstairs."

He checked his watch. "It's been more than five minutes."

"Please. It hasn't been that bad, has it?"

Bill gave me a disgruntled look. I smiled and took hold of the curved banister and started climbing. He followed. "You have a nice ass, you know," he said, just to get even.

We reached the top of the stairs. It was lovely up here. The railing ran along the length of the hallway, and one could look down below into the foyer. "Where was your room?" I asked Bill.

He took me to it. It was down at the end of the hall, well out of the way. "When I was born, so late after my brother, my father couldn't stand my crying. So he had my mother put me down here."

"Your father sounds so delightful." I grimaced.

"I'll try to remember something good about him."

We were in Bill's room now. It was actually two rooms, a bedroom and a sitting room. "My crib used to be in there," Bill explained, "and my mother would sleep in here. Until I got older. Then I slept here and used the smaller room for my closet."

"Big closet."

"I had lots of toys."

"You had a train set."

"Yes. Much more trouble than it was worth. The cars kept falling off the track. That's one thing I'll never get my kids."

"But you're not going to get married, so how can you have kids?"

He gave me a look, then a smile. "I'll explain it later, perhaps just before you and Michael get married."

There was a door next to Bill's bedroom. "What's this?" I asked.

"It leads up to the attic."

We took it and discovered that the attic had been remodeled so that now it served as a playroom. Back down a flight, the two bedrooms closest to Bill's had been guest bedrooms in his time, though one of them must have been mine when I lived here. I still couldn't remember. "Then there's Alan's bedroom," Bill said.

We walked into what had been Alan's bedroom. "Look what they've done," Bill noted. "They've combined Alan's bedroom with my parents' and made a huge master suite. I'll have to tell Alan about this."

We walked through and discovered a spacious bathroom, or I guess one must call it bath area now, with its Jacuzzi and sauna. "Clever," Bill said. "They've combined Alan's bathroom with my parents' bathroom."

"So Alan's bathroom and your parents' were back to back."

"Yes. I always envied him having a bathroom because I had to get up and go down the hall, and I was so scared late at night that some monster was going to attack me on my way back and forth. I almost would have preferred to wet the bed."

"He must have been able to hear everything that went on in your parents' room," I noted.

"I don't quite see Alan as an eavesdropper," Bill chided.

I didn't see him that way either. But if his parents argued, he probably couldn't help but hear. Whereas, Bill was all the way at the other end of the house. He wouldn't have heard a thing.

We were out in the upper hallway again. I could see in my mind's eye William and Sarah Townsend arguing, coming out of their bedroom, Alan alerted by their loud voices, Townsend driving Sarah toward the stairs, she backing up to them until there was nothing to do but fall.

We were at the head of the stairs ourselves now. They were such broad, sweeping stairs, with carpeting down the center of them to let the wood show. "This is where your mother fell," I stated.

"Yes." Bill sighed deeply. "I thought it was all part of a bad dream. You know how sometimes you're half awake, half asleep? I heard noises that even now I can't distinguish. And then the thump, thump, thump, and I knew someone had fallen down the stairs. This I knew because, when my father and mother weren't home, I'd send my roller skates crashing down the stairs just to see them go. I was awake then, wide awake. But I was afraid to move. You see, oh god, this is so awful to admit, I hoped it was my father. I hoped he wouldn't be around anymore because I was so afraid of him.

"What a wish to make for the Christmas season, eh? And I always thought later that that's why my mother died. It was God getting even with me for wishing my father dead. I can't tell you the guilt I lived with. You see, I knew that I had killed the one person I loved most in all the world. And I couldn't even confide in Alan because he was so devastated by the loss. Our mother—oh Becky, she was such a wonderful woman, so sort of crazy and happy and patient and, well, motherly. When she died, it was the end of life for both of us."

"Did your father push your mother down the stairs?"

"Alan believes he did," Bill quietly admitted. "I don't

know. It's all so vague. I keep thinking if only I could remember what the screaming before the thumps was about. I've often thought of going to a hypnotist and finding out, really finding out what I remember. But there's so much I would be afraid of discovering."

"I agree with you there," I said. "We all have secrets better left covered. But if you and Alan hated your father so, how come you weren't grateful three years later when your stepmother killed him?"

Bill looked at me strangely. "What peculiar little beast is hidden within you, Becky Belski?" he wondered.

"I'm sorry," I apologized. "Vengeance is mine, sayeth the Lord, and all that. And really who suffered for the second murder? Everyone but your father."

"That's the only good thing about death, isn't it? You're past suffering. Come on, let's get out of here."

We started down the steps, but I stopped, so Bill stopped. "What is it?" he asked. "For reasons you must understand now, I don't like to tarry on these stairs."

I didn't want to tarry either, but something had just come back to me. I looked quizzically at Bill. "You know, it occurs to me that the perfect place to put a Christmas tree in this house would be right there in the foyer, at the foot of the stairs."

"Yes," Bill confirmed. "That's where we always had it."

"So that's how your father got away with the excuse that your mother tripped while carrying presents down to it."

Bill said nothing.

"And when he came down these steps that day and saw that your stepmother had turned on the lights of the Christmas tree—"

"Let's go, Becky. Let's go now!"

24

BILL raced down the stairs and pushed out the front door. I gave a look of apology to the very proper ladies and rushed out the door after him. I caught up with him on the sidewalk. "Your father was in one of his rages. Your stepmother sent you and Elizabeth to the kitchen," I continued. "She wanted you away from the reach of your father's temper. And you two huddled in the kitchen while she shot him."

"Give me the keys to your fucking car."

"It's my car. I'll drive," I told him. I took out my keys and opened the passenger door for him. Then I went around and got into the driver's seat. Instead of starting the car, I dropped the keys back into the bag. "After she shot him, you and Elizabeth ran into the study and saw your father lying there dead. You were hysterical. Your stepmother sent you across the street to the Mellon house. But what I don't understand, Bill, is why didn't she send Elizabeth across the street with you? Why keep Elizabeth there in that house with a dead man?"

Bill slumped back into the seat, his jaw slack, his eyes

glazed. "It was so long ago. It doesn't matter. It really doesn't matter. I've lived with the lies so long they're part of me now, aren't they?"

"What lies, Bill? What happened that day? You were old enough to remember. It wasn't as if you were asleep, as you were when your mother died. You know what happened when your father was shot. Please, please tell me. I have to know."

He looked at me then, so very, very sadly. "You're part of her, aren't you? You have something to do with Jane Peters?"

"I just want to know the truth about her, that's all."

"The truth." Bill looked at his hands. "Which truth?"

"What happened?"

"What don't you know?" he wondered absently. "We were all going to be together until the weekend, when I would have to return to boarding school. Between visiting my grandmother and my friends, we did all the Christmas things together. My stepmother took us sledding and skating; we made Christmas cookies; she played the piano and we sang carols. She wanted me to have fun at home. She wanted me to write to Alan, to let Alan know that she wasn't all bad. Oh, she didn't say it in those words. She'd just say to me, 'Tell Alan he can come home, that he's very welcome here, that I'm not some monster.' But it wasn't only for Alan that she made this holiday. She was just that sort of person. Like at Easter she would hide Easter eggs around the lawn, that's after we spent hours decorating them. And we would get baskets under our beds. She wanted to be a good mother, not only to her own daughter but to me.

"I don't know what went on between her and my father. My father was always the outsider in any case, because of his violent outbursts. If one was smart, one stayed out of his way. She didn't have that option. She was married to him.

"Like that last day. Who knows what set him off? He was at the top of the stairs. He saw the lights on the Christmas tree. He started screaming. I remember looking up those stairs and wishing he would fall down them. God, I hated that man.

"But he didn't fall down. He came down the steps and demanded to know why we had turned the Christmas lights on before dark. He started hollering about how the tree should have been taken down, the electric rates, all sorts of garbage. And my stepmother tried to convince him that there was nothing wrong with enjoying the holiday season a few days longer. He started up again about how the tree should have been taken down on New Year's Day. He called my stepmother a variety of names, all pointing to her lack of breeding. And then, when she didn't scream back, but just stayed away from him with the two of us, that seemed to enrage him more. So he picked up the Christmas tree, literally picked up this huge eight-foot tree and threw it against the wall.

"Everything smashed. The glass, the bulbs, the trinkets. It made a hideous sound. But that wasn't enough for my father. He grabbed a gun from the table drawer and started shooting up the tree. Elizabeth started screaming. I placed my hand over her mouth and thought, oh my god, he's going to turn the gun on us. I don't know how my stepmother did it, but she had enough sense about her to say, 'Bill, take Elizabeth into the kitchen and stay there.'

"So there we stayed, listening to them. After the shots died, my stepmother said something about this being the last step. She wanted a divorce. And my father said he'd see her dead before he'd pay her a penny in any divorce settlement. Then she sort of yelped, as if she had been struck or something. We didn't know. Elizabeth tugged at me, saying we had to defend Mommy or he would kill her. I wanted to call the police, but Elizabeth said there wasn't time. We were both in a panic. So we decided to see what was happening, and maybe we could do something about it. We snuck out of the kitchen, through the dining room and into the living room. From there we could see my father and my stepmother. He was so close to her, we were afraid he would do to her what he had done to the Christmas tree.

"I was paralyzed with fear. But Elizabeth darted forward, and I followed her, knowing we had to do something. We ran into the study. Neither my stepmother nor my father was paying any attention to us. And that's when the shots rang out. Six shots. Bang bang bang bang bang bang, just like that, one after another.

"Everything stopped. My father fell dead at my stepmother's feet."

"But how did your stepmother manage to get her hands on a gun?"

Bill looked straight at me. "My stepmother didn't kill my father. Elizabeth did."

25

"YOU'RE lying!" was my instinctive response.

"I've been lying all these years," Bill replied. "Now I'm telling the truth. Finally. Yes, I was in the house when it happened; and yes, Elizabeth, not Jane, shot my father. That's the truth, Becky."

"How did she get the gun?"

"From the dining room display case. While I was watching my stepmother and my father in horror, Elizabeth must have run back and grabbed a gun to defend her mother. I didn't see it in her hands, even when she ran past me to come to her mother's aid. I didn't even see the revolver when she fired. She just stood there, and like in the pictures she went bang bang bang until the gun was empty.

"My father fell, and we didn't know what to do. We all stared at him. He was just lying there. Blood was seeping out all over him. We none of us moved. Finally, my stepmother took a tentative step toward him and said, 'I think he's dead.' That's when Elizabeth dropped the gun.

"She stood like—like a zombie, not seeing, not speaking.

Her mother went over to her and tried to talk to her, but Elizabeth was stiff, like wood. Then my stepmother looked at me, as if maybe I would know what to do. But all I could do was start crying.

"I don't know when Jane made her decision to take Elizabeth's crime on herself. We were all in a state of shock, Elizabeth most of all. She was just standing there, staring at the body. I remember my stepmother taking hold of me and saying, 'Listen, Billy, there's something we have to do now so that Elizabeth won't get into trouble. We have to make sure that everyone thinks I killed your father.' So that's how our cover-up began.

"I remember crying all through it. It was Jane who thought of switching guns. She took the one from the study's bookshelf and placed it in the display case in the dining room. I was the one who suggested washing Elizabeth's hands well because I was into all these crime shows and I knew that she would have traces of powder on her hands from firing the gun.

"And it was always hurry, hurry, hurry because we knew we had to call the police, call an ambulance. We were worried someone had heard the shots. Then Jane said to me that I should run across the street to Jelly's house and tell her that my stepmother had just shot my father. She made me promise never ever to tell the truth to anyone under any circumstances.

"I didn't want to leave her. Especially I didn't want to leave Elizabeth. But my stepmother said I had to go to Jelly's and pretend I was over there the whole morning. Jelly would lie for us. No one must know that I was there in the house with them when it happened. 'Then the police won't be able to question you. They can't make you tell them what really happened. For Elizabeth, Billy. We have to do this for Elizabeth.' Who was still at that time totally out of it.

"So I ran over to Jelly's and told her what my stepmother said about how she shot my father and that my stepmother didn't want me involved. Besides, I had been in the kitchen all the time, I hadn't seen anything. I told Jelly all the lies Jane told me to tell her. And Jelly, being the good sort that she is, never said anything about me being there. But she did ask me where Elizabeth was, and I told her Elizabeth had been in the kitchen with me when it happened. 'Thank God!' Jelly said. So I knew that the best thing to do was to keep quiet.

"I don't know what my stepmother said to Elizabeth. All I know is that the next time I saw Elizabeth—and that was later that night, when Jelly thought I was sleeping—my stepsister was in bed, playing with her dolls. I asked her how she was feeling, what had happened when the police came and everything. Elizabeth told me that her mommy had shot my daddy and she was very sad about it. Then she just went back to playing with her dolls. And it occurred to me that we were not only going to lie to the police, our friends, and the rest of the world, Elizabeth and I were also going to lie to each other.

"Then Alan came home, and he took care of everything. I felt safe as soon as he arrived."

"You told him that Elizabeth shot your father."

"No," Bill said. "Not then. I was so confused. I had made this promise to my stepmother and it was like we were all in this together. I did tell him that I had been in the house when it happened, in the kitchen with Elizabeth, but that Jane didn't want me involved, so she sent me over here and told me never to tell anyone I was in the house. Alan said that it was a good thing our stepmother had done, that it was better no one ever knew I had been in the house. 'But what about Elizabeth?' I asked. And then Alan told me that Elizabeth was still in shock. A doctor had seen her and had ascertained that she had no memory of anything that took place in that house that day.

"I didn't believe it. I thought Elizabeth, like me, was telling people exactly what her mother told her to tell people. But I never had a chance to see Elizabeth again because

Alan took me to the Mortons and Elizabeth stayed with Jelly until my stepmother was let out on bail."

"That was a dumb thing for your stepmother to do, to lie like that," I said. "She should have told the police the truth. You could have verified it. They wouldn't have done anything to a little girl."

"That's what I said to her, Becky. Not in those words, but something like, 'They won't hurt Elizabeth.' But Jane said, 'This marriage has already destroyed me. I don't want it to destroy my daughter too.' I was so young then, I didn't know what she meant. But later when I thought about it I assumed Jane thought Elizabeth would be known as a murderer all her life." Bill sighed. "It weighed on me, though, knowing what had happened and not being able to say anything. Years later, when I was sixteen, I was out at a party and got so drunk. I came home to Alan. He had a place in Chicago then, on the lake. We used to watch the waves together from his window. But this night, if I had seen a wave, I would have puked. I remember being dizzy and sick and thinking I was going to die. Have you ever been that drunk?"

"No," I admitted.

"Anyway, I told Alan I had a final confession to make, and he humored me. That's when I confessed to him that Elizabeth shot our father.

"I think that's the only time in my life that I've ever really stunned him. He just sat there with his mouth hanging open. That sobered me up more than anything. I asked him what we should do. And he said there was nothing we could do. See, I thought we could get Jane Peters a new trial. But Alan said she wasn't in prison anymore and, if we told now, what would be the point of her sacrifice? 'You'd be hurting her and you'd be hurting Elizabeth.' I could see he had a point. So I never said anything more about it. But it's always bothered me, nagged away at me. What should I have done?"

The question was rhetorical, so I didn't answer. I was still trying to digest the fact that I was a murderer. Yet, I couldn't make the connection. I still didn't remember one damned thing about that day. But I was angry. I was definitely angry at my mother for doing something so stupid. What difference would it really have made to my life if both she and Billy had told the truth, that I killed William Townsend?

I would never know. I suppose she might have been right, that it could have branded me forever. Yet it would have been just as easy for us to move away, where no one knew William Townsend or cared about his murder. Instead, she made this ultimate sacrifice of hers. She could have changed her story at any time. But maybe her lawyer told her he could get her off. And hadn't Alan said something to Jelly about my mother only having to serve a few years? Maybe she figured it would be worth it, that Winnie would take care of me for those years, and then we could resume our life together.

But it hadn't turned out that way. My mother never made it out of prison, not alive at least, something Alan failed to tell Bill the night of Bill's confession. And I had lived a life of supreme indifference to her. She sacrificed everything for me, and yet to me she was just a vague memory.

"Becky," Bill said. He waited while I tried to collect myself from the recesses of my mind. "Do you now have whatever you were after from the moment we met?"

I looked at him. "Oh, Bill," I said. I reached out for him and drew his hand to me.

He pulled away but smiled slightly. "You're a strange, strange woman," he told me. "What was it you were after? Tell me. You at least owe me that much."

"I didn't see you just to get information. I really enjoy being with you. I always have."

"You always have. That makes it sound like a long-standing relationship."

"Very long-standing." I put my hand on his and looked up into his eyes. "I'm Elizabeth Peters."

26

"WHY didn't you tell me!" Bill demanded to know. "Why spend months leading me on, snooping around, whatever you were doing?"

"What should I have told you? I'm Elizabeth Peters? Please fill in the blanks? Bill, I don't remember anything about that day, even now that you've relived the entire catastrophe. It's a total blank for me. If I asked you any questions at all, it would have been about how my mother came to shoot your father. What would you have thought? That I was still pretending? Still covering up?

"Besides, I didn't even know what I was looking for when I first met you. Your name was on the list that Daryl Aberdeen gave us. You were one of their friends. When I saw your name, it brought back all sorts of pleasant memories. Like playing catch. I remember that so well, Bill, playing catch with you. I had no idea how involved I was going to become, as I tried to understand the truth of what happened back then. I had no idea there was going to be a mutual attraction between us. And I didn't mean to cause you any pain by bringing this all back. But the more I found out, the more curious I became." I smiled wryly. "Talk about killing the cat."

Bill stared sternly at me. "You don't remember shooting my father?"

I shook my head. "Not one bit of it, not being in the kitchen, not grabbing the gun, not running to my mother's defense. I can't even remember your father tossing the Christmas tree against the wall, nor taking pot shots at it. The only thing I can remember about your father—and I don't even know if this memory comes from the day of the shooting—I see him as a dark figure on the stairs. That's it. His was the shadow that overwhelmed me in my sleep. But until now, I never associated his shadow with anything more than the usual night creatures that inhabit all bad dreams."

"Jesus. My sister." He smiled, then laughed. "After all this, should we catch up on old times?"

"I think we've already done enough reminiscing."

But we hadn't. Not really. I took my car keys out of my purse and started the engine. We drove to a coffee shop and sat there for hours, just talking, talking, talking. "You know, Bill," I finally said, "there's still so much I don't understand. All the legal switcheroos. What brought them on? Who got my mother her lawyer? Couldn't she have mounted a better defense?"

Bill shook his head. "I don't know anything about that. Alan might, though. As I said, when he came home from school, he took over. You could approach him about it." He smiled and ran his finger around the rim of the coffee cup. "I have an idea," he said. "When you marry, let me give you away."

"Michael would just love that," I recoiled. Then we both burst out laughing.

It was only when I got home that the good feeling of being with Bill left me. Then I had to stare at the mirror and come face to face with the fact that I was a murderer. I had taken another person's life.

I tried to conjure up the horror of it. I made the effort of putting myself back into that house with my mother, Bill, and my stepfather. I went over the events in my mind exactly as Bill related them. And I came up empty.

Obviously, I was never meant to be an actor because I could not emote myself into the part of a murderer. Although the images of my early years were now definitely tarnished, I still saw myself as Becky McKennah, running home to my mother with my report card from the Sioux Bluffs elementary school. I saw Winnie baking cookies, bicycling with me, going to the PTA open house. Nowhere in my childhood could I find the place where I stored this nightmare. I only saw it reflected in my mother's sad eyes at her trial for second-degree murder.

In essence, I guess, I had not only murdered my stepfather, I had murdered my mother. She offered her life for mine. And the gods took her up on it.

I spent the night trying to piece all of my mother's actions together. I still couldn't understand why she did it. What made her take that instant decision to claim my crime? She must have known I would get off. I wouldn't even have been charged. And yet she sacrificed her freedom and her inheritance by confessing to the police.

I wondered then when she had changed her plea from self-defense to guilty with mitigation. Was it the six bullets I had put into William Townsend's body that caused her to drop self-defense? Was it some deal her lawyer worked out with the prosecuting attorney? And how had I ended up in the arms of Winnie McKennah?

Bill was right. The only one who might have all those answers, aside from my mother's lawyer, who probably wouldn't talk, was Alan Townsend. It wasn't until the early morning hours that I became determined to see Alan that very day. It was also in those wee hours that I wondered about Michael. I would have to tell him about all of this, and

I worried about what this new information would do to our marriage plans, nebulous as they were. Michael might be stalwart, but how would his mother react? I had a feeling my being a murderer might upset Mrs. Rosen more than my being Christian.

Somehow, despite the somersaults of my mind, I fell asleep about three and didn't wake until my usual ten. When I lifted the shade, the sun was shining. It would be a perfect day. Why ruin it by seeing Alan?

Face it, I finally had to tell myself. It isn't Alan you're afraid of. It's what he might tell you.

Okay, but Alan was pretty scary in his own right. He was not Bill. He wasn't exactly a warm person, one who would be willing to open up, except with his children. And I wasn't his child.

I stopped thinking. Sometimes one just has to cut off the mind and act. So I hopped into the shower, then out again to put on this atrocious gray wool skirt that Winnie McKennah forced me to buy when I was going off to school. She assured me it would be suitable for all sorts of occasions, like tea with the dean of women. Well, they no longer had a dean of women, but I was still stuck with the skirt. I always wore it when I wanted to look respectably dull.

I put on my black turtleneck with it and wrapped a scarf around my neck, then slung my wool jacket over me. I was ready for the trek downtown. I took the el, mainly because I lived near the Davis Street station. It was the usual slow ride into town. I used the time to try to formulate the sort of questions I was going to ask Alan Townsend. That's if I could get in to see him.

His office was in the McCormick building, right on the river. The elevator whisked me up to his floor, and I found myself stepping out onto thick carpeting and the soft sound of money. I thought of my mother then, working in this office, meeting William Townsend, starting her affair with him. He must have seemed like an answer to her dreams. And that's the trouble with us women. When we look to men to be the answer to our dreams, we usually end up with nightmares.

I was politely directed to Alan Townsend's office. It seemed as if he had an entire wing. He definitely had two receptionists guarding the beginning of his inner sanctum. They were much like palace guards with their "Halt, who goes there?" My name was relayed up the line, and I was ushered into the inner reception area, where an older woman took my name, writing it down carefully. Then she looked up to ask, "Do you have an appointment?"

"No," I confessed. "But he just might see me."

No intercom here, the gray angel rose from her desk, knocked discreetly on the door and entered the holy of holies. The door closed. It opened less than a minute later, and she beckoned me inside.

27

ALAN Townsend was standing against the window. "Come in, Ms. Belski," he said. "How pleasant to see you again."

His absolute lack of inflection led me to believe he couldn't have cared less. But he indicated I should take a chair in the cozy sitting area, and he sat down with me. "Coffee? Tea?" he wondered.

"Nothing, thank you," I replied.

He nodded at the woman, and she departed. We were left alone in this certainly soundproofed office. Alan sat back and crossed his legs. He got in the opening shot. "I'm glad you told Bill the truth before I had to."

I looked up, surprised.

"You're not the only one who has—um, shall we say resources, if you'll pardon my pun. That time at the house. When you said your name was Becky and that you were in computers, I knew instantly who you were. Of course, then I had you checked out to make sure. But—"

"You had been sending checks to Winnie McKennah all those years for her Becky, and she must have told you about my studying computers."

"Yes," he agreed. "Well, since we're both busy people, perhaps we should come right to the point of why you're here. Bill came over last night and told me what happened. I wondered how you were going to worm it out of him. You did a good job of it. Poor Bill was always the sensitive one."

"Obviously," I said, a little too coldly.

Alan smiled. "I honestly didn't know that you were the one who shot my father until Bill told me many years later. Since I assume this is going to go nowhere outside this room, may I say, if they had a medal for dealing out death, I would have given it to you."

"You hated your father."

" 'Hate' is too weak a word."

"He killed your mother."

"Yes. At least that's my supposition. I heard them arguing; and I was worried about her, wondering whether I should burst into their room and save her. But then she left the master bedroom and talked about getting away for a while, with the children. He was following her. There were shouts as their 'conversation' deteriorated. Then I heard her fall. When I came out of my bedroom, my father was standing at the edge of the stairs, hanging onto the banister, looking down at her. I knew from the way she landed that she was dead."

"Why didn't you tell the police?"

"And say what? That they had been arguing before she fell? How could I prove that he pushed her? He could simply claim they were arguing, and she fell in the heat of it. It was like your mother's case. My father didn't actually physically wallop anyone. He just intimidated people, bullied them, humiliated them. A case of the tongue being mightier than the fist. Physical violence is something the courts can understand. But not mental violence. That's beyond the capacity of our justice system. As your mother found out."

"Why did you lie at my mother's trial? Why did you tell the judge that everything was always so hunky-dory at home?"

"At that time, I believed your mother killed my father. I wanted to see her put away."

"But why?" I leaned forward to ask. "You've already admitted to me that your father was a bastard."

"Why should I have done anything to help your mother? It was your mother my parents were arguing about when my mother took her fatal fall. It was your mother who eight months later moved into my mother's house, took over my mother's things. Jane Peters slept with my father before my mother died; she slept with him after; she married him. How do I know my mother's fall wasn't their plot to get rid of her?"

"My mother wouldn't have—"

"According to Bill, you don't even remember your mother," Alan said harshly.

I sat back, defeated.

"I remember your mother very well. She was one of those helpful people, always there, always so sweet, while plotting, planning, conniving behind those beautiful brown eyes, serving my mother hors d'oeuvres at the Christmas party, when everyone in the room knew she was screwing my father. The gall of it. And then she moved into my mother's house and expected to be part of our circle of friends, people who had watched her help destroy my mother?"

"Jelly Mellon liked her," I said defensively.

"Jelly Mellon was and is a nymphomaniac. Even then, she was beyond the pale of our crowd. Now, of course, she's taken the one unforgivable step. I suppose it's okay to sleep with someone else's husband. But the line is obviously drawn at a son-in-law. She found a kindred soul in your mother."

"But Billy liked my mother. You're the one who never gave her a chance."

"Did Bill ever tell you about the zoo he used to keep in the backyard? Bill likes most living creatures. He's my brother and I love him for his goodness. But for him to say he was fond of your mother means nothing to me.''

I sighed. ''You're unrelenting in your hatred, aren't you?''

He smiled coldly. ''I do know how to bear a grudge. Now, if you don't mind—''

''Just one second, please. Why did my mother change her plea from self-defense to guilty of second-degree murder?''

''I suppose she must have thought she was guilty.''

''She didn't have a source of income except what came from your father, so who paid for her lawyer?''

Alan was silent for a minute before he said, ''I did.''

''But you hated her.''

''Let's just say there were legal matters that had to be cleared up so that life could continue to run smoothly. It was pointed out to your mother that she had very little going for her, should she choose to continue her plea of innocence. She wasn't innocent. We had witnesses who would testify as to her having an affair with my father when he was still married, spending exorbitant amounts of money on clothes, cars, and restaurants. In other words, we had witnesses who could paint her as the money-grubbing tramp she was. We made that very clear to her.''

''You and the prosecuting attorney, or you and the lawyer you hired for her?'' I shot back at him.

He smiled grimly. ''On the other hand, if she pleaded guilty and signed some papers, she could try her hand with a judge for a suspended sentence. She could bring whatever witnesses she wanted into court, and we wouldn't help the prosecutor find contrary witnesses.''

''Except for you and your perjury.''

''I've already explained that to you. Besides, the defense counsel and the prosecuting attorney had a deal. Should the judge not be taken in by your mother's heartfelt testimony, should he not give her a lenient sentence, your mother would serve no more than five years in jail. So for her agreement to certain matters, she had a chance at anything from probation to a suspended sentence to five years' jail time."

I sat there thinking for a minute, trying to figure out how things were presented to my mother, what sort of panic she must have been in, how worried she must have been about me and her. "Exactly what papers did she sign?" I asked.

"Well," Alan said, "I suppose it doesn't matter now if I tell you. For signing away all rights to the Townsend estate—"

"Which she would have gotten if she had been found not guilty," I pointed out quickly.

"She wouldn't have gotten anything if she had been found guilty of any of the charges against her because they were all felonies committed during a murder or manslaughter, whatever the charge was going to turn out to be," Alan argued. "I was more than generous with her. She signed away any claim to the Townsend estate. In exchange, I paid her legal expenses, all debts, I promised her a lump sum when she was released from prison. And I took custody of you," he ended softly.

"You what?" I was shocked.

"Well, something had to be done with you." He pushed his chair back from the coffee table. "It all makes sense now. It didn't at the time. Jane kept saying that she didn't want anyone to speak to you or Bill. The first thing she asked of her attorney was that you two be protected. Bill was hysterical, given to crying fits. We all knew you were in a state of shock. Only Jane and Bill knew why. I just assumed it was the shock of seeing someone dead. I asked Jane if she had some relative you should go to. She said she wanted you placed somewhere where no one would ever be able to remind you of what happened." Alan shrugged. "Where was I going to find such a place?" Then he smiled. "It was funny because I was discussing the problem with Winnie McKennah, whom I had known forever. She was more of a permanent fixture than the office furniture. And she offered to take you.

"I was dumbfounded, of course. None of us ever thought of Winnie as having any personal feelings, but she let her hair down that day. She told me, a young kid really, how she had always wanted to get married and have a family, but it never happened. She knew you. She had met you a few times when you were here with your mother. She would take you as her own and leave the Chicago area. You'd never have to hear about your mother or the Townsends again.

"So I offered the deal to Jane. I had found someone who would take you, but she wanted to keep you. I would send you a generous monthly support check up to and including college, should you choose to go. But Jane had to sign away her rights to you. In effect, she had to give you up for adoption."

"Is that what Winnie McKennah asked my mother to do?" I wondered.

"No," Alan admitted. "But she was afraid of taking you in and then losing you. That was true enough."

"And you were all for the adoption deal because you knew that would destroy my mother completely," I judged.

"Yes," he admitted, "as much as my mother's death destroyed me."

I sighed. "No wonder she didn't live past her prison sentence. Why would she want to? Thanks to you, she had nothing left."

"She had plenty to look forward to," Alan disagreed. "She had the money I was going to give her when she got out. And what makes you think that money wasn't more important to her than you were?"

"You!—" I held myself back. That's what he wanted, for me to become an emotional, hysterical woman. I would have to disappoint him. I smiled as coldly as he. "But you never had to pay my mother anything, did you?"

He didn't answer. He just sat there, staring at me. He didn't feel any guilt. He didn't feel anything.

"You know, Alan, I think you're probably as big a bastard as your father ever was."

"No," he chose to disagree. "No one could be quite as monstrous as my father. Look, Becky, or Elizabeth, or whatever you're going to call yourself now, none of us really escaped from what happened back then. Bill won't marry; I married out of social necessity; you've been chasing shadows. But what's important to remember is that we've all moved on. We've made some sort of life for ourselves. We're wounded, but we're walking. Bill says you're getting married again. So forget all this. Go on with your life. Have children. Try to be happy."

"When I have children, I'll think about my mother having me."

He turned away. "There's nothing more I can do for you." He stood and walked back to his desk.

I stood also. "I don't think you treated my mother fairly, Alan. Just remember, you're not the only one who can bear a grudge."

"Is that a threat?"

I didn't say anything more. Let him sweat it out. Big joke. What could I do that would bother him? It was all over. My mother was dead. His mother was dead. William Townsend was dead. Everyone had gotten away with murder. Including me.

28

WITH Christmas drawing closer, I became more and more depressed. This would be the first Christmas I'd spent without my adoptive mother. This was also the season when Sarah Townsend fell to her death down that staircase, when my mother confessed to my stepfather's murder. Why had my mind settled on these three facts instead of happier occasions?

Michael noticed. I went to several Christmas parties with him and tried to be of good cheer. But it was definitely forced joviality, and he was aggrieved. I tried to convince him that it had nothing to do with him. I explained that something had happened in my life that was turning me inside out. He wanted to know what it was, but I wasn't ready to tell him.

I consulted Bill Townsend. He said I should tell Michael, and the sooner the better. "A burden shared is a burden halved," he assured me. This was probably how he had felt after confessing to Alan what he knew of their father's murder. I dragged my pain after me much as Santa Claus drags his sack, but with definitely less joy.

"Someday," Bill said, "you're going to have to simply say good-bye. Drop it. Let it settle into the quicksand of your mind."

But saying good-bye was exactly what I had never done. I had said good-bye to Winnie McKennah, and that was painful enough. She had been the best mother a girl could hope for, and things were right between us. But I had never said good-bye to Jane Peters. I didn't even know where my mother was buried. In prison? In the Chicago area? If that's where she came from.

I decided to make that my Christmas project. I would find her grave and lay a wreath on it.

Nat was surprised to see me in the office. "Do you still work here?"

"Ho, ho, ho," I responded.

"Did you bring your gift for the grab bag?"

I had forgotten. "Tomorrow," I promised him. I sat down at my terminal and began to check the records for Jane Peters, death of. I came up empty.

So I resorted to a rather old-fashioned tool. I called the state prison in Dwight, where my mother had been housed. "Women's Correctional Center, Merry Christmas!" someone cheerfully answered the phone.

I didn't think there could be a merry Christmas in prison. Certainly, there wasn't for several clerks, when I asked them to dig up information on my mother for me. Their complaints about it being such an old case, that they would prefer getting ready for the Christmas party that afternoon, left me cold. I told them I'd wait in my office to hear from them.

Their Christmas party was at four. I heard from them at 3:50. "We don't have a death certificate for Jane Peters Townsend," one of the women reported.

"Well, who would have it?" I wondered.

"Probably the county clerk where she lived after she was released from prison."

"Excuse me?"

"She was in perfect health when she left here in 1968."

"Are you sure?"

"That's what it says on her release form."

My fingers tensed while my heart leapt. "And do you have an address for her?"

They did. As I wrote it down, my pencil snapped, and I had to grab for a pen. Bathed in an unbecoming film of sweat, I hung up the phone.

Alan Townsend had lied to me. He knew, he must have known that my mother was still alive. Did Winnie McKennah know too? Had she lied to me all those years ago when I asked her about my real mother? God!

I was ready to pick up the phone right then and there to call Alan Townsend. To call him every name in the book.

But there were more important things to do. I had my mother's first address. From there I could track her down.

It took me three days. After her release from prison, she was on probation for three years. During this time she worked as a reservations clerk for United Airlines. After her period of supervision was completed, she moved to Tucson, Arizona, where she owned a small boutique that sold Indian jewelry and tiles to the tourist trade. She had never remarried. She had no other children. She lived in one of those fake adobe condominiums on the outskirts of Tucson, and she looked older than her fifty-one years. I know. I spent a day following her. I even went into her shop and bought myself a silver ring. I looked into her eyes and tried to discover if she was happy. But it was the Christmas season, and Tucson was full of tourists escaping from the north. She was too busy to be happy. As she waited on me, she was merely polite.

"Is there something else I can help you with?" my mother asked me. I was holding my credit card, and she was trying to hand me the box with the ring in it. I smiled at her, the sweet kind of smile you would offer a friend. She looked at me as if I were—strange. "Not right now," I told her.

When she closed up the shop that night, rather late, probably to get the Christmas trade, I was there. She recognized me from before and probably thought, "Oh, oh, a crazy."

"Jane," I said to her, just so she'd know that I knew her.

She peered at me then, as if trying to place me. She smiled slightly the way you do when someone knows you but you can't for the life of you remember her. "Yes?" she asked. She had a gentle voice.

I let out what I thought was going to be a little sigh, but it turned into a sob. She stepped toward me, as if wanting to help but still not knowing whether I was some insane stranger. I held out my hand. I was wearing the ring I had bought earlier. She took my hand. My mother took my hand. And then I did start crying. We stood there on the street like total idiots, me crying, Jane probably wondering how the hell she had gotten into this mess.

I took my hand away, pulled a Kleenex from my pocket, and wiped my eyes. "I'm Becky Belski," I announced. She gave that slight smile again. "I used to be Becky McKennah before my marriage."

Her smile dropped as her mouth fell open.

"I'm Elizabeth. Mommy."

Why did I call her Mommy? What a nut. At my age no one calls her mother Mommy. Yet the last time I had seen her she was Mommy to me.

The smile came again and it grew wider. She stepped closer to me and touched my hair. "Elizabeth," she said softly, and I knew her voice. This was my mother.

What a time we had that evening. She wanted to know everything, but I wanted to know everything too. The conversation was very disjointed and yet everything seemed to come together rather nicely. I told her how and why I had found her, but she wasn't really interested in that. She wanted to know all about me, my childhood, how Winnie had treated me, what my life was like from the moment we were separated.

Then I had to chide her. "You shouldn't have done it, you know."

She shook her head and shrugged.

"I didn't remember a thing. I still don't."

"I'm glad for that," she said.

"Why did you let me go? There must have been other alternatives," I pointed out.

She sighed. "There were. And I had time in prison to think of all of them." She smiled, then lowered her head. "I had so many regrets. But Alan said—"

"Alan!" I almost snarled.

She reached across to me and took my hand. "When I got out of prison and wondered if I should go back on the deal, Alan said you were happy. I thought to myself, well, I've signed this paper, giving custody to Winnie. What if I try to get you back and she refuses to relinquish you? Then we would face a court battle. The judge would have to decide whether you should be living with the fine, upstanding Winnie McKennah or the scurrilous, murdering Jane Peters. Did I do the wrong thing for your life?"

I thought it over. "No," I had to admit.

"Then that's all that matters."

"No, it isn't all that matters. I don't like the way you were treated."

"Elizabeth, it was so long ago. I'd rather just forget it. I have my shop, I have my friends. I do have a life here. And now"—she looked at me longingly—"I have you?" As if she had to ask.

"You're damn right you do!" I assured her.

She frowned. "I can't believe Winnie let you talk like that."

I laughed. I had a mother again!

And I had some unfinished business back in Chicago. On the flight home I thought things through. Every path my mind took led me to the conclusion that somehow my mother and I had been cheated. I know that life cheats everybody, but it seems that we, as a pair, had been more wronged than most. All these years we had been deprived of each other. No, I couldn't say I had really suffered, though even now my attitude toward Winnie McKennah was becoming more ambivalent. Surely, she knew that my mother was still alive. As much as I loved her, it was cruel of Winnie to keep my mother and me apart.

But Winnie wanted a daughter named Becky. I fulfilled that hope. My mother wanted wealth and security. For a time she had had both. But she paid for her dream by losing it all. She spent time in prison for a murder she didn't commit. And by doing so, she lost the money from the Townsend estate that was rightfully hers. I knew what her inheritance would have been because I had obtained a copy of William Townsend's will. A third of it was to go to his spouse Jane Peters Townsend.

What exactly was a third of William Townsend II's estate worth?

Alan Townsend held the paper on which my mother signed away her portion of the estate. But why should that paper hold up in court when it was based on the false premise that my mother killed William Townsend II? She didn't do it!

The day after I came back from Tucson, I arose with a renewed interest in life and what it was bound to bring. I made a careful judgment of what I should wear on that special day. I settled on the suit Nat had me buy for our first meeting with Bellini Reese, which was also the first time I laid eyes on my beloved Michael Rosen. The suit certainly should photograph well.

Throwing caution—and money—to the wind, I hailed a cab and had it take me downtown to the law offices of Cohen, Kahn, Cohn and Kahane. I discovered that Michael was in conference with Mr. Reese. "Thank you," I told Bellini's secretary. And then I pushed through the closed doors, while she plaintively called, "You can't go in there."

Bellini was certainly shocked to see me, unannounced as I was. Michael was horrified. "Becky!" Bellini enthused. "Is there something we can do for you?"

"Yes. I'm sorry to tell you, Bellini, but Michael won't be

able to work for you from now on. Come, Michael," I turned to my darling to say.

Michael was so stunned that he not only followed my directions, he held onto his files. That certainly must be a first.

I took Michael by the elbow and dragged him out of Bellini's office. Bellini called after us, "I hope you'll let me handle your divorce when the time comes." I don't know which of us he was speaking to.

"Becky, I'm going to kill you for this," Michael said under his breath as we entered the elevator on our way down to his floor.

"No, you're not."

"Yes, I am."

"No, you're not, Michael! Remember all your talk about wanting that one big case that would put your name in lights?" We got off on his floor and entered his office. When I had kicked his door closed, I threw my hands around his neck and gave him a hug and a kiss. His response was less than enthusiastic.

"Do you know how many lawyers don't have jobs out there?" he sort of shrieked. "What are we going to live on?"

"Michael, I've got a case for you that'll go down in Cook County history. So sit at your desk, take out your legal pad, and start writing!"

With reluctance he sat down and reached for one of his well-sharpened pencils. He didn't begin to smile until I was five minutes into my recital. By the time I finished, roughly two hours later, he was beaming.

Of course, I had to undergo his interrogation, his probes and feints. But I at least maintained my composure. Michael was falling all over himself in delight. "I should have worn my gray pinstripe," he said, after he called the first reporter on his list. And then, "Do you have any idea of what your mother's reaction to this is going to be?" he cautioned.

"I don't know what it'll be, Michael, because I didn't

discuss with her what I'm about to do. But I'm going to take the chance that she'll be pleased. And rich, after this is all over."

Michael finished calling the reporters. By that time Bellini had phoned, wondering when Michael was going to get his ass on up there. "I'm sorry, Bellini, but I've got a hot one here," Michael said before he hung up. I was so proud of him.

We took Michael's car north to the suburbs. We were pleased to see that the press had already arrived. I wondered if there was a statute of limitations on Alan's perjury. But I dismissed that thought from my mind as I tried to smile and look gracious with flashbulbs popping in my face and the cameras running.

All that stopped when we entered the Kenilworth police station. The policeman on duty looked at the two of us and asked, "Is there anything I can do for you?"

I stepped forward bravely. "Yes. I'd like to confess to a murder."